# Northern Lights

**KAY D. RIZZO**

Nampa, Idaho | Oshawa, Ontario, Canada
www.pacificpress.com

Cover design by Gerald Lee Monks
Cover resources from Lars Justinen
Inside design by Kristin Hansen-Mellish



The author assumes full responsibility for the accuracy of all facts and quotations as cited in this book.



Additional copies of this book may be obtained by calling toll-free 1-800-765-6955 or online at http://www.adventistbookcenter.com.

Library of Congress Cataloging-in-Publication Data:

Rizzo, Kay D., 1943-
Northern Lights / by Kay D. Rizzo.
pages cm
ISBN 13: 978-0-8163-4678-3 (pbk.)
ISBN 10: 0-8163-4678-X (pbk.)
1. Christian stories. 2. Love stories. I. Title.
PS3568.I836N67 2013
813'.54—dc23
2013033105

November 2013

# Dedication

I dedicate this book to my heavenly Father:

Thank You for bringing my husband of fifty years into my life. He's my greatest cheerleader, my unfailing inspiration, and the hero of every story I write. Richard, your love warms me through life's dark times and causes me to dance in the sunlight.

# Acknowledgments

Thank you! Thank you! Thank you!

- Richard Rizzo, KX7U, for your stalwart encouragement, for the fun "plotting trips" to the mountains, and for your exceptional knowledge of ham radio and Morse code;

- Lieutenant Colonel James Milburn, for sharing your military insights and your enthusiastic endorsement of the "read";

- Ruthie Milburn for your editing skills getting the manuscript "up to snuff";

- Flora Smith, my high school English teacher, for demonstrating courage, determination, grace under fire, and a love for literature that took me beyond the Five Little Peppers and How They Grew series;

- Elizabeth Eshbach for sharing your husband's experiences building the Alaskan Highway;

- And to all the other WWII "brains" I picked while researching the story. Your personal experiences made the era come alive.

# Contents


| | | |
|---|---|---|
| | Prologue | 7 |
| 1. | The Letter | 13 |
| 2. | Blizzard Conditions | 23 |
| 3. | Family Dinner | 27 |
| 4. | Face-off on Maynard Mountain | 37 |
| 5. | The Journey North | 43 |
| 6. | Winter's Chill | 55 |
| 7. | The Big Freeze | 59 |
| 8. | Deep Water | 69 |
| 9. | No Early Thaw | 73 |
| 10. | Out in the Cold | 81 |
| 11. | Change of Plans | 85 |
| 12. | Declaration of War | 97 |
| 13. | A Tug-of-War | 101 |
| 14. | A Stroke of Luck | 109 |
| 15. | Code: SOS | 111 |
| 16. | No Holiday for Sabotage | 123 |
| 17. | The Prisoner | 131 |
| 18. | A Daring Challenge | 137 |
| 19. | A Day of Revelation | 155 |
| 20. | Stranded in a Blizzard | 169 |
| 21. | A Time for Contemplation | 181 |
| 22. | A Time of Peace | 191 |
| 23. | Choices of the Heart | 199 |
| 24. | The Desires of Your Heart | 207 |

# Prologue

*I know the plans I have for you . . . plans to prosper you and not to harm you.*
*—Jeremiah 29:11, NIV*

## The Bering Sea: January 1911

Hours before the first black wave slammed against the bow of the eighty-foot fishing boat, Captain Marko Petrov heard the voices. The gnawing pain in his arthritic knee was deafened by the Sirens' song of doom. The devil's breeding ground for monster storms is what the natives called the waters off the Aleutian chain. Helmsman Alex Kopitzke, the beardless, pimple-faced grandson of Petrov's lifelong friend and confidant, One-legged Pete, stood at the helm. Poor old Pete had joined the landlubbers after he lost his left leg to diabetes.

The captain hauled out his gold-encased pocket watch, checked the time, and made the appropriate notation in the vessel's log. He glanced up when he heard scraping outside the door. The handle turned and first mate Owen Swenson angled his six-foot frame through the narrow opening. No words were exchanged as the first mate shed his foul-weather gear and the beefy five-foot-seven-inch Petrov donned his sealskin mackinaw and rubberized yellow slicker. The captain then jammed a matching rain hat over his thinning gray hair. More at home in the elements of the sea than those on land, the taciturn seaman stepped out of the protective confines of the bridge and onto the deck. A cold, wet wind slapped his salt-and-pepper-bearded face. The voices echoed through the night.

Only a shiftless or inexperienced Alaskan seaman ignored the dangers inherent on the brine. Yet despite the risk, a surprising number of North Pacific fishermen became blasé about maintaining basic safety rules aboard ship when a storm threatened. They ignored weather reports, turned off emergency radios, and stowed life rafts in the pilothouse. But Captain Marko Petrov respected the mischief lodged in the arms of a wave. In the twenty years of fishing for Pacific cod in the Bering Sea, he had studied La Mer's capricious nature. In return, she sent the voices to forewarn him of pending tragedy—when he took the time to listen to his demanding mistress.

Her lessons had been hard learned. Marko's father had ignored the voices the night a rogue wave broadsided the *Fedik* and washed the boy's father into the Bering Sea, never to surface again. Another night, minutes before an angry wave smashed into the sturdy craft and flooded the pilothouse, the young captain had turned a deaf ear to the voices. Obviously, only the grace of an unseen God had spared his life and the lives of his crew, and Marko vowed to never again ignore the voices.

Despite the relative calm of the water's surface illuminated by the wolf moon on this chilly night, he heard the voices. Though there was no visual evidence of an approaching storm, the captain hunkered deep in the collar of his mackinaw and threaded his way to the galley, where he found Herman Yedifsky adding Tabasco sauce to the stew bubbling on the cast-iron woodstove. Whether making a stew or a goulash from leftovers, Tabasco sauce and minced garlic were staples in Herman's daily fare. Only the morning oatmeal was spared the assault.

Captain Marko Petrov stomped his feet on the bristled mat inside the galley. The welcoming aroma of freshly baked gingersnaps cooling on the counter met him. "Came to warn you. I think we're in for a big one tonight."

"The voices, skipper?" A deeply spiritual man, Herman "Tiny" Yedifsky trusted the skipper's "voices." For more than thirty years, Tiny had fed the crew aboard the *Fedik,* first hiring on with Anton Petrov, and then with his son, Marko. Six feet tall and well over 250 pounds, Tiny ruled his kingdom with a yard-long wooden spoon. No one crossed the mild-mannered giant. "Ah, the voices."

"Thought I'd give you a heads-up, old friend." The captain edged toward the cooling cookies and stuffed a handful into the inside pocket of his mackinaw. Pretending not to notice, Tiny grinned.

"Gotta go." Petrov popped a cookie into his mouth and gave his friend a mock salute. On his way out of the galley, he called over his shoulder, "Gotta warn the men."

Before the door clicked shut behind the skipper, Tiny had fastened the cast-iron lid on the stew pot and stashed the gingersnaps in a watertight container. If the captain's voices were accurate, which they always were, Tiny knew his emergency supply of hardtack, a bowl of hot stew, and a few gingersnaps would warm the innards of the crew during the long, cold night ahead.

On deck, the *Fedik's* ten-man crew fastened every hatch and checked every porthole. To the north, a few darkened clouds rode the horizon as the crew secured every loose item on the deck and lashed down anything that could break loose and become a lethal projectile during high winds.

Following a thorough inspection of the vessel, the captain climbed the steps to the pilothouse. Before opening the door, he gazed out at the deceptively calm water and sighed. All was as ready as it could be, and yet the voices continued. A simple man, Marko left nothing to chance. He was certain nothing happened by accident, that there was a purpose to everything and everyone under the heavens. He never doubted that somewhere overhead beyond the canopy of stars, a Hand directed his life and the lives of his crew. While he joked about the voices coming from his mistress, La Mer, he believed that a Divine Being sent the warnings he dared not ignore.

During storm or calm, the spiritual lessons learned at the feet of his Russian Orthodox grandmother had governed Petrov during his years at sea. Out of habit, yet laced with concern, he recited the traditional sailor's prayer.

> O God, the protector of all who trust in Thee, without whom nothing is strong, nothing is holy; Increase and multiply upon us Thy mercy; that, Thou being our ruler and guide, we may so pass through things temporal, that we finally lose not the things eternal. Lighten our darkness, we beseech Thee, O Lord; and by Thy great mercy defend us from all perils and dangers of this night. Grant this, O heavenly Father, for the sake of Jesus Christ our Lord. Amen.

He'd barely whispered his amen when a forty-foot wave broadsided the vessel. A sudden impetuous gust of wind followed. The ship pitched and rolled like driftwood in the surf. *Boom!* A second rogue wave shook the craft to its timbers, this time against portside. A third turbulent surge hit the stern, plunging the boat forward.

The waves tossed the lumbering fishing boat as if it were a toy. "We're going down," Captain Petrov muttered as he snatched the wheel from the young helmsman's control. "This time, we're going down."

The demons of the deep toyed with the *Fedik* as the captain struggled to maintain his course toward Amaknak Island. Though it seemed like hours, the terrifying maelstrom lasted far less time. Suddenly, a crew-member, soggy hair plastered against his forehead, his slicker dripping with saltwater, burst into the pilothouse. "Skipper! Look starboard!"

The captain peered out into the storm. Petrov's breath caught in his throat. In the churning debris floated an overturned boat.

"Boatswain, prepare a skiff." Captain Petrov guided the craft as close to the wreckage as he dared. One of the seamen trained the *Fedik's* spot-light on what was left of a hull that appeared to be about forty feet long. The *Fedik* circled the overturned boat to assess the damages. Despite the tossing waves, the men aboard the *Fedik* lined the railing of the deck hop-ing to spot any survivors. None could be seen. And to the captain, the voices continued to croon their melody of death and destruction.

Suddenly, the wind grew still; a foreboding calm descended on the waters. The captain gave the wheel to the helmsman and went on deck. During the lull in the storm, the men heard the cry of a terrified infant. *Impossible,* the captain thought. *Are the voices toying with me?* When a sec-ond, more insistent wail filled the night air, he had no doubt but that a young child had somehow survived the storm. Two of his crew turned toward him, their bodies tense for action. Petrov gave a nod and within minutes the men were rowing the skiff toward the wreckage.

As the skipper waited impatiently for news, he gripped the wooden railing. *Are my imaginings playing tricks on me? Am I merely hearing the "voices" once again? Is there a baby crying or not?* He held his breath and watched as his men searched through the rubble. Suddenly, one of the men straight-ened and shouted as he lifted a sodden bundle above his head. "A baby! It's alive!"

Cheers filled the air as the rescuers returned to the *Fedik*. When one of the rescuers placed the squalling infant in the crusty captain's arms, the men hooted with delight.

"You look good as a daddy, Captain!" Kopitzke shouted. "You missed your calling."

The captain gazed down at the child, who was wailing in protest. His heart warmed. Years earlier, when he chose La Mer to be his mistress, Petrov dismissed any dreams of loving and marrying a real woman or holding his own flesh and blood in his arms. With his own father at sea during his childhood, he knew the harsh and lonely life he and his mother had endured, and he had vowed never to do the same to his own family. But that vow hadn't silenced the yearnings in his heart. With the tenderness of a seasoned grandpa, Petrov whispered, "How did you survive the storm, little one?"

For an instant, the infant gazed up into the grizzled face of the captain but quickly returned to voicing his discomfort.

"His folks lashed him to the forecastle," one of his rescuers shouted above the child's cry. "That's what kept him from being washed into the drink."

"You are truly a gift from God," the captain murmured. "A miracle. God must have a great and mighty plan for you, little one."

"I'll take 'im, Cap'n." Tiny pushed his way from the back of the hovering ring of sailors. "I grew up the oldest of eleven young'uns. I know what he needs."

When one of the other seamen objected, Tiny challenged, "Have you ever changed a dy-dee?" He glared menacingly at the challenger. "I didn't think so. Now make way, men. I need to get this little one out of that soaking wet blanket and into the warmth of my galley."

Though shivering from the frigid waters of the Arctic, the baby stopped screaming long enough to reach up and tug at the man's grizzled beard. Tiny laughed. "See? He knows when he's in good hands."

The youngest crewmember called out, "How do you know it's a he?"

"I just do. Only a male child could raise such a ruckus." Tiny turned and headed to the mess hall.

"So what are you going to name him?" one of the men called after the cook.

Tiny paused at the hatchway and glanced toward the captain. "Cap'n?"

Petrov smiled. "I was thinking we should call him Mouzeza. It's a

Russian name that means 'drawn from the deep.' "

Tiny nodded and touched the side of the child's face with his finger. "Mouzeza. How do you like your new name, l'il fella?" Gently, the cook teased his beard from the baby's grasp. "Talk about luck. This child was born under a lucky star."

"Luck had nothing to do with it, my friend," the captain corrected. "You wait; you'll see. This child is part of a grand design, a divine plan that goes far beyond this night."

Tiny disappeared through the door into the galley, babe in arms, and the sailors ambled back to their stations; Captain Petrov rested his elbows against the railing and gazed into the night. The storm had passed. The moon, peering out from behind a lingering cloud, traced a luminescent pathway across the surface of the water, illuminating the remains of the sinking vessel. For a moment, the captain listened and then heaved a satisfied sigh. The voices of the sea had grown silent once more.

# Chapter 1: The Letter

*It takes two to write a letter.*
*—Elizabeth Drew*

## Seattle, Washington: November 1941

A bone-chilling rain soaked western Washington—normal weather for late November. Gray clouds hung low over the newly snow-blanketed Wenatchee Mountains to the east while rain pelted the city of Seattle. Before leaving for Bellwood International Import/Export Ltd., cryptologist Elizabeth Ames had resisted the urge to call in sick. It would have been the perfect morning to slip into a pair of flannel pajamas and snuggle down in front of a crackling fire with a bowl of Golden Delicious apples and a good Agatha Christie novel. However, she knew as head operator of the company's ship-to-shore communications department that her skills would be needed to guide one or more of her father's merchant ships safely to shore.

*Always responsible, that's me.* Elizabeth gazed into the foggy grayness beyond the icy raindrops pelting the radio-room window. Behind her, the steady *clickity-clack* of shortwave chatter supplied a backdrop of normalcy to the chaotic discord churning through her brain. Idly she brushed aside from her left cheek a lock of her Rita Hayworth red curls, which frizzed more than usual in the damp weather. A light sprinkle of freckles bridged her nose, standing out in soft contrast to her pale, porcelain skin.

Liz watched but didn't see the parade of semitrucks lumbering across the wooden docks below the window, spraying muddy water onto the dockworkers in their rubberized gear. The intricate choreography performed by the longshoremen and their giant cranes as they lifted, towed, and shifted massive wooden crates from exotic ports of call onto boxcars going only God and the dock foreman knew where, usually fascinated her. But not today—not when her world threatened to shatter into a heap of finely cut crystal.

Despite Hitler's troops surging across Europe and the Tiger of Malaya's invasion of Malaya and Singapore, the United States shipping industry boomed. The Great Depression was fading into a painful memory as money had begun to flow once again, causing Americans to clamor for foreign-made goods. Through diplomacy and subterfuge, the United States had maintained a distance from what political pundits were calling World War II. Yet Europe's unrest made thinking Americans wonder how long President Roosevelt could hold out against the Axis threat spreading around the world.

As inevitable as the country's involvement in these international conflicts appeared to be, Liz had her own personal battle to fight. The glass in the window reflected a seething bitterness in her steel-gray eyes; less obvious was the pent-up anger seething in her heart. She swiped away an uninvited tear sliding down her cheek and gritted her teeth against a sudden wave of nausea. Steam wafted up from the mug of hot tea she gripped with her left hand. The aroma of cinnamon and nutmeg did nothing to cheer her spirits. The reason for her discontent was the unopened onionskin airmail envelope clutched in her right hand addressed to *Elizabeth Ames, Bellwood International Import/Export Ltd., Seattle, Washington.*

*Leave it to Alan to make his first communication since he joined the army as impersonal as possible,* she thought. The carefully formed address denied her the basic respect of addressing her as Mrs. Elizabeth Ames, the woman he had vowed to love "till death do us part."

This wasn't the way Liz had planned her life. Whenever she played with her favorite paper dolls as a child, her boy and girl dolls would meet, fall in love, marry, and have three babies and would always live happily ever after. But since meeting the silent, mysterious engineer Alan Ames, Elizabeth had begun to wonder if "happily ever after" could ever really happen.

The young couple had waltzed through the first three steps of her fantasy—meet, fall in love, marry. *What happened to the fourth and the fifth steps? Where does love go,* she wondered, *when it abandons the human heart? Is it incinerated in the searing heat of angry words; does it wither away to dust from neglect; or does it freeze into an icy block of unspoken accusations?* Despite the warmth of her avocado-green sweater, she hugged herself against a shiver that skittered the length of her spine.

Instinctively, the woman glanced over her shoulder at the row of clocks mounted on the wall above the ship-to-shore communication station and set for each of the planet's different time zones. It was 10:48 A.M. Pacific Time. She'd spent half of her morning break clutching the unopened envelope and looking but not seeing the dreary world beyond the office window. Sooner or later she'd have to read the dreaded letter. Sooner or later she'd have to discover what Alan had written.

There was so much Liz didn't know about her husband of four years. In Alan's absence, Elizabeth had begun to wonder if she'd ever really known him. She knew his favorite color was green; he preferred Duke Ellington to Bing Crosby; apple pie to lemon meringue—all superficial trivia. But she wondered what went on inside his head. What was truly important to him? It hurt to realize she hadn't a clue. *Does anyone intimately know the real Alan Ames?* she asked herself during the seven months since he had enlisted in the military. Worse yet, she hadn't a clue where he might have gone. She glanced down at the envelope. Neither the postmark nor the series of military codes and numbers in the return address space revealed his whereabouts.

It had been the evening of her parents' thirtieth wedding anniversary party that Alan, a licensed architect and civil engineer, announced his intention to join the United States Army Corps of Engineers. He didn't try to make his action sound noble or patriotic, merely matter-of-fact. What he didn't mention to her or to their family and friends was that he'd resigned from his job with Washington State's highway department that afternoon and intended to leave for basic training the same evening.

The word *stunned* didn't adequately describe Liz's reaction. His abrupt pronouncement silenced the celebration. Confused, she shot a quick glance toward Alan's equally startled mother. His parents, who'd driven north from Portland for her parents' party, appeared as confused as she. Without further explanation, Alan grabbed his trench coat and headed for their Hudson coupe, leaving Liz behind to sputter an awkward apology to her parents and their guests and run to catch up with him. Silently, she climbed into the passenger side of the car and closed the door.

"Alan?" She studied Alan's profile as he put the car into reverse and backed out of the driveway. From the set of his jaw, she knew he had no intention of explaining himself. The short ride home from the hotel ballroom to their two-bedroom Craftsman-style bungalow overlooking Puget Sound seemed interminable.

Alan parked the coupe in the driveway and strode into the house, leaving a bewildered Liz to open her own car door. She followed him inside the house. In the hallway, she tossed her purse onto the antique, hand-carved, mahogany console table beside the front door—the first piece of furniture they'd purchased as husband and wife. As she did, she caught a glimpse of her reflection in the wood-framed mirror above the console. Fear darkened her face; fury welled up in her eyes. She clutched her shaking hands to her stomach to stay the inner volcano threatening to erupt. Liz knew how much Alan hated when she "ranted," as he called her emotional outbursts. Determined this was one fight he couldn't avoid, Liz slammed the front door behind her with more force than she'd intended. The leaded glass in the door rattled.

"Alan, talk to me. What is going on? What have I ever done to deserve such public humiliation? I am your wife, or at least I was the last time I read our marriage license." Liz winced at the unexpected shrillness of her voice. She paused. *Now is the time to be rational.* She took a deep breath. *Rational? How can I be rational at such a time? Surely if there ever were a time for tears . . .*

Alan paused for an instant, his left hand poised on the knob of the bathroom door. He shook his head and heaved a heavy sigh. As the air escaped his lungs, his shoulders sagged and his resolve appeared to waver. As he turned toward her, the expression in his brown eyes was unfathomable. He opened his mouth to retaliate, and then clamped it shut and entered the green-and-white tiled bathroom.

Before he could close the door, she stopped it with her left arm. The door banged against the wall. Without glancing her way, he removed his brown canvas travel bag from the closet beside the medicine chest. Slowly, item by item, he dropped his toothbrush, a can of tooth powder, and his shaving equipment into the bag. Careful not to touch her, he wordlessly pushed past and crossed the hallway to their bedroom.

Frozen with disbelief, Liz watched him jam several changes of skivvies and T-shirts into the bag, and then, without a glance her way, stride out the front door to a taxi parked by the curb in front of their house. It was the first she'd noticed the taxi. *Was it there when we got home from the party?* She didn't think so. She realized he must have called the taxi from the hotel before making his announcement. That he would have called for a taxi before he told her he was leaving stabbed her to the quick.

"Alan! Help me understand what you're doing! Just once, can't we talk this out?" She shouted from the porch as he climbed into the cab. Like an errant child caught stealing candy from the neighborhood grocer, the cab leaped forward and bounded down the sleepy, suburban street.

"Alan, don't run away! Please, say something. Scream at me! Shout! Let's have an old fashioned, top-of-the lungs battle royal." Liz collapsed onto the porch floor and buried her face in her knees. She thought as she had so many times before, *If only once we could fight and then passionately make up like other married couples.* As she sank back onto her haunches, Liz knew that would never happen—not with Alan. Alan never let go of his self-control—in front of her or in front of anyone, for that matter. Yet even as the yellow vehicle disappeared from view, her husband's ever-present censure following the death of their infant son, Lanny, silently screamed at her. Her fault! With Alan, everything was always her fault.

"If you'd been at home caring for our son instead of leaving him with a babysitter while you trotted off to work for your father . . . If you had quit your job when Lanny was born and cared for him as a mother should . . ." Although Alan never completed his accusations, she knew what he was saying. "Our son would be alive today."

*And maybe he's right,* she'd thought so many times since that fateful afternoon when the telephone call from the babysitter caught her leaving the office. That their only son had died for no apparent reason flashed through her brain for the hundred-thousandth-millionth time as Liz stared at the unopened envelope. "Oh, dear God! I can't do this. Please, I can't do this."

Liz wasn't a woman who'd ever felt the need to pray to a God she couldn't see, touch, or hear. Even after her son's death, the grieving mother left the praying to her maternal grandmother, Grandma Keating.

The address on the hated envelope swam before her eyes. She ignored the steady tap of Brad Lucas, her communications assistant, sending and receiving Morse code from a cargo ship approaching the Port of Seattle.

*I can't cry! I can't cry!* Liz swiped at a tear sliding down the side of her nose. She took a ragged breath and exhaled slowly. *Look on the bright side,* she told herself. *Despite the loneliness you've endured, the subsequent months without conflict since Alan left have been a blessing in an odd sort of way.* She had begun to heal—at least that's what she told herself while seated in front of the fireplace, wrapped in the quilt Grandma Keating had given as a wedding gift. Yet, despite the cozy warmth of the fire, a block of ice had surrounded her tortured heart and refused to melt.

It wasn't that her family were not there for her. They were. On weekends Liz's well-meaning mother orchestrated a variety of family activities to keep her grieving daughter from becoming a recluse. Despite her mother's most heroic resocialization attempts for her elder daughter, Liz preferred her evenings of solitude overlooking the Sound from the porch of her tiny Craftsman cottage.

As time passed, Liz had begun to laugh again at the silly jokes her co-worker Brad cracked and his weirdly accurate imitations of famous people such as President Roosevelt, Cary Grant, Mae West, and England's Winston Churchill. When she realized it had been at least two weeks since she'd awakened from the debilitating nightmare of running toward but not being able to reach her crying son, Liz actually breathed an awkward prayer of thanksgiving. *Yes,* she decided. *I've definitely begun to heal, in spite of your silence, Alan Randolph Ames!*

And almost a year after the fateful day her son had died, Liz vowed to never again become the whimpering, tearful person she'd been in the days and weeks following the graveside funeral. She would put her loss of Lanny and of Alan behind her; she would move on! In her heart she knew she'd done everything she could to properly care for her son. *Mrs. Lake was a responsible babysitter,* Liz reminded herself. *Lanny died while sleeping in his crib. Sometimes that happens to infants no matter what adult is caring for them,* she again reminded herself. She took a sip of hot tea from the mug cozied in her hands.

"Hey, what's wrong? Bad news?" Brad flicked the switch to broadcast the incoming Morse code throughout the state-of-the-art maritime radio room. "Is the letter from that husband of yours?" The slight young man, barely out of trade school, had a sympathetic heart and wisdom beyond his years. That helped to offset his tendency to be more than a little nosy. While she never discussed Alan's departure with Brad or with any other employee at her father's firm, she knew how fast gossip spread throughout the tight-knit company.

"Looks like it." Liz stuffed the envelope into the pocket of her green-and-brown-plaid wool skirt and idly ran one hand along the wide box pleats as if to smooth out the pesky wrinkle the letter had added to her day.

"Aren't you going to read it?" Brad raked his fingers through his sandy blond hair and stretched. "Go ahead. Take a longer break if you need to, or better yet, go home. You could be coming down with the flu or something. I'll be OK for another half hour or so. Robert should be here by then." Robert Gross had taken and passed his advance radio license and was waiting for the actual notification to arrive in the mail from D.C.

"Thanks, but I'm doing fine." She braved a strained smile. "You know Rob can't go on-air until his license arrives from the FCC." She glanced down at her pocket. "Don't worry. I'll be fine. I will read the letter eventually."

Brad shrugged, clamped a yellow #2 pencil, cigarlike, between his teeth, and quipped in his best W. C. Fields imitation, "There's no time like the present, my little chickadee."

One corner of Liz's mouth lifted into a grin, but her heart remained heavy. Brad continued with his impersonation. "They say married people live longer. Personally, I think it just seems longer . . ."

"SOS! SOS!" A sudden flurry of Morse code interrupted Brad's banter. "CQD VNL. CALLING ALL STATIONS. DANGER." VNL were the call letters for the *Vancouver Lady,* one of Liz's father's larger merchant marine ships. "R—JAPANESE SUB APPROACHING STARBOARD. GIVE COURSE OF ACTION—SK."

Brad keyed in a quick "R," signaling to Sammy Chan that he'd received the operator's transmission. Immediately, the unsettling message took priority over Alan's unopened letter in both of the radio operators' minds. From the rhythm of Sammy Chan's excited "fist," Liz could tell the young mariner, whom she'd trained for the job, was nervous. The woman's ability to recognize each of her father's radio operators' identities as well as mood from the first dots or dashes transmitted almost superseded her exceptional speed at keying. To accurately copy and send fifty words per minute outranked most of her peers by several words—an invaluable skill when faced with a ship-to-shore emergency. And this appeared to be an emergency.

Throughout the summer months of 1941, Japanese submarines harassed privately owned merchant ships crossing the Pacific. Cargo ships flying the flags of European countries had been torpedoed. Up to this point, flying the neutral flag of the United States had protected the Bellwood's mariners from being hijacked or sunk, but no one knew when the tide would change. As the ship operator's coding ended, Liz immediately transmitted, "R—THIS IS K7UV, GIVE LOCATION—SK."

"R—K7UV—LATITUDE 46 DEGREES, 54 MINUTES NORTH; LONGITUDE 126 DEGREES, 42 MINUTES WEST—SK."

She shot a quick glance at the floor-to-ceiling world map on the wall behind her station. "R—YOU'RE ON COURSE, VNL. ANY RADIO CONTACT WITH SUB?—SK."

"R—TRIED, BUT NO REPLY—SK."

"R—CAN YOU IDENTIFY SUB?—SK."

"R—NEGATIVE. CAN ONLY SEE RED DOT PAINTED ON SIDE OF CRAFT—SK."

A third signal interrupted their transmissions. "BK—BREAK! BREAK! THIS IS COAST GUARD CUTTER 117, MONITORING VNL'S TRAFFIC. WE'RE FIVE NAUTICAL MILES FROM VNL, AND ON OUR WAY. WILL CONTINUE TO MONITOR TRAFFIC—SK."

"R—VNL, DID YOU RECEIVE TRANSMISSION?—SK," Liz tapped to the operator on the *Vancouver Lady.*

"R," was his reply.

Liz heaved a relieved sigh and coded back, "R—TELL CAPTAIN GRAYSON TO HOLD A STEADY COURSE. HELP IS ON THE WAY, SAMMY—SK." After coding a quick thanks to the Coast Guard cutter, Liz cranked her neck from side to side to unseat a painful crick in her neck.

Static electricity crackled throughout the radio room as Liz and Brad silently stared at the radio, deciphering the series of dots and dashes transmitting between the Coast Guard cutter and the *Vancouver Lady.* That the cutter's radio operator couldn't establish radio contact with the Japanese submarine made the threat of the enemy submarine more ominous. "R—CAPTAIN OF THE UNIDENTIFIED JAPANESE SUBMARINE,

WE KNOW YOU COPY. BACK OFF!—SK," the cutter operator tapped. "THE *VANCOUVER LADY* SAILS UNDER THE FLAG OF THE UNITED STATES OF AMERICA—SK."

To the merchant ship's operator, the Coast Guard added, "HOLD FAST—VL WE WILL MAKE EYEBALL CONTACT WITH YOU IN 5 MINUTES—SK."

An immediate reply from the threatened vessel followed. "R—THE SUB IS PREPARING TO DIVE. I REPEAT—THE JAPANESE SUB IS PREPARING TO DIVE!—SK."

The relief evident in Sammy Chan's "fist" brought satisfied grins to Liz and Brad's faces.

"Hot-doggie!" Brad leaped from his chair, swept a startled Liz into his arms, and broke into an impromptu tango. In the middle of a dip, the door to the radio room flew open. Richard Bellwood's six-foot-five-inch frame filled the entryway. By the scowl on his face, Liz knew her father had jumped to an entirely wrong conclusion.

"Sir!" Brad froze. Liz, still trapped in the dip, grasped Brad's biceps to keep from falling to the floor.

The young radioman stumbled through an explanation as he righted the owner's daughter to her feet. "Did you hear? We just defended the *Vancouver Lady*'s honor, sir." Instantly, Brad realized his words had come out wrong. "I mean, sir, the Coast Guard scared off a Japanese submarine harassing the *Vancouver Lady*."

Richard Bellwood's bushy red eyebrows narrowed into a tight crease. "I know what you mean, young man. However, I would appreciate it if you would unhand my daughter—my married daughter, I might add!"

"Yes, er, yes, of course, sir." The flustered young man returned Liz to her feet, released her waist, and snapped to attention. Bristling at the unspoken implications in her father's voice, Liz shot an angry glare at her father, silently daring him to pursue the subject further. "Was there something you wanted, Dad?"

Taken aback by his elder daughter's brisk tone, Richard sputtered, "Yes, er, Lizzie, your mother insists you come to dinner tonight. Your sister Anne and her fiancé will be there, as will Grandma Keating."

Liz tilted her chin defiantly, sending a sidelong grin at the pale-faced young man quivering by her side. "Brad could use a good home-cooked meal. Couldn't you, Brad? Do you think Mom would mind if I bring a guest?"

Both the company owner and the short, wiry, radio operator stared at her as if she were a cockroach crawling out from under an icebox at midday. Brad nervously pushed his wire-rimmed glasses higher on the bridge of his nose. "No! No! Thanks anyway. Uh, I, uh, I've got, uh, plans tonight. Maybe another time."

A self-satisfied smile crept across Liz's face. She hadn't really imagined Brad would accept her dinner invitation, but she knew the idea of her asking the young man to dinner had irked her father.

"Oh, that's too bad," she cooed. "Grandma Keating would love your W. C. Fields imitation, as well as your impersonations of *The Shadow* and of *The Lone Ranger.* Those are Grandma Keating's favorite radio shows. But maybe you can come to visit another time."

Imitating the sweeping glamour and grace of the radiant Hollywood starlet Loretta Young, Liz tilted her chin upward, flipped her cascade of titian curls away from her neck, and breezed out of the radio room. Once she knew she was beyond the two men's vision, she took a deep breath and rushed down the corridor to what she jokingly called her "inner sanctum."

Since her father didn't employ many women beyond the necessary secretarial staff, the pink-and-white-tiled ladies' room had always afforded her a modicum of privacy. Whenever tempers flared or egos clashed in the radio room, which sometimes happened, she would wait out the storm in what she thought of as her porcelain retreat.

As a teenager, working summers for her father, she'd once camped out in the ladies' room for thirty minutes to avoid the unwanted attentions of a love-struck college radio apprentice. It was here where she'd retreated following her first kiss; where she'd wept before leaving home for college; where she'd contemplated Alan's marriage proposal; and where she had released pent-up tears after losing her son. But on this soggy November morning in 1941, it was here she finally generated the courage to read Alan's letter and when, after reading it, her heart seemed to stop beating.

# Chapter 2: Blizzard Conditions

*When you have to make a choice and don't make it, that is in itself a choice.*
*—William James*

## Whittier, Alaska: November 1941

Captain Alan Ames started awake at the off-key shrill outside his bedroom window—morning reveille. His dream of fishing for salmon on the Columbia River evaporated into reality. Numbed by too little sleep, Alan's mind scrambled to identify his surroundings—Alaska! He squinted at his bedside clock—5:00 A.M.

"Five more minutes, please. Just five more minutes!" He groaned, rolled over and plastered a second pillow against his exposed ear. Outside the ice-coated window beside his bed, the nonstop roar of the wind accompanied a second rendition of the hated wake-up call.

Alan could hear the grumbling and swearing of the sleepy inhabitants beyond the flimsy plywood wall separating his eight-foot-square officer's quarters from the other men in the austere, makeshift barracks. Now fully awake, he dashed for the officers' showers. He knew the warm water would quickly turn frigid once the men began taking their showers.

*What am I doing here?* he asked himself for the thousandth time, as a stream of rusty, tepid water sprayed down on his military-cut hair. Months earlier in Seattle, the idea of joining the Army Corps of Engineers had sounded exciting to the young civil engineer. At that time, he would have done anything to escape the restraints of his marriage to Liz. No matter how irrational he knew his thinking had become, Alan couldn't erase the conviction that if Liz had properly cared for their son, Lanny still would be alive. His own mother had always been there for him, not gallivanting off to some job. Was it too much to wish the same for his son?

The family didn't need Liz's salary. While the Pacific Northwest had been hit especially hard by the Great Depression, especially his father-in-law's maritime industry, Alan, a civil engineer, had been in great demand by the government's recovery process.

The subzero wind howled around the corners of the shower tent and seeped through the tiniest of slits in the canvas. Alan ran the scratchy, military-issued towel over his shivering, bare skin until his chest and thighs glowed a healthy pink.

Shipping out to Alaska had not been his goal as he slogged his way through basic training and then qualified for officers' school in the Army Corps of Engineers. An army recruitment officer in Seattle had assured him when he enlisted that, with his engineering degree, Alan would be able to cherry-pick his assignments. *Cherry-pick—right!* Alan groaned.

He'd barely completed his training when he found himself on a troop train heading for Seattle. *What irony,* he thought. *Right back where I started.* Upon reaching the city, he resisted the temptation to call Liz. Simmering anger and niggling guilt outweighed his growing desire to hear her voice. A pelting spray of icy rain forced Alan to raise the collar of his peacoat as the troop ship glided north, past Bellwood International Import/Export Ltd. He glanced toward the radio-room window, hoping to catch a glimpse of his estranged wife. Many times since he had left home, Alan had regretted the hasty decision he'd made. For a moment, he wished he could turn back the clock. For an instant, he ached to feel her reassuring arms about his waist and her warm breath tickling his bare chest.

Settling into the routine of army life on the Alaska coast proved to be easier than he had imagined. The nearby, sympathetic ear of a saucy, nineteen-year-old blonde named Trudy helped. With Trudy, Alan found he could relax—no pressure, no grand expectations, no retrospective soul-searching, and no recriminations. These few moments of escape made the long days overseeing the backbreaking work of digging a tunnel through a mountain of granite more bearable to the confused young captain.



As the lead field engineer on the tunnel project, Alan knew one miscalculation on his part could bring down the mountain on dozens of workers. That the largest and newest backhoe had broken down for the second time in one week; that the fuel line for his main earth mover froze and cracked again; and that a new storm threatened to slow down the progress on the tunnel faded into insignificance during the few treasured moments he and Trudy shared at the end of each day.

The dimple-cheeked, blond, blue-eyed girl could always tease a smile out of Alan's customarily dour countenance. Alone in his quarters each evening, Alan couldn't shake the fact that as delightfully delicious as Trudy Dahl's attention and attributes may be, he had a wife waiting for him in Seattle. Considering himself an honorable man, Alan knew he must walk a fine line between adultery and innocent flirtation—assuming such a line existed.

# Chapter 3: Family Dinner

*The hardest thing in life is to know which bridge to cross and which to burn.*
*—David Russell*

## Seattle, Washington: November 1941

Liz's pasted-on smile survived the tomatoes stuffed with capers and toasted breadcrumbs; the corn chowder; the oven-warm, whole-wheat rolls with butter; and the seasoned Coho salmon with asparagus spears and baby carrots alongside. Despite the jazz of Duke Ellington coming from the console radio in the parlor, the tortured woman wondered how long she could keep the mask in place in spite of the throbbing pain in her heart. A quick glimpse at herself in the mirror above her mother's highly polished mahogany buffet revealed what Liz already suspected. Her eyes were red; her face, pale and gaunt; and her expression, haunted. Most of her curls had escaped the snood at the nape of her neck.

The family members gathered around Kay Bellwood's elegantly appointed dinner table pretended not to notice. But Liz knew they had. Sooner or later someone, probably her mother, would comment on how "tired" Liz appeared, a polite way of saying the young woman looked less than her usual spiffy self. And then, Katherine would scold Richard for overworking their daughter. Yet despite her mother's concern, Liz knew that nothing would upset Katherine Bellwood more than revealing the family's imperfections in front of a non–family member like Fred, fiancé of her younger sister Anne. The arrival of Alan's letter would definitely fit into her mother's imperfection category.

Grandma Keating's presence at the table was Liz's only hope of surviving the evening. Liz could depend on her grandmother, a retired college writing teacher, to entertain family and guests alike with tales of her latest outrageous antics, which effectively kept the attention off her distraught granddaughter. How the woman could be so intelligent and still manage to get tangled in so many bizarre situations was a mystery to the entire family. Personally, Liz believed the humor was in her grandmother's gift of artful storytelling more than the events being reported. Wispy gray curls haloed the older woman's animated face. Sea-green eyes danced above the pair of half-glasses perched on the tip of her nose.

"Imagine my embarrassment when I went to smooth the back of my skirt before sitting down at my desk and found no skirt to smooth! You wouldn't believe it. I'd traipsed the entire length of the main corridor of the college and into a classroom of aspiring writers with the back of my skirt firmly tucked into the waistband of my baby blue silk undergarments!" The gray-haired professor leaned forward, her dinner fork and her punch line balanced like a baton in the hand of an orchestra conductor. "The moment was a bit too cheeky for my taste."

"Mother! We have a guest dining with us tonight." At the older woman's earthy reference to a human body part, Katherine nervously dotted her lips with her linen table napkin and rolled her eyes toward the blushing young man seated next to her younger daughter.

"Bosh! Fred is about to become a member of the family, aren't you, son?" Grandma cast a smart, satisfied grin toward the embarrassed young man, who promptly choked on a spear of asparagus. "You need to know what kind of a family you are joining, right?"

Even though Grandma Keating was Katherine's own mother, the uptight hostess cast an imploring "do something" glance toward Richard, seated at the far end of the table and sputtering with laughter. Poor Anne giggled nervously into her napkin.

"Grandma! You're making this up!" Liz gasped. She could vividly imagine the students' reactions to her grandmother's embarrassing dilemma.

"I most certainly am not," Grandma defended.

"What did you do next, Grandma?" Anne asked.



"Anne, stop encouraging her!" Katherine interjected in a stage whisper. But Grandma Keating did not relinquish her stage time.

"I've discovered I can learn valuable lessons from every painful or embarrassing experience in my life." Grandma Keating glanced toward Liz. "My lesson in this instance is, I now check the back of my skirt before I exit the ladies' facilities."

Liz laughed aloud, despite her mother's displeasure. She'd also caught her precious grandmother's subliminal message. "And then, what did you do, Grandma?"

"I laughed at myself, straightened my confounded skirt, of course, and proceeded to teach my class. What else could I do?"

"And your writing assignment for the class that day must have been to write about 'Your Most Embarrassing Moment'?" Liz's dad's shoulders heaved with laughter.

"You are right, dear Richard. I couldn't pass up a made-to-order teaching opportunity, now could I?" Grandma Keating shot him an impish grin.

Determined to change the conversation to a more refined topic, the forever-gracious Katherine produced the practiced smile of a thousand hostesses who'd found themselves trapped in such an awkward moment. "Is anyone ready for dessert?" she asked. "Tonight you have a choice of either Gertie's famous boysenberry tarts or her equally delicious lemon meringue pie."

Over the years, Gertie, the Bellwood's live-in cook, housekeeper, and all-around confidante, had cared for the two girls while Katherine indulged in her passion for charity work. Round and cuddly, Gertie owned more calico Mother Hubbard aprons than Liz's mother owned silk dresses imported from France. After living twenty years in America, Gertie still spoke with a heavy German accent. During her teenage years, Liz had tried to correct the woman's pronunciation of words to no avail. However, the woman's baking skills were phenomenal in any language. The only foods more delicious than her buttery, flaky piecrusts were her weekly batch of chewy oatmeal-raisin cookies. As Gertie patiently waited to take requests, the Swiss-made grandfather clock in the hallway gonged seven times.

"Oh, Mama," Anne dabbed her lips with her napkin. "Fred and I really must leave. We have tickets to the symphony. They're performing Debussy tonight, my favorite." Anne turned toward her crestfallen fiancé, who obviously preferred a piece of Gertie's lemon meringue pie to the composer's "Quartet in G Minor." Copying her mother's placating tone, the girl patted her fiancé's hand. "Don't worry, darling. After the concert, we'll slip home for a piece of pie."

Katherine smiled indulgently. "Fred, I'll have Gertie pack a few boysenberry tarts for you to take home as well."

The resigned young man nodded a grateful thank-you, rose to his feet, and assisted Anne from her chair.

"Have fun, you two," Grandma called as the couple disappeared beyond the dining room doors. "Give old Debussy my love. I do so remember our weekend together in Minsk . . ."

"Mother! Claude Debussy was a little before your time!" Katherine chided.

"Are you sure, my child?" Grandma teased. "I had a life before you were born, you know."

Katherine waited until the dining room doors closed behind the couple and then leaned forward, both elbows on the table. "And now, Elizabeth, what is going on? Your father said he walked into the radio room and found you and Bradley in a compromising, er, situation. And what about the letter from Alan?"

Liz's face deepened to the shade of a ripe pomegranate. This was the moment she'd dreaded. How predictable for her mother to mention Brad's impromptu dance before asking about the letter. The young woman glanced toward her grandmother for rescue. Grandma Keating's face was wreathed with concern, but she remained silent. With no one coming to her rescue, Liz took a deep breath.

"First, Dad walked into the radio room when Brad became a little overexuberant after a Japanese sub backed off from the *Vancouver Lady.* That's all. A quick, two-step tango—nothing more to it."

Dad cleared his throat. "That boy doesn't know how close he came to being fired for that little shenanigan!"

"Daddy! Don't you dare! Brad's a peach of a guy. He's never been anything but a gentleman with me, I assure you. In fact, he's like a little brother." Liz set her jaw in defiance.

Richard held his ground. "Bradley is a man, not a boy! And he has an obvious crush on you, Elizabeth. I see it even if you don't."

"Your father's right, Elizabeth," Katherine continued. "A woman in your position must guard against possible rumors. You are a married woman, even if your spouse is gallivanting off who knows where. You vowed, 'till death do us part.' " She paused meaningfully and raised an eyebrow.

Liz dropped her head. A loose curl tumbled forward, teasing the left side of her face. "Mama, I am keenly aware of the vows I made before God when I said 'I do.' "

"In our family, a married couple works out their problems—together. They don't run away from them!" she continued. "You aren't considering divorce, are you? Has Alan given you, uh, biblical grounds for divorce?" Katherine could barely think, let alone speak of the possibility of adultery.

Liz stared down at the curl of whipping cream atop the slice of lemon meringue pie Gertie had set before her. How could the distraught young woman tell her prim and proper mother, a proud member of Seattle's higher society, about the contents of Alan's letter?

Grandma Keating laid a comforting hand on her granddaughter's forearm. "Now, Katherine, be kind. Lizzie hasn't betrayed her marriage vows. Liz isn't a teenager to berate for kissing a pimple-face boy on the porch swing. She's a twenty-six-year-old woman who can deal with her own marriage as she sees fit."

"Thank you, Grandma." Liz's voice broke. "But sooner or later you'll all need to know." She took a deep breath. "Today I received a letter from Alan, the first since he left. It seems he's been sent to Alaska, of all places."

Katherine snorted in disbelief. "Alaska? What's in Alaska besides snow, igloos, and salmon? Smells fishy to me!"

"Now, Katherine, it is possible . . ." Her father cast a compassionate glance toward his elder daughter. "The government is concerned that the Japanese aggression will spread north to the Bering Sea and the Aleutian Islands. Their subs and their patrol boats are constantly harassing our merchant ships. My guess is they are building roads or something to move troops and equipment along the Pacific coastline."

Katherine tightened her lips and sniffed. Her eyes hardened as they always did whenever Richard sided with one of their daughters instead of with her. Noting the silent battle between her parents, Liz took a deep breath. *I can make it through the evening—one way or another.* She glanced toward her mother. *What a way to end the day.* From the moment the mail carrier delivered Alan's letter, Liz felt like she'd fallen into the vortex of a deadly maelstrom.

"What did your husband say, Elizabeth, dear?" Grandma urged.

"He's met a woman named Trudy." Liz's voice broke.

"Trudy?" Katherine demanded. "Men!"

"Katherine, you are leaping to unwarranted conclusions." Grandma's voice remained patient and calm, as if she were instructing a freshman English student on the correct tense of a verb. "I believe Liz said Alan only mentioned meeting a woman named Trudy. That hardly implies a sordid, Hollywood-style love affair."

Like a teenager being corrected in front of friends, Katherine's eyes flashed with fury. "Where there's smoke, there's usually fire, Mother! Just the fact that Alan mentioned the woman means there's more to their relationship than casually conversing with the proprietor of the local general store! Certainly, even you find it suspicious that the first letter Liz receives from her husband in seven months mentions another woman."

"Actually, you may be right, Mother." Liz inhaled deeply. "Alan wrote that if I want a divorce, he'd gladly give me legal cause, which, to me, implies he might not have done so as yet. At least, that's what I'd like to think."

"Oh my!" Katherine patted her lips with her napkin. "This happens only in other people's families, not to the Bellwoods."

"Bellwoods or not." Liz flipped her napkin onto the table. "What does it actually matter? Alan wants a divorce. He suggested I could get a six-week 'quickie' divorce either in Mexico or in Reno, Nevada."

"He's probably right, honey," Richard began. "I presume his reference to legal cause implies adultery charges, since a divorce other than in Nevada is possible only for adultery, physical abuse, or desertion, the latter which takes seven years to establish."

"Nevada? Quickie divorce? Adultery? Listen to the both of you!" Katherine's face suffused with color. "The women in our family do not divorce their men!" She turned to Grandma Keating. "Tell her, Mother! When John lost his job at the lumber mill during the Great Depression and left my sister Lydia and their five children to fend for themselves, Lydia didn't run out and file divorce papers. And she stuck it out until he returned home. At one point, she picked gooseberries to keep food on the table for those children. If it hadn't been for your father's largess . . ."

Richard stiffened; his eyes narrowed. "Katherine!"

But the woman barely noticed. "And then there's your second cousin,

Sissy. Why that woman traipsed after her husband Ralph from Seattle to Wichita, east to Baltimore, and back to Albuquerque. They lived in a twenty-foot house trailer, hauled behind a rusty Model A Ford. Their baby daughter Helen slept in a wooden crate in the backseat between stacks of spare automobile tires in case of flats."

At the mention of her cousin's baby, a razor-sharp knife blade sliced through the last of Liz's self-control. If Alan had asked her, she would have followed him to the Atlantic and beyond. For him, she would have lived in a canvas tent in the north woods. But he hadn't asked. She buried her face in her hands.

"Katherine, how can you be so insensitive!" Grandma wrapped her arms around her granddaughter's shoulders. "To bring up Sissy's baby! You obviously haven't a clue how devastating it is to lose a child, and now, possibly lose a husband as well." She tenderly held the sobbing woman. "There, there, honey. Katherine, when your ten-year-old brother Manny died in the quarry accident, I thought I'd die too. Do you know I still have nightmares of being buried under a rockslide—forty-five years after the fact?" Grandma stroked the younger woman's tousle of curls and cooed like a mother dove comforting her young. "Even today, every ten-year-old boy I see brings pain to my heart."

Katherine sniffed into her napkin. "I'm sorry, Mother. I didn't mean to hurt you or my daughter. I was only trying to—to— Oh, obviously, I can't do anything right in this family!" The woman leaped to her feet and fled from the table.

Liz's dad stared after his weeping wife and then back at Liz. "I'm sorry, Liz. Your mother didn't mean to hurt you. You know that, don't you? Katherine lives in a world of black and white; right and wrong; there are no shades of gray in her thinking." He heaved a sigh. "The important thing you must remember is that she loves you deeply. I know your mother. Whatever you decide to do, she'll become your strongest supporter. And now, if you ladies will excuse me, I need to go and comfort her."

Grandma Keating waved away Liz's father. "Go. You have always been able to reason with Katherine better than I." Without a word, Grandma helped Liz from the table and led her into the parlor. "Come, child, sit on the sofa beside me. My honey-bunny, you've been carrying much too heavy a burden for far too long."

To have Grandma Keating call her by her endearing childhood nickname brought a fresh round of tears. Liz crumpled into her grandmother's arms and sobbed. For more than an hour, her grandmother listened as Liz wept over the loss of Lanny, the death of her marriage, and the demise of her dreams. Finally, the young woman ran out of tears.

"I don't know what to do, Grandma. This isn't how I pictured my life to be. All I ever wanted was a vine-covered cottage, three perfect children, and a husband who loved and cared for me. When I met Alan, I thought I would have that and more. What went wrong?"

Grandma brushed the curls away from Liz's moist face. "Life went wrong, my dear. Life seldom plays by the rules we imagine. Life just happens. Jesus promised that in this world there would be troubles."

"Well, He was certainly right about that!" Liz knew little about Jesus Christ. She'd celebrated the Christmas Baby born in a manger, and the Man who had been martyred on a Roman cross, but that was the limit of her interest and her knowledge.

"Here! You read the letter." Liz shoved the crumpled envelope into her grandmother's wrinkled hands. "Read it and tell me what to do. Should I encourage Alan to commit adultery so I have legal cause for seeking a divorce? Or should I stick to my knitting and wait for him to come to his senses?" She threw her head back against the sofa and stared at the ceiling. "But what if he never does? I don't want to spend the rest of my life alone. Maybe I should forget our marriage ever existed." She covered her eyes with her hands. "Maybe I just married the wrong guy."

"Wait, wait, wait a minute, darling, while you are married to Alan, he is the only man for you—not the right man, not the wrong man, but the only man. That's what marriage is about—fidelity." Grandma handed Liz one of the lace-edged embroidered handkerchiefs the older woman kept tucked in the bosom of her silk-flowered dress. "As to what you should do next, only you and God can decide that, my dear—not your mother, not your father, not even me. Remember what Great-Great-Grandma Harris used to say, 'Only the spoon knows what's in the kettle'? No one outside your marriage really knows what you should do."

Liz sat up and blew her nose on the embroidered hankie. "But I thought your Bible spoke against divorce?"

"My Bible? It's your Bible too, you know. Jesus did speak about divorce. He said that 'because of your hardened hearts, you may divorce in the case of infidelity.' And for the most part, the laws of our country uphold that principle."

"What about this Trudy person? You said I shouldn't jump to a conclusion regarding her, but what other conclusion is there? Besides, if I encourage Alan to commit adultery with this woman, wouldn't I be sinning as well, by aiding and abetting?"

"Good question, my dear." Grandma pursed her lips thoughtfully. "But first you need to decide whether or not you want to repair your marriage."

"Yes, yes, I do."

"Right now, it looks as if you have only a partial picture of the situation, kind of like one of my favorite jigsaw puzzles of Mount Rainier. Sounds like you need to locate the missing pieces before you can get a clear picture of what you are facing."

Liz shook her head and sighed. "Look at Alan's letter. How am I supposed to fit all the puzzle pieces together from that one page? What would you do?"

Grandma Keating took Liz's face in her hands. "You're a resourceful young woman. If I were you, the first thing I'd do is ask God for wisdom. I know He'll guide you. He does me."

"But, Grandma, your God doesn't always make things clear . . ."

"My God? He wants to be your God, too, honey-bunny. He makes the important things abundantly clear. If you ask Him, you will know what to do when the time is right." Grandma Keating kissed her granddaughter on the cheek. "In the meantime, I need a slice of Gertie's lemon meringue pie. How about you?"

# Chapter 4: Face-off on Maynard Mountain

*Winter must be cold for those with no warm memories.*
*—Terry McKay*

## Whittier, Alaska: November 1941

Captain Alan Ames focused his binoculars on the seven men, suspended on ropes, chipping away at the face of Mount Maynard. Shards of granite fell earthward like hail to the syncopated cadence of the hammering pick axes. The sound reverberated across the valley floor of the Chugach National Forest. Junior officer of the army's 177th Engineering Corps, Alan shook his head in disgust. *Whoever said, "There's a right way and a wrong way and the army's way," couldn't have been more correct,* Alan thought.

"Facing off" the surface stone of the mountain had proven to be a more difficult task than the elite Army Corps survey team from Washington, D.C., had calculated. Laying fourteen miles of track and opening a tunnel through a couple of mountains hadn't seemed like much of a problem when viewed on a wall map in some three-star-general's Washington office. Faced with a combination of unrealistic goals, poor planning, and Alaska's short building season, along with the inevitable strife between the Army Corps of Engineers and the civilian construction firm the government flew in from Boston, Massachusetts, they had tunneled less than one hundred feet into the mountain.

The young engineer glanced down at the campsite below—if one could call a barely cleared and leveled airstrip, a couple of army Quonset huts, a cluster of tents, and a couple of plywood shacks a campsite. He sighed. Alan was exhausted; his men were exhausted. Even the citizens of the small town of Whittier that had been chosen to be the terminus for the railroad spur were exhausted.

To survive in the unfriendly terrain, "tunnelers," as the workers were called, had needed to develop the skills of longshoremen, carpenters, seamen, and architects before the digging could begin. The army and the civilian population of Whittier had worked around the clock to build an adequate loading dock for unloading supply ships at what would be the beginning of the railhead. But no matter how hard or how fast or how long the men worked, the certainty of a fast-approaching winter of heavy snows and brutal subzero temperatures loomed in everyone's minds, especially in the mind of Captain Ames.

Alan had to admit that running off to join the army no longer seemed like a very mature way to handle his marital problems—kind of like a kid running away to join the circus. And being assigned to the wilds of Alaska wasn't how he had envisioned his military experience to begin. *Building airport runways on tropical islands in the Pacific would have been nice,* he thought, *but no. I have to land an impossible assignment in the wilds of Alaska!*

Alan became a civil engineer partly because he enjoyed outdoor life. As a child, he loved hiking in the backcountry of eastern Oregon and Washington. *How unlike Liz,* he thought. For her, "roughing it" was anything short of a stay at the European-inspired Mayflower Park Hotel in downtown Seattle. Taking a stroll on Mercer Island was her idea of adventure, that and a night listening to jazz greats at Seattle's Jackson Street. *At this moment, even I'd welcome the comforts of a luxury honeymoon suite overlooking Puget Sound,* he admitted. He tucked his leather-gloved hands beneath his armpits and turned his back on the incessant wind.

Alan had studied the history of the army's tunnel project. Years earlier, Otto Ohlson had proposed a route through Maynard Mountain as a shortcut to a deep-water port. But the railroad manager's plans got lost in the army's dusty archives until 1941. With a warring Japan less than a leap across the straits from the Aleutian Islands, the military geniuses in Washington realized the present railway between Anchorage and Seward would be a prime target for saboteurs.

The U.S. Army needed a shipping facility protected from the open sea. Also, the existing railway's roadbed between Anchorage and Seward with its wooden bridges, numerous tunnels, and steep grades through the Kenai Mountains slowed supply trains to a crawl and was too remote for the army to protect and maintain. The proposed route to Anchorage through Maynard Mountain would be seventy miles shorter and would terminate at a protected port, decreasing the exposure of American ships to Japanese subs. On paper, the plan looked ideal.

In March 1941, the Department of the Interior appropriated $5.3 million to build the proposed rail tunnels, fourteen miles of track, and the terminus site in Whittier. By April, 151 men, 137 military, had hiked from Turnagain Arm to Whittier to begin the project of clearing a trail through the brush and trees up the side of Mount Maynard. In late August, Alan arrived in time for the "face-off" of the surface stone on the proposed Maynard tunnel.

The twenty-seven-year-old engineer tapped the tunnel's rolled-up blueprints against a nearby boulder. Mulling his discontent, Alan didn't hear the crunch of military boots on the loose rocks until his commanding officer, Colonel Anton Anderson, stood directly behind him.

"Hello, Captain!" The project's lead engineer, who measured his words with precision, stepped up beside him.

"Sir." Alan snapped a proper salute.

"What progress is your crew making this morning?" The officer raised his binoculars to his eyes to study the workmen dangling on ropes off the face of the mountain.

"About the same as yesterday, sir. We should finish facing off by Friday."

"Friday?" The colonel shook his head. "That's not what I was hoping to hear, Captain Ames. We've got to dig that tunnel portal and construct a protective snowshed before the first snow falls!"

"Yes, sir." Alan had heard all this before. Anderson did tend to repeat such information as if instructing grade-schoolers.

"The local people say that by the end of the month, the snow will pile deep at the foot of the mountain. Without a snowshed, access to the tunnel will be blocked 'til spring."

"Yes, sir."

"With winter storms looming, I'm thinking of working teams round the clock on twelve-hour shifts." Lowering his binoculars, Colonel Anderson ran his tongue along the inside of his left cheek and rocked back on his heels. "What do you think?"

Alan lifted one eyebrow. "Is that wise, sir? The men are exhausted."

"I know. But I have those whining Boston Beaners breathing down my neck at every turn. Just because they constructed a subway system through downtown Boston, the United States government thinks these city slickers can complete similar projects up here in the north woods." The officer snarled. "Always complaining about something, they are. Cheeky too. If you ask me, they just keep getting in the way of real progress."

"Yes, sir." *Boston Beaners? City slickers?* Alan smirked at the Colonel's use of colloquialisms.

The colonel focused his binoculars on the workmen a second time and shook his head. "Another thing, Captain, I don't like the number of breakdowns we've had on the equipment lately. Something's fishy in Denmark, if you ask me. Could be sabotage."

"Sabotage, sir?" Alan shot a quick glance toward his superior.

The colonel again remained silent for several seconds. "Sabotage. The evidence points to sabotage instead of simple chance."

Alan had to admit that the thought wasn't new to him either. "But who, sir? Who would—"

"The Japanese, perhaps. Also, we have several Aleuts on base who might object to our desecrating their sacred mountain. And what about that Dahl fella? Do you think he might purposely try to slow down progress on the tunnel by sabotaging the big rigs?"

"Oh, no sir. Mr. Dahl is as trustworthy as they come, sir."

The colonel grinned. "Well, if anyone should know, I guess you would, with all the time you're spending with his daughter."

"I—er—uh . . ." Alan floundered; his face reddened.

"Repeatedly over the years, I've seen that little flirtations can be damaging even to strong marriages." He rocked back on his heels and asked, "You are married, aren't you, son?"

"Er, yes, sir."

"Thought so. A word to the wise should be sufficient. As to the possible sabotage, keep on the lookout for strange coincidences or any unusual behavior."

"Yes, sir."

"I'm depending on you, Ames." The colonel turned on his heel and headed back down the path to the camp base.

"Yes, sir." *That was a strange conversation,* Alan mused. How out of character it was for the spit-and-polish army colonel to give personal advice to a subordinate officer. Alan blew warmth into his gloved hands. *If it's this cold in November, how cold will it be come January?*

# Chapter 5: The Journey North

*Man proposes; God disposes.*
*—Thomas à Kempis*

## Seattle, Washington: November 1941

Liz agreed, under duress, to spend the night at her parents' home. The hours dragged by: Liz couldn't sleep, couldn't cry, couldn't pray. Instead of reaching the throne of God, her prayers bounced off the ceiling of her pink-and-white childhood bedroom. The distraught young woman heard no voice from heaven telling her what to do, and she saw no message written on her mirror giving her instructions. One undeniable fact, however, was clear to her with the arrival of daylight: she knew she couldn't make a rational decision without filling in the missing pieces to her strained marriage. She determined she wouldn't give up on her marriage without a fight—Trudy or no Trudy.

Perhaps it was the cocoon of innocence Liz stepped into when she entered her childhood bedroom; perhaps it was the Baby Ruth candy bar wrappers and love notes pressed between the pages of her college yearbooks; perhaps it was the bridal shower invitation in the lingerie drawer alongside the crumbling orchid bouquet from her wedding day. Whatever the reason, Liz emerged from her childhood bedroom the next morning with a plan.

By the time Liz arrived at her parents' dining room for breakfast, the table was set with French rose-print Limoges china. The crystal goblets filled with ice water and a slice of lemon testified that Gertie had been working on the family's breakfast since before dawn. Liz waited until Gertie had placed a stack of freshly made pancakes on each plate before making her announcement.

"You want to do what?" Richard Bellwood's baritone voice bellowed. "Are you crazy? A woman can't go traipsing off alone to the wilds of Alaska! And at this time of year! That's rough territory up there."

"Dad, I'll be fine. I can handle myself, I assure you." While Liz maintained an exterior of confidence and control, inside she quivered like a skinny first-grader on the first day of school. Reason told her that Father was right. Traipsing off to Alaska, as he put it, had to be one of her more harebrained ideas; yet she knew it was the only way she could learn whether her marriage could survive.

Fork in one hand and a knife poised over Gertie's syrupy blueberry pancakes, Richard Bellwood stared at his older daughter in total disbelief. "Where did you get this crazy idea?"

"Well, Grandma Keating . . ."

"Your Grandmother Keating! I should have known!" He jammed his fork into a square of pancake, stuffed it into his mouth, and chewed vigorously. Before he could swallow, Liz's mother swept into the room, her electric-blue caftan wafting behind her.

"Grandma Keating? What has my mother done this time?" the woman asked.

Dad leaped to his feet to seat his wife. "Your mother has put a cockamamie idea in our daughter's head to go to Alaska to confront Alan!"

Always deaf to her surroundings, Gertie entered the room and poured steaming hot herbal tea into Katherine's china teacup. The woman had been privy to numerous family feuds. She knew they'd "kiss and make up" in the end. They always did.

"My mother did what?"

Liz concentrated on steadying her hand as she poured the hot maple syrup over her stack of pancakes. "No, Daddy. No, Mother. That's not what happened. Grandma merely suggested I not make any hasty moves until I had gathered all the facts. Staying here in Seattle is not going to give them to me." Liz carefully set the pitcher of syrup on its saucer. "Actually, it was you, Mom, who reminded me that the women in our family don't quit and run without a fight."

"I—I—I didn't mean that you should . . ." Katherine sputtered. Liz swallowed a devilish grin. Her mother was seldom at a loss for words.

"I know. I know." Liz heaved a sigh. She hated to cause pain for two of the most important people in her life, but in this case, pain was inevitable. "I can't leave things between Alan and me in limbo. I need to know for certain if there's any hope for us—for our marriage."

"Darling, be reasonable. Alaska is no place for a lady. They say there are seven men to every woman." Katherine shot her elder daughter her best you-know-what-that-means look.

Knowing her next remarks would draw blood between her parents, Liz paused a moment before continuing. "Mother, I grew up around men at the docks. I know how to take care of myself."

"Richard! See! I knew it! It's your fault! You raised her to be the son you never had, and now, now look at the results. Who knows what those low-life longshoremen taught our innocent little daughter!"

"Mother!" Liz clicked her tongue in disgust. She tapped the edge of her plate with her spoon. "Those longshoremen put this expensive china on your table. They've been nothing short of gentlemanly at all times, I assure you!"

"Richard, do something!" Katherine's hands fluttered as if she were drying her nail polish.

Liz's father leaned threateningly across the table toward his daughter. "I won't allow it!"

"You won't allow it?" Liz leaped to her feet. "I am a married woman of twenty-six, which is adequately above the age of consent in all forty-eight states, I believe!"

"I'll fire you! I am your boss, you know." When he pounded the table with his fist, her mother's favorite sugar bowl jumped in response.

"No, you won't, because I'll quit first!" Liz set her jaw in the best Bellwood tradition. Two sets of stormy gray eyes flashed across the table at one another. Liz was the first to give.

"Please understand, Daddy, this is something I must do. I need your help and support, not your censure." Her voice faltered. "As far as money is concerned, I have plenty in my savings account." When she called him Daddy, Richard softened.

"It isn't the money. You know it isn't the money." He swallowed hard and sank into his chair. She watched as her father considered her words.

After a long pause, he stated, "I have always been here for you. And I always will be." He studied her eyes for several seconds. "When do you plan to leave? You couldn't have picked a worse time to travel to Alaska—what with winter storms and all. And I'll have to get someone to fill in for you until you return."

"Well, I'm certainly not postponing my trip until spring. By then, Alan and this Trudy person might have disappeared into the wilderness. As for finding a replacement for me, Brad would be a great supervisor. He's faithful and loyal to a fault. Oh yeah, Daddy, if you could help me close up my house before I go, I would appreciate it."

"I can take care of that for you, Princess. I just wish I could go with you. But with that big shipment coming in from Bombay, and another from Turkey . . ." He glanced toward his wife and noted the fear in her eyes.

Katherine hesitated for a moment. Liz could read the conflict on her mother's face. "I suppose I could clear my social calendar to go with you, honey."

Knowing how much Katherine hated boating of any kind, even during good weather, Liz giggled. "It's all right, Daddy, Mama. This is something I have to do alone, I'm afraid. Besides, I have no idea how soon I'll be able to return to Seattle, bad weather and all. I'm hoping to be back before Christmas."

Katherine heaved a relieved sigh.

Her father gently touched Liz's forearm. "I'm sorry, Princess. I don't like letting you down."

"No, Daddy, you aren't letting me down. I really do believe in what I am about to do. I have to give Alan and my marriage one last chance."

Richard cleared his throat. Tears glistened in his eyes. "The least I can do is book you on the Alaska Steamship Company's *Sitka Sue*. It's not a luxury liner, but the accommodations will cover your basic needs. I know the captain. He'll take good care of you. Plus, I'll pay you to deliver a packet of contracts to my representative in Whittier."

"Oh, Daddy, thank you!" Liz leaped to her feet and wrapped her arms around his neck. "You are the best father in the whole world." She straightened. "And Mama, you are so precious too. Your offer is truly appreciated, but don't worry, I'll be OK. I won't do anything stupid, I promise. So, how soon can I leave, Daddy?"

"If this isn't stupid enough," he mumbled under his breath. "The sooner the better, I would think, considering the storm patterns at this time of year." Richard knitted his brow. "*Hmm,* let's see, today is November 16. The *Sitka Sue* is scheduled to sail on the twentieth."

"I can do that." A jolt of adrenaline shot through Liz. Her eyes brightened. While the trip to Alaska wouldn't be a luxury cruise, finally coming face to face with Alan and working out their future encouraged her.

★ ★ ★ ★ ★

The early Thanksgiving celebration proved to be a solemn occasion for the Bellwood family. Even Gertie couldn't suppress her tears as she served her famous pumpkin pies topped with thick whipped cream. Later that evening, the family gathered in the parlor to listen to President Roosevelt's weekly address. They were encouraged to know that the nation was staying neutral in the growing conflict. That Japan's ambassador had arrived in Washington to negotiate peace talks between the two countries canceled any doubts Liz's father might have had regarding a change in policy.

As Liz drove home to her and Alan's little cottage, she questioned whether the long journey to Alaska would be worth it. Would it actually save her marriage? Was there a marriage left to save? *Yet, doing something is far better than just waiting for life to happen,* she decided.

The next morning, heavy storm clouds threatened to dump their contents on the city as the Bellwood family, Grandma Keating, and Gertie gathered at Pier 17 to see Liz off on the *Sitka Sue.* With trepidation, Liz eyed the small ocean-going freighter loaded with foodstuff and household goods for Anchorage. It was nowhere near the "looker" of any of her father's ships. She shook her head and sighed. *In for a penny; in for a pound.*

From the *Sitka Sue*'s narrow, paint-chipped deck, Liz waved goodbye to her loved ones. As the ship eased away from the pier, self-doubts arose. *Is this the beginning of a fool's errand? If Alan's love for me has dissolved to the point where he would suggest divorce, what hope can there be for our marriage? No!* Liz told herself firmly. *It's not like I'm leaving Seattle forever,* she reminded herself. *At the latest, I'll be home before Christmas.*

Creature comforts aboard the *Sitka Sue* were meager at best. Yet Liz was grateful to find that the closet-sized stateroom had a fold-up cot, a four-drawer chest, a straight-backed wooden chair, a private toilet, and a sink. When Liz opened her leather suitcase and found a small Bible atop her yellow-daisy flannel pajamas, a weepy smile crossed her face. "Grandma," she whispered.

Liz spent the first hours at sea shivering beneath a scratchy wool blanket on her narrow cot. Feeling chilled, she donned two pair of wool stockings under her brown wool snow pants and added a bulky brown tweed overcoat. She pulled a hand-knitted wool cloche on her head and slipped out of her stateroom onto the deck. Sharp, needle-piercing ice crystals pelted her face as she watched the freighter maneuver the fjords and islands along the coast.

Liz filled her days by pacing the deck of the *Sitka Sue,* retiring to her quarters to read the underlined passages in her grandmother's Bible, or taking short, fitful naps. Night after night, she faced the cold northwesterly winds and stared into the darkness. Docking at Ketchikan brought memories of her first trip to Alaska, one she'd taken with her father. Standing at the railing, she could almost hear her dad's voice regaling her with stories about his first excursion to what the Aleuts called "the great land." Liz remembered feeling very grown up at seven years old. He'd called her his little princess. Little princess? Hardly a little princess anymore, at least in her husband's eyes. An unexpected wave of nostalgia washed over her. The disturbing juxtaposition of memories brought fresh tears to her eyes, which instantly froze on her cheeks.

Liz breathed into her fur-lined leather gloves to warm her fingers. The tip of her nose stung from the biting temperatures, and her nose started to run. She reached into an overcoat pocket for a handkerchief and asked herself the same three questions she'd asked herself countless times: *Is the failure of my marriage my fault? Could I have saved Lanny's life? Could I have done more to help Alan open up to me?*

With the Ketchikan freight unloaded, the *Sitka Sue*'s powerful engines growled to life once more and continued northward. When the dinner bell sounded, Liz reluctantly made her way to the mess hall. As the only female on board, she sensed that her presence dampened the crew's usual camaraderie. While Captain Clark and First Mate Jake Mendota attempted to engage her in conversation, Liz knew both men found the task difficult. As a result, she would swallow her meal as quickly as possible and escape to her cabin. Later, after the crew disappeared to their posts, she'd resume her nightly haunting of the deck with her ever-present companion—guilt.

By the time the *Sitka Sue* docked at Skagway, Liz was eager to use her land legs once again. Ramshackle gambling halls, garishly painted brothels, and boarded-up bars—ghosts of the Klondike Gold Rush of 1897—dotted the small community. Fighting the stiff breeze as she walked along the main street, Liz recalled why the native tribes had named Skagway the "windy place with white-capped water." Chilled, despite her heavy, wool coat and leather boots, she ducked into a general store. Along the back wall were shelves of used books. As she ran her gloved fingers over the dusty tomes, she found a tattered copy of Jack London's *The Call of the Wild.* She smiled. It had been years since she'd read the adventure classic.

As she placed the book on the scarred wooden counter, a short sprightly man with a grizzled beard, shaggy hair, and gold wire-rimmed glasses perched on the end of his nose popped up from behind a stack of wooden crates loaded with Washington apples. "Find something you'd like?" His smile broadened into a yellow-toothed grin.

Startled, she stepped back from the counter. "Yes, sir."

He picked up the slim volume and eyed the book's tattered cover. "Ah, one of my favorites. Did you know this is the town Mr. London wrote about in this here book? Originally, he called it *The Sleeping Wolf.* Don't know why some New York publisher changed its name." The store owner picked up a well-chewed pipe and stuffed it in his mouth. "My pappy used to lift a pint or two with Mr. London at the Kodiak Bar just down the street. I'd sit on the floor at the men's feet and listen. Oh what yarns Mr. London could weave about the South Seas, Europe, and, of course, the Northwest."

"Really? How exciting."

Encouraged by her interest, the old man continued. "Mr. London had a bad case of Klondike Fever, he did. Couldn't stay in one place too long. I heard he lived out his days in northern California."

Fascinated, Liz enjoyed the salt-and-pepper-haired merchant's ramblings until the horn of the *Sitka Sue* pierced her reverie. Stuffing the book beneath her heavy coat, she waved goodbye to the shop owner, and then half slipped, half ran along the icy boardwalk to the dock. She had no desire to be left behind in Skagway.

"You made it!" At the top of the ramp, the ship's middle-aged captain greeted her with a jovial laugh. "So how did you like Skagway? I was afraid we'd have to send out a search party for you."

"A couple of times I would have welcomed a rescue team. I don't know how many snowbanks I landed in." She laughed as she brushed caked-on snow from the collar and elbows of her coat. She slipped *The Call of the Wild* from inside her coat.

Captain Clark glanced down at the book in her hands. "Ah, my favorite. For me, London's later books lacked the passion of this one."

"Well, I'm looking forward to reading it if you can guarantee me a smooth cruise from here to Whittier."

"That, my dear, is highly unlikely at this time of year." Over his shoulder, the final deafening horn bellowed. The captain glanced toward the bridge, touched the brim of his hat, and bowed slightly. "Gotta go. Have a delightful read, my dear."

As Captain Clark promised, the crossing to Prince William Sound was anything but placid. The freighter slowly maneuvered in and around the icebergs in the bay. Liz cringed each time ominous scrapes and booms came from far below the ship. Liz hibernated in her cabin with her book, a kerosene lantern, and a jumble of ideas of what she would say to Alan when she saw him again.

For eight days and nine nights after her departure from Seattle, Liz's spirits, like the waves thumping against the hull of the *Sitka Sue,* rose with anticipation and fell with anxiety. The captain dropped anchor at the far end of the Cook Inlet, near the isolated settlement of Whittier, a town hardly large enough for skiffs and small fishing boats. Snow-capped mountains surrounded the partially constructed dock and warehouse. The few weather-beaten houses in town had hunkered down for winter in what appeared to be a giant snow bowl. The *Sitka Sue* would be the last merchant ship bearing foodstuff and building supplies from the States until spring.

"Mrs. Ames." A blond seaman named Hector strode the length of the wooden deck to where she waited, her two massive suitcases packed. She'd slung the strap of her leather carry-on case over her left shoulder. "Mrs. Ames, I'm here to help you with your luggage. The captain received a transmission from your father this morning. His general manager, Mr. Ralph Lorry, will meet you at the dock."

"Oh, that won't be necessary. I think I can manage." She reached toward the larger case.

"No, I insist." The young man took the handle of the smallest case from her grasp. "I do hope you found your time aboard the *Sitka Sue* tolerable despite our primitive accommodations. We men aren't used to having a woman on board, you know."

The young man's awkward attempt at conversation brought a smile to her face. "The accommodations were more than adequate and everyone treated me with grace and proper deference," she assured him.

Hector heaved a sigh of relief. Liz was certain that the captain had stressed to the crew how important it was that the daughter of Richard Bellwood enjoy her cruise on his freighter. "Did you know that the town of Whittier was named after the poet John Greenleaf Whittier?"

"Indeed."

The young man continued. "The U.S. Army has a military camp just outside town. They're digging a railway tunnel that will connect Whittier with Anchorage. It will shorten the trip by seventy miles, so they say," Hector continued. "Eventually, both trucks and trains will run through the tunnel at the same time. Can you imagine?"

"That will be one impressive tunnel." Liz gazed at the construction site visible halfway up the mountainside. *So that's why Alan has been deployed to Alaska,* she thought. "Where do you call home, Hector, when you're not sailing on the *Sitka Sue,* that is?"

"I hail from Kansas City, Kansas, ma'am."

"Kansas City?" Her voice rose in surprise.

"Yes, ma'am. It was during the Great Depression. My dad hit the rails immediately after my mom's funeral. I was ten. Six months later, I left my Aunt Meta's farm and set out to find him. Never did. But I ended up in Seattle, where I signed on with the *Sitka Sue.* Captain Clark has been like a dad to me."

Liz wondered how to respond without patronizing the boy. "I do wish the cook would share the recipe for his corn chowder. It is delicious. I could have eaten it three times a day every day."

"I'll see what I can do." Hector beamed with pride. "The captain has a reputation of serving hearty, robust meals to his crew. Food is important to him. He says a ship operates on its belly. Oh, I almost forgot. Captain Clark told me to remind you that the *Sitka Sue* sails in eight days, on December 15—ready or not."

"Oh, I'll be ready. Trust me, I've had enough ice and snow this week to last a lifetime. I think I'll be ready to move to San Diego or El Paso—somewhere warm—when I get back home." She shivered dramatically.

The young man laughed. "It does get mighty cold in these parts, but I like it."

Liz followed Hector as he lugged her suitcases down the gangplank. They'd barely stepped onto the pier when a black Chevy truck, coated in an oatmeal-thick layer of mud, pulled to a stop in front of them. A colossus of a man, sporting thick brown canvas pants, sealskin mukluks, and a red-and-black checked woolen jacket, hopped out of the vehicle. His shock of gray hair, matching mustache, and chest-length beard blew in the stiff midday breeze. She watched him lumber around the idling vehicle and fling open the truck's passenger door. The canyonwide grin on the man's face matched the twinkle in his indigo blue eyes.

"Welcome to Alaska, Mrs. Ames. I'm Ralph Lorry, local manager for Bellwood International." He grabbed her hand and vigorously shook it as if priming the family's backyard water pump. "Here! Let me get that luggage for you." Before she or Hector could respond, Mr. Lorry tossed her cases into the bed of the truck with the ease of a major league baseball pitcher lobbing a strike over home plate.

"First things first. I'll deposit you and your luggage at Miz Mabel's boardinghouse—the cleanest hotel north of Juneau. Then I'll send a message to your papa, letting him know you arrived in Whittier safe and sound." He glanced down at the brown leather boots with the stacked Cuban heels on her feet. "You might want to get yourself a pair of fur-lined boots before you travel much farther in Alaska. For that matter, my daughters might have an extra pair to loan you. What size do you wear?"

"Uh, er, six and a half."

"Perfect." He glanced at the heavy brown packet of papers she clutched in her hand. "I take it those documents are for me?"

"Er, yes, sir. Thank you, sir."

The man took the packet from her hands, helped her into the cab, and closed the door, after which he ran around the front of the truck and climbed aboard. "If *Sitka Sue* hadn't docked before the end of the week, I think your dad would have stowed away in the first military flight north. He's been mighty concerned about you."

Liz laughed. "I'll bet he's been hounding you. Dads are like that, you know—protective of their little girls." All the nights when she paced the deck of the *Sitka Sue,* feeling so terribly alone, it comforted her to know she'd never been far from her father's thoughts or out of his heart.

"Hey, I do the same whenever any of my five baby girls go traipsing off to who knows where." Mr. Lorry shifted the idling truck into gear. The vehicle lurched forward.

"You have five daughters? What are their names? How old are they?"

At the mention of his children, Mr. Lorry's chest seemed to expand an additional six inches. "Well, let me see. There's Ethel—the oldest. She's thirty-two. She's given me six grandsons. She and her hubby, Ben, live here in town. And next there's Beatrice—age thirty, wife and mother of three girls. Betty is twenty-five and a mother of a boy and a girl. Connie is twenty-two, and my baby, Ruthie, is twenty. Both are single and attending the University of Washington in Seattle."

"You are truly blessed, Mr. Lorry." Liz fidgeted with one of her gloves. All the talk of babies and grandchildren had made her uncomfortable. *Just another childhood dream gone awry,* she thought.

"The greatest blessing in my life is my wife, Katrina—a gem of a woman. My beard may be gray and my steps are slowing down, but to her, I'm still the young buck who sang 'K-K-K-Katy' outside her bedroom window during the blizzard of 1906."

Liz smiled at the idea of this mountain of a man crooning to his beloved from a giant snowbank.

"Her father chased me with a broom." Mr. Lorry's beard danced with merriment. "Let me tell you, my wife's father was a very big man!"

Liz blinked in surprise. *How much bigger could Katrina's father have been than the man the woman married?* Liz wondered. "You've been married a long time, and you obviously still love her. That's amazing. What's your secret?"

Mr. Lorry's stomach jiggled with laughter. "Living in Alaska. It's impossible to run away from your problems when the snow is eight feet deep outside your cabin door. Of course, there are those who 'split the sheets,' that's what we, in these parts, call separatin'. Happens to some couples after a particularly long and frigid winter. But as Katrina and I figure, you can either freeze up for seven months, or you can resolve your differences. That's when you get to kiss and make up. How do you think we produced five gorgeous daughters?"

*If only it were that simple.* Liz blinked back a rush of tears as she stared at the fog steaming the inside of the truck's windshield. *Oh, Alan, am I making a fool of myself?* she wondered.

"Life is hard north of the fifty-ninth parallel. That fact alone brings people together. We need one another to survive, one another and God." While Lorry continued his upbeat monologue, Liz studied the man's weathered profile. The interwoven laugh wrinkles appeared to be a road map to hard-earned wisdom.

"I have good news for you, Mrs. Ames. I've been told that that wayward husband of yours is out at the base."

She started in surprise. Just how much had her father told this stranger?

"The U.S. Army has a temporary military camp north of Whittier. One day it will be the main headquarters for rail and shipping operations in Alaska." Lorry cast her a sideways glance. "While you settle in at Miz Mabel's, I'll send a message to your dad and pick up a pair of those mukluks for you. But first, I'll drive you to the military headquarters here in town. Who knows? By suppertime you may be happily reunited with Mr. Ames." The man pursed his lips thoughtfully. "He's one lucky man to have a wife willing to travel so far to be with him. By the way, Captain Clark meant what he said about sailing on December 15. If you intend to return on the *Sitka Sue,* you'd better have your business in Alaska settled by then, or you'll be spending the winter here in Whittier with us."

# Chapter 6: Winter's Chill

*Destiny is not a matter of chance, but of choice.*
*—William Jennings Bryan*

## Base Camp, Maynard Mountain: December 1941

An engineer to the core, Captain Alan Ames detested the slightest schedule variation to interrupt his carefully calculated plans—human or otherwise. If his life had been on the track he planned, he'd be living in Seattle with Liz and their children. Instead of freezing in army fatigues, he'd be wrapped in a tartan lounging robe. Instead of stomping out the numbness in his semifrozen toes, he'd be basking in his favorite club chair and sipping a cup of hot tea. An Irish setter would be lying at his feet. Beside him, the fireplace mantel would tout a row of awards granted to the most successful engineering firm in the Pacific Northwest. From the perspective of a college freshman, his ten-year-plan had appeared quite reasonable.

Instead, the man found himself in frigid Alaska trying to untangle yet another unexplained on-the-job mishap. This time it was a burst fuel pump on one of the army's largest bulldozers. Equipment breakdowns, broken tools, shipment delays, fire damage to the newly built shipping dock in Whittier, and a weeklong blizzard—it had been one delay after another to slow down the dig into the side of the mountain.

With all the snafus and on-the-job malfunctions, Alan began to wonder if his superior officer might be right. It could be sabotage, or, as the native population of Whittier believed, the tunnel project might be cursed. Moeshe Jones, Alan's buddy and civilian coworker, suggested as much the morning after the snow tent collapsed outside the freshly dug entrance to the tunnel. But then, Alan knew that Moeshe, a demolition expert hired out of Seward, believed everything that happened—good or bad—was due to divine will.

"Perhaps Someone is trying to tell you something." Moeshe cast a dramatic gaze heavenward and then stirred his mug of hot tomato soup. "Perhaps the scarring of the Aleut's holy mountain is offensive to the Aleut gods."

"That's ridiculous!" Alan scoffed. "The gods, no matter who they might be, have better things to do with their time than to sabotage this project." Under his breath, he added, "Like snatching tiny babies from their parents' arms."

The army officer straightened his shoulders. "The God of the pale skins is always on the side of right, correct? This tunnel and the subsequent railway connection to Anchorage will give the U.S. military a way to fortify our defenses of the Alaskan territory. That has to be God's will, don't you think?"

Remaining silent, Moeshe took a second sip of the hot liquid in his mug. "Ouch! I always burn my tongue. I guess I'm not patient enough for hot drinks. By the way, where's Lowell this morning?"

Alan glanced about as if the missing coworker might suddenly appear. "Don't know. Did he call in sick? He looked a little pale yesterday. If he didn't report to the infirmary, he should have."

*Another delay,* Alan thought. Without the team's third man, a second-year student whom he barely remembered from his days at the University of Washington's College of Engineering, not as much would be accomplished as Alan had hoped. *Could frequent illnesses in camp also be part of the enemy's plan to derail the project? Sabotage via the digestive tract?* Alan chuckled aloud at a thought he considered ludicrous.

Hired as diggers on the tunnel, many Inuit and Aleut tribesmen abhorred what they believed to be a desecration of their land. Workmen brought in from Seward also objected to the army's main shipping port being relocated from Seward to Whittier. Add a Japanese sympathizer or two, and there was room to suspect sabotage in every accident, breakdown, or on-the-job slowdown not attributed directly to the weather.

But as yet, Alan and his team could find no definitive evidence of mischief beyond the subzero Arctic temperatures, low enough to crack the block of any fuel-driven engine.

Captain Ames wrapped his fingers around his steaming mug. He lifted the cup to his nose, closed his eyes, and slowly inhaled the warm steam. Childhood memories of building snow forts, making snow angels, and fierce snowball fights with neighborhood pals flashed through his mind. *Ah, to be a kid again when snow meant playtime, and ice was made for fun,* he mused.

From down the hill toward camp, he heard his name called. It was Anderson's desk sergeant. "Captain Ames! Captain Ames! You're wanted in the colonel's office, pronto."

# Chapter 7: The Big Freeze

*When I can look Life in the eyes,*
*Grown calm and very coldly wise,*
*Life will have given me the Truth,*
*And taken in exchange—my youth.*
*—Sara Teasdale*

## Whittier, Alaska: December 1941

Seated on a straight-backed wooden chair in a claustrophobic six-by-six-foot waiting area outside the major's office, Liz studied the envelope containing the letter of introduction written by her father to the U.S. Army officer in charge. The bold ink scrawl fit the forceful nature of its author. She glanced through the small dust-covered window of the army-gray Quonset hut to spot Ralph Lorry idling his truck engine in the parking lot. She'd tried to assure him that she had a license to drive, that he didn't have to wait for her, but the man stubbornly assured her that he would wait for her "to finish her business," as he put it. At first, she thought his determination to treat her like a hothouse orchid came from wanting to please his boss, her father. But after listening a while to the gentle giant, Liz realized Ralph Lorry would have treated any woman with the same respectful deference.

Liz removed her brown leather gloves and stuffed them into the pockets of her overcoat.

"Mrs. Ames." A corporal, with military-short, blond hair, stepped through the entry to the inner office and held open the door for her. "Major Judd will see you now."

Noting the corporal's rigid military stance and emotionless expression, Liz suppressed a wild urge to giggle and snap off a whimsical salute. Lately, when she pictured Alan in the army, she realized he was a natural for the regimented lifestyle he'd chosen. Gracefully, she rose to her feet and brushed past the young man and into the major's office. A dusty, eight-paned office window and two small desk lamps supplied the only sources of light in the disorganized office. Thumbtacks nailed a configuration of geological maps of Alaska to one wall. A second wall sported an array of blueprints tacked to a massive corkboard along with scraps of notepaper of all sizes. The otherwise sparse décor of the major's office also included several manila folders atop a scarred metal desk and two paint-chipped, straight-backed gray desk chairs, one behind the desk and one in front. To one side, beneath a stack of bulging manila folders, a well-worn, wooden desk occupied the left wall. Her eyes were drawn to the up-to-date, ship-to-shore, shortwave radio station on the desktop as well.

Beneath the wooden table were four cardboard packing boxes laden with what Liz immediately recognized as a treasure trove of electronic radio equipment parts. Clocks set for the world's time zones dotted the wall above the radio station. Above the clocks hung the requisite Klaxon emergency light and the accompanying horn set to notify the operator of urgent incoming traffic. On the far end of the row of clocks hung a giant calendar with a Currier and Ives print of a New England Christmas scene complete with horses, a sleigh, top-hatted gentlemen, and hoop-skirted ladies. Days one through five of the month of December had been crossed off with red crayon.

Beneath this scene of disorganized efficiency, a barely controlled chaos of papers, folders, and military handbooks cluttered the tabletop, giving the humble radio station a slightly distressing aura. Liz shifted her attention to the radio operator seated at the station. The man's strong square shoulders beneath a wrinkled military shirt matched the general ambience of the room. By the gold oak leaf on the man's uniform, she identified the radio operator to be a major. Liz judged the officer with the five o'clock shadow to be in his early to mid-thirties.

Major Judd pushed his chair away from the table, stood, and turned to face her. He towered over her five feet seven inches by an easy six inches.

His deep brown eyes contained a vaguely disconcerting warmth that drew her inexplicably to him. Stunned by her initial reaction to this stranger, Liz continued to stare. He smiled with amusement.

"Does the station pass inspection, ma'am?"

"Uh, you are Major Judd?" She stammered like a star-struck schoolgirl. *Of course he is, you nitwit,* she silently scolded. *Who else would he be?* "Sorry. I expected you to be much older."

"Some mornings I feel much older, I assure you, especially in the northernmost wasteland. And you must be my savior!"

"I beg your pardon?" When she extended her right hand in greeting, he held it a bit longer than was socially correct. She blinked in surprise as electricity traveled from his hand through hers and through to the length of her arm. Never had she experienced such an instant attraction to anyone, even when she had first met Alan. Liz found herself reluctant to break the startling connection. She found herself wondering if her bulky tweed overcoat looked too schoolmarmish.

"Mrs. Ames, it is a pleasure to meet you." He continued to hold her hand. "Your father notified me that you were coming. He also said you are a crackerjack radio technician. Forty to fifty words per minute—whew! That's really flying. I'm lucky to break thirty-five. And yes, I am Major William Judd."

"Sir?" She slipped her hand from his grasp. Removing her father's letter from her coat pocket, she handed it to him. "Here's a letter of introduction. You may know my father."

"No, not really." The officer glanced at the envelope. "Your father has contacted me by radio several times in the last week to tell me you would be arriving on the *Sitka Sue,* that you were searching for your husband. Otherwise, we've never met. However, I've notified Colonel Anderson. Captain Ames is on his way into town from our base camp north of town."

"Thank you, but how does finding my husband make me your savior?"

"Well—" The major ran his fingers through his shock of honey brown hair. "Last week my head radio man, Andy, slipped and fell while hiking on a nearby glacier. He had to be flown to Anchorage for emergency surgery on his leg."

Liz immediately saw where this was going. "Surely, the army has more than one backup operator."

The officer raised his hands in surrender. "My second technician, Chuck, is in bed with double pneumonia; and Freddie, his backup, eloped while on home leave and missed his return travel connections out of Portland. The earliest Andy and his broken leg can get here is a week from tomorrow. As for Chuck, I haven't a clue as to when he will be well enough to work again."

"You are in a tight spot, Major."

"As you can see, I've been living here 'round the clock since last Tuesday." He gestured toward a cot and a bedroll behind the office door. "We've been shorthanded since the Army Corps of Engineers commandeered all available enlisted men to work on the tunnel."

Liz glanced toward the radio equipment. "You have an interesting setup here." While the station lacked the sophistication of her father's equipment, she had operated a similar rig during her early days at her Bellwood International.

"Your father swears you're a top-notch radio operator."

"I can maneuver my way around most pieces of electronic radio equipment." She paused and glanced at the radio log. The entries were as neat as the office was messy. "But, Major, as you probably already know, next Saturday I am scheduled to head back to Seattle on the *Sitka Sue*. Until then, I'd be glad to give you some relief time."

The man's eyes lit up. "Relief? How soon? Like right now? Can you take over for an hour or two while I get a shower and shave and perhaps a hot breakfast?"

"Breakfast? Breakfast was hours ago. When was the last time you ate a decent meal, Major?" Liz shook off the thought of how much she sounded like Gertie or Grandma Keating.

"Since it looks like we'll be working together for the next few days, please call me Will. As to a regular meal, Corporal Smythe has been bringing me cold sandwiches from Mabel's place. Along with a bottomless pot of hot stew, I'm doing fine." The wide grin coursing his face disarmed her once again.

"OK, Major, er, Will, take a five-hour break. I'll cover for you. Because I've never before run an army field office, is there anything I should know before you abandon me to the military jungle?"

"As to the military jungle, nothing much happening in that area. You are in Alaska, you know, where our Saturday evening fun is watching icicles melt." A grin swept across his face followed by a slight frown. "You said you do know how to work with this setup . . ."

Liz grinned. She could operate this station in her sleep. "Don't worry. I think I can manage."

Will started toward the door. "Don't worry. Corporal Smythe will take care of any military business that may come in while I'm gone. You just man the radio, or should I say woman the radio." His quirky grin fell easily into place. "If something comes up you can't handle, Smythe can find me at Miz Mabel's."

"Aye, aye, Major." She snapped off a smart salute.

The officer laughed as he hauled on his heavy military overcoat. "That's navy talk, Mrs. Ames. You're in the army now. Try, 'Yes, sir.' "

Suddenly, she remembered her waiting driver. "Oh, I forgot. I left Mr. Lorry in the parking area with his truck engine running. Please tell him I'll be staying here for a while."

"Sure. I'll let him know. By the way, in these cold temperatures, everyone keeps the engines of their vehicles running, twenty-four hours a day."

"Really?"

"Really. Turn 'em off and the engines freeze up. Thanks again, Mrs. Ames. You don't realize what a lifesaver you are."

"You are welcome to call me Liz. And seriously, I am glad I can be of service to my country while I'm in Alaska. Now get out of here." She laughed and waved him away.

After the door closed behind the major, the room felt shabbier and colder. She removed her cloche hat, stuffed a few wisps of auburn hair into the chignon at the back of her neck, and settled in at the radio desk. As she got oriented to the radio setup, Corporal Smythe knocked on the door.

"Would you like a hot drink, ma'am? The major said you might." Again, the young man's straight-backed military stance produced a giggle from Liz.

"I'm sorry, corporal. I'm not laughing at you, honest. I'm just not accustomed to military decorum. Please relax; you make me nervous."

"Sorry, ma'am."

"It's OK. You seem so out of place with your, er, surroundings."

"Yes, ma'am." The corporal lifted his chin a trifle higher.

She smiled at the obvious pride he took in his military demeanor. "How did you come to be in Alaska? The luck of the draw?"

"Hardly, ma'am. I got a little tipsy in New Orleans one Saturday night and kissed the daughter of my commanding officer. The next thing I knew, I was aboard a ship for Alaska." He glanced about the office and shrugged. "As you can see, Major Judd doesn't always operate by army protocol, but he is fair and easy to work for."

"That's good to know." Incoming code from headquarters in Washington, D.C., ended their conversation. The corporal waited while Liz transcribed the message into the log.

"Anything important?" the young man asked.

"Just something about a shipment of lumber being stalled in Seward. Nothing that can't wait until Major Judd gets a hot meal and a short nap." She scribbled the message onto a piece of notepaper and handed it to the corporal. "Here, put this where the major will find it."

"Major Judd usually puts messages in this box." He pointed to a wire basket buried under a stack of outdated *Stars and Stripes* magazines.

"Gotcha. I knew that." Liz chuckled as she moved the magazines to an empty spot on the floor beside the table.

The corporal gave a nervous little laugh. "Will there be anything else, ma'am?"

"No, thank you. Wait! I could use a fresh pitcher of water and a clean glass."

"Yes, ma'am."

Being surrounded by familiar equipment comforted the woman. For the moment, she could table her anxiety regarding her inevitable meeting with Alan and dedicate her attention to the world of shortwave ham radio. By the time Corporal Smythe returned with the pitcher of water and a clean glass, the surface of the radio table had taken on a modified semblance of order. In the process, Liz had categorized several government manuals according to date of issue and stacked them on the floor beside the table.

During the first four hours of her shift, three messages came in: one from army headquarters in Maryland about curtailing unscheduled leaves, a second from a military base in northern California asking if they'd spotted any foreign vessels along the coast, and a third from the local construction site reporting that Captain Ames was in the field and would arrive in Whittier at 1800 hours.

Liz wondered what Alan's reaction would be when he learned of her arrival in Alaska. She glanced at the local time. Her insides quivered at the prospect of seeing him again. Now that it was about to happen, what would she say to him? She'd spent so many nights pacing the deck of the *Sitka Sue* planning her speech. She couldn't mess up now. Yet she couldn't remember a thing she had practiced.

At 1500 hours, Corporal Smythe's replacement arrived. Private First Class Andrew Epps identified himself and quickly retreated to the outer office.

When Liz finished organizing the radio station to her liking, she resisted the urge to do the same with the materials on the major's desk. *Unrequested help must be given only in moderation,* she reminded herself.

Five hours passed quickly. Before she knew it, a refreshed, clean-shaven, Major William Judd bounded into the office, carrying a picnic basket, which he informed her contained two stoneware mugs, a jug of potato-white-bean soup, and a basket of homemade sugar donuts. Draped over his arm was a red-and-white checked tablecloth. Matching napkins lay atop the food in the basket.

"Hungry?" Will didn't wait for an answer. "Thought you would be. Miz Mabel insisted I offer you something to eat before sending you back to the boardinghouse to rest."

"Did you get some rest, Colonel?"

"Will, call me Will. I'm not a colonel, Mrs. Ames. I'm only a major. And yes, I slept like a baby! Thanks for asking. You told me to call you Liz or Elizabeth?"

"I answer to either. Sorry. One army rank is pretty much the same to me as another." She laughed nervously. "I've dealt only with the navy hierarchy, I'm afraid."

"OK, Elizabeth, how about some chow? That's the same regardless of one's branch of service, right?" He strode over to his desk and with one hand swept aside half of the stacks of manila folders to make room for the food. Without warning, the stack slid off the desktop onto the floor. Immediately, both Liz and Will attempted to retrieve the folders.

"Here, let me help," she volunteered.

"No, I've got 'em," he insisted. Simultaneously dropping to their knees, they bonked foreheads.

"Ouch!" Liz rubbed her head.



3—N.L.

"Are you all right?"

"I think so."

His face was inches from hers. Their eyes met. For an instant, they stared, transfixed. First to recover, Liz stuffed the folders she'd collected into his hands. "Here." She leaped to her feet.

Visibly shaken, the major stood to his feet and deliberately set the folders at the opposite end of the desk. "Mabel's soup smells delicious. It's the best north of the Canadian border."

"It sure does." Liz's knees quivered, and she held on to the edge of the desk for balance. Heightened color filled her cheeks. She swallowed hard.

Will turned away. Neither spoke while he poured the steaming hot soup into the mugs. "Elizabeth, shall we eat?" He gestured toward the chair on the front side of the desk and dropped into his chair behind the desk. "I had a crush on an Elizabeth in the first grade—red hair, freckles, *hmm*." A grin spread across his face as he glanced across the desk at her. "Elizabeth, are you sure you never lived in Omaha?"

Liz took a spoonful of the chowder stew into her mouth. "No, afraid not. I'm a native of Seattle, Washington. I've developed webbed feet from all the rain to prove it—convenient when swimming in the Sound."

Will laughed. "Webbed feet, eh? Well, we relocated Nebraskans claim that if we learned we had less than a year to live, we'd move back to Nebraska."

"Why?" she queried.

"Because living six months in Nebraska would seem like a whole lot longer."

Laughing, Liz choked on her soup. He started toward her to help her. She waved him away. "No, no, I'm fine."

They ate in companionable silence for several minutes.

"Ready for a donut?" He reached into the basket and removed an old-fashioned cake donut dripping with chocolate icing.

"Sure. I don't usually eat my dessert before finishing my main course, but I'm in Alaska, so why not be adventurous?" She took the donut from him and bit into it. "*M-m-m-m!* I never could resist chocolate. Alan, that's my husband, says I'm addicted."

Will grinned and pointed. "Oops! You have a little frosting on your face."



"Where? Here?" She dabbed the left side of her mouth with her napkin.

"No, it's more over here." Will reached across the desk with his napkin to whisk away the frosting from the corner of her lips. Suddenly, the office door burst open and slammed against the back wall.

"Sir?" Private Epps stepped into the office. "Captain Ames is here to see—"

Before the young man could finish his sentence, an agitated Alan brushed past the private, halted inches behind Liz's chair, and snapped off a salute.

"Sir! Captain Ames reporting as ordered, sir!" Alan's eye never strayed toward the startled woman nor showed any sign of acknowledging her presence.

"Alan!" Liz slipped out of her chair and attempted to slip her arms about his waist. His arms remained rigid at his side; his eyes faced forward. "Alan," she whispered again. When he didn't respond, she stepped back, her face crimson with humiliation.

Will rose from his chair. "At ease, Captain. Please feel free to greet your wife appropriately."

Alan cast a sideways glance toward Liz. "Is that an order, Major?"

"No. No, of course not." The major cleared his throat. "It's simply the proper thing to do, Captain, after she traveled so many miles to be with you."

"I didn't invite her to come to Alaska, sir. She came on her own." Alan's clipped reply sent a new rush of color into Liz's cheeks.

The major's eyes flashed with irritation. "Nonetheless, Elizabeth is here and deserves a respectful greeting!"

Alan's eyes narrowed as he shifted his gaze from the major, to his wife, and then back again. "Elizabeth, is it? Well, well, well! In Whittier only a few hours, and you are already on a first-name basis with one of my superior officers? You do work fast, Lizzy, my girl. How many other men have you had buzzing around you since I joined the army?"

The major responded icily. "Elizabeth, er, your wife filled in for me on the radio this afternoon while I went back to my quarters for a short nap. My radio man broke a— Why am I explaining myself to you, Captain?"

"I don't know, Major. Perhaps you should tell me," Alan responded defiantly.

Mortified by her husband's string of insinuations, Liz stared at the two men poised tensely across the desktop. While she didn't know about Major

Judd, Alan was behaving totally out of character, challenging his superior officer. *Does Alan hate me so much as to humiliate me like this?* Her emotions shifted from embarrassment, to pain, to fury. Liz stiffened her shoulders and burst out defiantly.

"Excuse me, gentlemen, but in case you forgot, I am in the room. I can speak for myself! First, Alan, it's so delightful to see you again. I hope my presence in Alaska doesn't upset your personal agenda too much. But if it does, so be it. I am here now." Liz's glare would have wilted the resolve of the most resistant crabgrass. "Don't worry, I won't be here any longer than necessary. I've arranged to return to Seattle on the *Sitka Sue* next week. In the meantime, I intend for us to clarify our situation."

She whipped about. "And you, Major Judd," her eyes flashed with determination, "it is obvious that you need my assistance. So, while I'm in Whittier, I will be happy to spell you off on the shortwave until one of your technicians returns or it's time for my ship to leave, whichever comes first. You can pay me or not. It doesn't matter. Consider it patriotism. I don't care, but I won't be treated like a whimpering pansy by either of you, gentlemen. Do you both understand?"

She shot a threatening glance at each of the men. Both hung their heads. "Now, Alan, you and I need to talk, preferably somewhere with privacy. Perhaps you have a vehicle at your disposal?"

Alan stood frozen to the spot. A plethora of emotions from surprise to petulance crossed the man's face.

"Well?" She prodded as she pulled her cloche over her hair and slipped into her woolen overcoat. When the major jumped to help her with the coat, she snapped, "I can do it myself!"

"Sorry," he mumbled. The major looked sufficiently chastised.

Alan shrugged his shoulders and gestured toward the open door. "Out front."

"Good. I'll be waiting for you there." She slung the strap of her leather purse over her shoulder, glanced at her wristwatch, and then turned to the major. "Major Judd, if you'll send your aide for me around zero three hundred hours, I'll relieve you once more."

# Chapter 8: Deep Water

*Since Knowledge is but Sorrow's spy, it is not safe to know.*
*—Sir William Davenant*

## Alaskan Wilderness: December 1941

Swathed in a double-layer caribou-skin parka, matching knee-length trousers, and three-layered *kamiks* protecting his feet, Irnig-Kesuk had shed the white man's world and returned into his childhood persona. In this garb, the man could pass for any one of a hundred Inuit seal hunters in the region. That is, he could pass for any native of the north until one looked past the brown-blackish facial hair and into the man's eyes—eyes as inscrutable as the midnight blue waters of the Bering Sea.

Irnig-Kesuk is what his Japanese shaman father called him. In the Aleut culture, a person goes by several names during his lifetime. His moniker changes to fit whatever circumstances in which he might find himself. *But then, what's in a name?* he thought. *If William Shakespeare, the pale skin's greatest author, couldn't adequately answer that question, why should I try?*

From infancy, Irnig-Kesuk had been groomed to follow in his adoptive father's footsteps as a shaman. But due to the generosity of a wealthy American who owned a fleet of fishing boats off the Aleutian Islands, the boy with the "stormy sea in his eyes" chose another path—that of the pale skins. Through high school and college, Irnig-Kesuk determined he would learn how to fit into the white man's world. Assimilation became his focus in life. He shaved his beard, cut his hair, and wore appropriate garments.

At the university, he learned to endure occasional racial slurs and learned easy rapport with white people. To survive, he'd learned to smile, flatter, and please. His plan worked: in a flash, he could morph from an Arctic fisherman to a member of Seattle's educated university crowd as needed.

That the Aleut natives didn't give their young lifelong names confused the European trappers and traders. Irnig-Kesuk learned to use this cultural idiosyncrasy to his advantage. He devised an identity game that allowed him to be known by different names to different folks. This flexibility he used to great advantage. After his recruitment by the United States government, Irnig-Kesuk used this skill to vanish into the shadowy life of a secret agent. When alone in the world of jade-green glaciers, treacherous crevasses, and blinding snowstorms, he thought of himself as Irnig-Kesuk, the son of deep water. It was here he felt most alive.

He'd hiked more than five miles from the military camp to the foot of the Whittier Glacier. After sloughing his caribou-skin backpack from his shoulders onto a nearby rock, he lifted his hands to the turbulent clouds and shouted into the wind, "Goddess of earth, wind, and sky, today I'll be whoever you want me to be!"

His only nemesis at the military camp was a fellow Aleut, one he'd known since childhood. Amarok was also a man of many names and talents. Only when around Irnig-Kesuk or other Aleuts, he called himself Amarok. From the first day Amarok arrived at the camp from Anchorage, the two men made a silent, tacit agreement to avoid one another.

Amarok possessed a gift Irnig-Kesuk did not. Amarok could "charm the bark off a seal," as their adoptive father often said. Even the taciturn Colonel Anderson warmed to Amarok's wit and humor. But what Irnig-Kesuk lacked in social skills, he prided himself in his tracking skills.

Something about Amarok's arrival at camp didn't feel right to Irnig-Kesuk. To protect the interests of his people and that of his assignment, Irnig-Kesuk made it his mission to track his fellow Aleut's nightly comings and goings from the military camp.

★ ★ ★ ★ ★

A fringe of wolverine fur protected Amarok's face and neck from the cascade of hoarfrost falling from the boughs of a western hemlock as he strung a roll of wire from his radio pack to a nearby tree branch. He set up a portable shortwave radio station, recharged his wind-up battery, and quickly tapped out a series of dots and dashes to his contact in Anchorage—all in less than three minutes. The brief time it took to send his coded message limited the possibility of any interception. He buried his face in his fur hood and waited for a reply. Within seconds, the reply came. "R—FREIGHTER CARRYING SNOWSHED REPAIR EQUIPMENT STALLED IN SEWARD. ENGINE TROUBLE—SK."

"R—GOOD JOB—UNTIL NEXT TUESDAY—SK."

Alone except for a stray moose or a late-hibernating bear, Amarok rocked back on his haunches, savoring for a moment another small victory for his cause. Then quickly rising to his feet, he reeled in the wire and stuffed the antenna into his backpack. With great care, he packed away the rest of his radio equipment. Satisfied his task was complete, he removed from his coat pocket a handkerchief containing a slice of sourdough bread and smoked herring. Amarok took a satisfying bite and allowed himself a slight smile. Week after week, he carried out his mission to create small glitches to impede the progress of the United States Army Corps of Engineers as they drilled into the sacred and majestic Maynard Mountain.

Amarok knew his superiors in Anchorage were pleased. His handler on the fishing boat off the coast of Seward was pleased too. He hoped his father would be as well, as would be his father's gods. Though as far as the gods were concerned, he could never be sure.

★ ★ ★ ★ ★

Behind a boulder of calved ice off the Whittier Glacier, Irnig-Kesuk lowered his binoculars. He pursed his lips and slowly shook his head. The man was not pleased at what he had seen, not pleased at all.

# Chapter 9: No Early Thaw

*Speak when you are angry*
*and you will make the best speech you will ever regret.*
*—Ambrose Bierce*

## Whittier, Alaska: December 1941

Liz stormed through the outer office, past a startled Private Epps, and out of the building. As she stepped out onto the slab of concrete beyond the door, a stinging wind whipped her knee-length coat about her pant legs. The frigid gust stung her cheeks and nose as she eyed the three vehicles idling in front of the Quonset. Two were rusting pickup trucks of undetermined age. The third was a boxy, brown-and-green utility rig further camouflaged beneath a thick layer of caked-on mud. *Which one is Alan driving? I'd feel rather foolish if I waited for him in the wrong vehicle.* She smiled despite her anger.

For a moment, Liz considered returning to the office to ask Private Epps for help, but decided she couldn't stand the humiliation following her dramatic exit. Choosing the military truck, she picked her way over and around chunks of ice and mounds of frozen mud toward the vehicle. *I've got to buy a pair of heavy boots,* Liz told herself as she caught the passenger side door handle to keep from falling. She opened the door and climbed into the oversized vehicle, the door hinges squeaking in protest as she yanked it closed behind her. The woman leaned her head against the back of the seat and closed her eyes, feeling emotionally drained and tense. Doubts flooded her mind. *What am I doing here? Is saving my marriage to Alan worth it? Why am I putting myself through this nightmare?*

She opened her eyes. Condensation coated the windshield and passenger side window, transforming the cab of the truck into a cocoon of sorts. "Hold it together, Elizabeth!" The sound of her own voice gave her courage. She continued her much-needed pep talk. "There's no escaping now. You've traveled a long way to do this. You must see this through, however painful it might prove to be."

A fresh determination heartened her. She folded her gloved hands in her lap and heaved a soul-cleansing sigh. *You're here now, so quit your complaining and ferret out the missing pieces you traveled so far to find. Even if you must go home without resolving the issues in your marriage, you will be equipped to better determine how to proceed with your life.*

Fifteen minutes passed. Just as she considered the possibility her husband had exited the building through a rear door, Alan emerged from the Quonset. He climbed into the driver's seat of the vehicle she'd chosen. Without a word, he shifted the truck into gear. The growl of the engine made conversation impossible. Liz held on to the sides of her seat with whitened knuckles as the vehicle bounced, leaped, and straddled potholes and ruts over the gravel roadway. She turned toward Alan. "Hey, slow down! Are you trying to kill us both?"

Alan ignored her, his eyes glued to the road ahead.

She studied the man seated beside her. Her husband had changed since she'd last seen him. His face was leaner and premature wrinkles creased his brow, but the familiar volcanic anger seemed still to smolder beneath the rigid set of his jaw. He'd changed; he wasn't the man she'd married.

Her eyes misted as she returned her gaze to her gloved hands tightly folded in her lap. An overwhelming sadness swept through her as she recognized that neither was she the young coed who loved to laugh and who had enjoyed the nickname of Busy-Lizzy.

The truck jerked to an abrupt halt in front of a gray, two-story boardinghouse. Warm rays of light slatted through the wooden shutters, down the steps, and onto a shoveled pathway. Planters piled high with freshly fallen snow appointed the porch railing.

Liz glanced at her husband, waiting for him to break the silence. He didn't. His left hand rested on the driver's door latch; his right, on the steering wheel. Finally, "Well, are you going to get out?" Alan asked, carefully avoiding her gaze.

She pressed her lips together in quiet determination. "Not until we talk."

"Talk? What is there to talk about? My letter said it all." Alan's gloved fingers tapped out a strident beat on the steering wheel.

"Why don't you begin with an explanation of the contents of your letter. Do you seriously want a divorce?"

Alan shrugged and turned to look out the driver's window. His right hand continued tapping the steering wheel.

Determined not to accept his silent treatment, Liz waited. *I can sit here as long as you can,* she thought. After a couple minutes of silence, she heaved a giant sigh. "I've come too far not to receive an explanation from you. Why? Why do you want a divorce?"

"Why not?" The irritating tapping resumed. The steamed windshield blotted out the world beyond, but instead of creating a sense of intimacy, Liz felt more isolated than ever from the stone-faced man at her side.

"Perhaps because we took vows before God to love one another 'till death do us part,' " she said, trying to stay calm. "And the last time I checked, we're both very much alive."

When Liz didn't elaborate, Alan finally turned to face her. His eyes were steel cold. "Look, Elizabeth, I have a new life here in Alaska, and, frankly, you are not a part of it." Determined not to waver, she waited. Finally, Alan shook his head sadly. "I'm sorry, Liz, but the truth is, I don't love you anymore. I'm not sure I ever did."

His words sliced into her heart; she inhaled sharply but did not reply.

"Aren't you going to say something?" he eventually demanded.

Liz took a deep breath. "What can I say?" A long pause followed. "Is it another woman? The one you mentioned in your letter?"

The tapping on the steering wheel stopped. Eventually, Alan said, "Sure, if you say so. If that's what it takes for me to regain my freedom."

"Freedom? You were free enough to walk out the door of our home without advance notice. You were free to join the army with no thought for me. You were free enough to leave me to maintain a mortgage and a car payment. You were free enough to abandon our marriage bed to dally with another woman! And now you feel free enough to say you don't love me and never did. What freedom is left for you to regain?"

The thought of the invisible third person in the relationship flashed into Liz's mind. She couldn't bring herself to say, let alone consider, that he might be sleeping with Trudy. "Did you mean it when you wrote that you're willing to give me biblical and legal reasons to file for a divorce?"

Alan ignored her question.

Liz reached across the icy chasm between them and touched his arm. Barely above a whisper, she asked, "As your wife, I do have a right to know." Alan remained silent.

"Regardless of what you might feel about me, I still love you, Alan. Also regardless of anything you might have done, I still love you. And if it will save our marriage, I am willing to stay here in Alaska or to follow you wherever else you might wish to go if it would rekindle your love for me."

He turned slowly to face her. Through clenched teeth, he hissed, "Go home, Elizabeth. Go back to your family in Seattle. They're all you ever cared about anyway. I don't need you here complicating my life."

"Complicating your life? Now I'm a complication? And what are you implying about my family? When did they become your problem?"

"I didn't say they were!"

"Oh?" Liz snatched her hand from his arm. Fighting a sudden urge to vomit, she swallowed hard. *Stay calm. You know the drill. Nothing's changed. He wants you to overreact so he can justify his irrational behavior.* "Alan, I don't know what to say except that my marriage vows included a for-better-and-for-worse clause. And while this may come under the category of 'worse,' I'm not a quitter. If there's even one slim ray of hope—"

"There isn't!" Alan cut in. "Don't you understand? I don't want to save any part of our marriage. I want to forget it ever happened!"

Another slash through her heart. She was surprised to find herself praying. *Oh God, help me!*

Instantly, a flood of pleasant memories rushed into Liz's consciousness: their first meeting when they literally ran into each other while rounding a corner in the college library stacks; their first date to a symposium on why Hitler would never invade Poland; their first kiss on the steps of the women's dormitory; their first muffin shared over cups of hot cocoa at College Town, the off-campus student hangout; the first trip to Seattle to meet her folks; the night he proposed to her on the porch swing at his parents' home in Portland. The list continued. Liz finally whispered, "Alan, do you really mean that?"

He pounded the steering wheel with his fist. "I don't know what I mean. I just know I can't deal with what our lives had become before I left Seattle. I just can't!"

The violence of his reply sent shivers down her spine. Alan had so seldom given voice to his emotions during their time together. She folded her arms tightly, cocooning deep into the collar of her overcoat as if for protection against his icy attack.

"Grandma Keating always says not to make a hasty decision when you're either hurt or angry. And frankly, right now, I'm both. So, as I see it, we have a week to talk and to think about the future of our marriage."

"Fine!" Alan snapped. "A week, a month, a year won't change my mind—and I'm tired of sitting here."

Liz wanted to snap back, but instead offered, "We can talk in my room."

He shook his head. "Right now, I want to get as far away from you as possible!" For emphasis, he gunned the engine. "Please leave! Besides, don't you need to get some sleep before you relieve Willy-boy?" The sarcasm in his voice couldn't be missed.

"Alan, you know that there's nothing between Major Judd and me. I met the man for the first time today, for pity's sake." Too furious to cry, she swiped at the tears welling up in her eyes. "Besides, the last thing I want complicating my life right now is another man!"

"Just go! Get out of here!"

"Fine! Gladly!" She swung open the door. A biting gust of wind slapped her in the face. She turned toward her husband. "When will I see you again? Tomorrow? Monday?"

"I don't know." He avoided her gaze.

"Fine!" Her pride hung in shreds about her soul. "When you're ready to talk, you know where to find me! But also know that if you don't come to talk with me, I will find you. You can't avoid the inevitable. Sooner or later this week, we will talk, I assure you!" She slid off the seat, onto the running board, and stepped down to the ground. The glass in the side window rattled as she slammed the door behind her, causing an avalanche of snow to cascade off the roof of the vehicle and onto her head and shoulders.

Frustrated with her less-than-dramatic exit, Liz stormed across the slippery pathway to the boardinghouse. "I won't look back! I won't look back," she muttered aloud as she scaled the porch's icy steps. She heard Alan shift the vehicle into reverse and tear away from the boardinghouse. He gunned the engine the entire length of the street.

Before opening the front door, the woman paused and inhaled the cleansing aroma of the freshly fallen snow. She wanted to catch her wits about her before meeting her new landlady. But her brief moment of solitude passed when the front door opened and a short, gray-haired woman of fifty or so, with apple-red cheeks and a body to match, appeared. An overfed tabby cat rubbed against the woman's ankles. Ready or not, the brisk north wind shoved Liz into the well-lit foyer.

"Welcome, Mrs. Ames. Ralph told me you'd be here soon. He left a pair of mukluks for you to use while you're in Whittier." She cast a quick disapproving glance at Liz's city boots. "Come. Come into the dining room and get warm. You must be freezing after sitting out there in the cold for so long. Was that your husband? Here, let me take your coat." The woman deftly stripped the overcoat from Liz's shoulders and hung it on a wooden peg behind the door. "There! You must be hungry. I saved you some supper."

"Thank you, but I'm not very—" Liz glanced toward the stairwell where she hoped she could make her escape.

"Nonsense. Here in Alaska, we eat to maintain enough padding against the cold. Call me Miz Mabel—not Miss or Mrs., but Miz. Everybody does, don't cha know?" The woman took Liz by the shoulders and guided her into a parlor papered in giant cabbage roses and overpopulated with carved mahogany furniture. They walked past a pink upholstered chintz sofa and into a comfortably cluttered dining room whose walls were papered with giant vines of ivy. The light from a chandelier glistened off the highly polished rosewood table surrounded by twelve intricately carved matching chairs. A white porcelain bowl of realistic looking wax fruit rested in the center of the table.

"I am so glad you're here, Mrs. Ames. I miss having a woman around the place, especially during the off-season. We've lots to talk about, you and I." Miz Mabel would not be deterred. "I just know we're going to be good friends."

Liz managed a weak smile. Desperate to distract the chatty woman from becoming too personal, the younger woman pointed at the center of the table. "The doily, did you crochet it?"

"Oh, goodness, no!" The woman donned a yellow-and-white gingham Mother Hubbard apron resting on the back of a side chair. "That's Grandma Duncan's handiwork. When winter sets in, we Whittier ladies each have our own ways to maintain our sanity 'til spring." The woman chuckled at her own joke. "Mine's reading. I'll bet you're a reader too. Anyways, while you're here, help yourself to the books in my little library at the foot of the stairs. But for now, it's time to eat. Sit! Sit!"

Intimidated by Miz Mabel's effusive presence, Liz obeyed. The woman scurried out of the room but continued the conversation from the nearby kitchen. "Ralph also dropped off a couple of jars of his wife's huckleberry jam. Katrina's yummy preserves win first prize every year at the state's annual fair in Anchorage, speaking of which, with this new tunnel being built, we gals will find it easier to attend.

"I hope you like mashed potatoes along with grilled salmon steaks with wild blueberry sauce." The door between the dining and kitchen swung open, and Miz Mabel appeared carrying a dinner plate and silverware clutched in one hand and a serving bowl of steaming hot mashed potatoes in the other. "These should stick to your ribs 'til morning. You are a tall drink of water. But then, everyone's tall next to me," she giggled. "From the looks of you, you could use a little food that will stick to those skinny ribs of yours if you're going to survive an Alaskan winter."

"Here, let me help you." Liz rose to her feet.

"Sit, my dear. Sit!" Miz Mabel ordered a second time. "I'm the only cook in this kitchen, that is, except for Abby, my hired girl. You dive into those potatoes while I bring the salmon and berry sauce from the kitchen." The woman seemed unaware of her agility to leap from one topic to the next without taking a breath. "Mr. Lorry, he is such a dear, inundated me with several salmon, all cleaned and ready to grill. What we don't eat fresh, I'll dry and smoke. I should have enough to last 'til spring. By the by, did you enjoy the potato soup Major Judd brought over to you?"

"Yes, ma'am." Liz's stomach growled from hunger. That soup and the bite of donut was the last she'd eaten since breakfast on the *Sitka Sue*.

"Good." Miz Mabel buzzed out of the room and returned with a large platter of food. "Grill a salmon steak, boil up a couple sides of carrots and peas, and there you have it—a meal fit for a king, or queen, as the case may be." Dimples of pleasure formed in the woman's cheeks. "Any Alaskan cook worth her salt knows at least twenty-five ways to serve salmon—

and caribou for that matter." She placed a basket of hot sourdough bread slices on the table.

"Hope you like the bread. No store-bought bread is served at my table. My great-grandfather, Pierre Horton, came to Skagway from New York City at the beginning of the Yukon Gold Rush. He brought with him the starter I still use for my sourdough. Can't think of anything I cherish as much as I do my starter dough."

Liz slathered a slice of the bread with butter and took a bite. "I can see why. As you probably know, Seattle is also famous for its sourdough, but your bread is exquisite. I love the texture of your crust."

*"Hmmph!"* She accepted the compliment as if it were naturally due her. "You know the definition of an Alaskan sourdough, don't you?"

Her mouth full of bread, Liz could only shake her head.

"An Alaskan sourdough is a guy who's sour because he's out of dough and can't go back to the States." Miz Mabel chuckled at her own joke.

Liz laughed and nodded.

With such a variety of good food on the plate before her, Liz barely knew what to try next. She chose a forkful of the potatoes. "*M-m-m,* these potatoes are delicious!" Liz closed her eyes to better savor the spud's delicate flavor.

Her hostess placed a tumbler of water on the table in front of her guest. "The secret is in the shallots. Plus, I use sea salt."

Liz ate another forkful of the fluffy spuds. "*M-m-m,* whatever you do, don't change your recipe." As Liz ate, Miz Mabel gave her a complete dossier on the lives of many of the citizens living in the tiny town of Whittier. The woman also regaled Liz with the tale of being snowbound at a lumber camp in the Yukon Territory where Miz Mabel met her first husband; then she went on to describe how she met each of her five husbands and how each man had died.

"Outlived them all, I did. That's why I'd be skeered to wed ag'in. To marry me, the poor guy would be signing his own death warrant," Miz Mabel chortled aloud. "But enough about me. You, dear girl, need to catch a nap so you can relieve the major at three."

Liz blinked in surprise. "How did you—"

"Why, honey, don't cha know? Nothing goes on in Whittier that Miz Mabel don't know about."

# Chapter 10: Out in the Cold

*I will not pretend to justify this espionage.*
*—Hermann Hesse*

## Alaskan Wilderness: December 1941

The reflection of the full moon on a fresh layer of snow guided the Inuit tracker north by northwest toward the army camp. A row of icy hemlocks created a bejeweled corridor—a bit like diamond-studded walls. Alone in the magic of nature's festival of winter, he could almost forget about the presence of the gravel road running parallel to the towering hemlocks on his left or the growling dump trucks and behemoth earth movers.

Amarok's foray to the foot of the Whittier Glacier had revived his spirits. While sending and receiving radio messages at the base of giant granite rocks that had tumbled to the valley floor over the eons of time, he'd spotted a brown bear, unusual for the season, several bald eagles, and a lone wolverine.

Grumbling from the Inuit's stomach spurred him forward—one snowshoe after the other, plowing through the snow without breaking a sweat. *If I increase my pace, I'll reach camp before the mess hall closes for the night,* he thought. *If not, I'll have to settle for eating smoked caribou jerky 'til morning.* As much as he respected the foods of his native heritage, he'd grown accustomed to the scintillating delights of army fare, at least when cooked by Mrs. Dahl and served by her lovely daughter, Trudy.

A vision of the ethereal blond girl-woman wafted like a translucent winged butterfly through his mind. He allowed a wisp of a smile to tweak the corners of his lips. More than once, he'd gone out of his way to attract her favor with his charm and wit. Often it earned him an extra oatmeal-raisin cookie beyond the two-per-person limit. *Back to business, Amarok! When this job is done, you will return to your village, marry the lovely Mikia, and purchase a fishing boat—perhaps an entire fleet—of your own with the money you've saved double-dipping into the American and Japanese war chests.*

A traditional Inuit blessing came to mind, *"May you have peace in your igloo, a plump woman in your furs, oil in your lamps, and seal meat in your larder."* The seal meat and the woman, yes, but Amarok wondered if he'd ever find peace in his igloo or in his heart. The risks he took for his foreign employers surely wouldn't give him much peace. *Don't eat a moose 'til you catch it,* Amarok reminded himself as he stepped up his pace.

The roar from the engine of an oncoming army truck sent Amarok scrambling behind a massive boulder beside the road. He peered through the branches of a nearby evergreen. *Whoever is driving that vehicle is traveling too fast for the road conditions.*

The speeding vehicle rounded a sharp bend, spun out on the curve, zigzagged several times, and came to a halt, hoodfirst into the nearest snowbank. The driver jammed the gears into reverse and gunned the engine. The gigantic rear tires spun helplessly on the road's icy surface. The irate driver persisted until the engine stalled. Frustrated, the man climbed out of the cab to inspect the situation.

When the officer stomped around the rear of the vehicle, Amarok gasped in surprise. *Captain Ames?* The Aleut had never seen his stoic, unflappable boss out of control. The captain hopped back into the truck and tried, in vain, to restart the engine. For a moment, Amarok considered going to the man's aid, but how could he explain his reason for hiking in the wilderness at this time of evening as well as carrying a heavy backpack of radio gear?

The captain climbed out of the cab a second time and kicked the left front tire in frustration. "That woman! That woman You gave me, God!" he shouted, his furious words echoing in the silence of the evening. Pulling his military parka tighter around his neck and his woolen cap down around his ears, Captain Ames stormed toward camp along the deep, rutted tracks made by military vehicles. The Aleut ducked from sight when the captain glanced over his shoulder at the howl of a wolf and its mate's return call.

When he was certain the pale skin could no longer see him, Amarok slowly rose to his feet. "May the gods protect the fool," he muttered. The Aleut followed at a discrete distance. He couldn't have the captain wander off into the night never to be seen again.

★ ★ ★ ★ ★

Neither the captain nor Amarok sensed another pair of curious eyes watching from a safe distance before silently joining the strange procession toward the military outpost.

# Chapter 11: Change of Plans

*Change is not made without inconvenience.*
—*Richard Hooker*

## Whittier, Alaska: December 1941

Liz gazed around the cozy guestroom that would be her home for the next week before she returned to Seattle on the *Sitka Sue*. Her luggage sat unopened atop a down-filled crazy quilt of reds, yellows, and oranges that covered the four-poster bed. A second quilt splashed with the blues, purples, and greens of the ocean hung on the white plastered wall above the bed's maple headboard. After opening her largest travel case, she removed her grandmother's Bible and placed it on a small maple dresser. A nightstand and an oak rocker sat on the other side of the bed beside a window. Crisp white Priscilla curtains edged the small window. English ivy planted in a white milk-glass bowl on the windowsill added an additional spot of color to the room.

After placing her smaller items of clothing into the dresser drawers, she hung the heavier items in the tiny closet near a woodstove—the room's only source of heat. Cheery red-and-yellow flames glowed behind the smoky glass in the door. Liz sat down in the rocker to remove her boots and her damp wool stockings.

*"Ooh!"* Liz groaned as she ran her fingers across the beginning of a blister on her right heel. Along with the pain, a wave of homesickness washed over her. Too keyed up to fall asleep, she opened her grandmother's

Bible. When she'd first found the Book in her luggage, the young woman had been irked with Grandma Keating. But today, after the harsh encounter she'd had with Alan and the unsettling one with Major Judd, the Bible represented home and love and security.

The place for religion in Liz's adult life had evolved into a CTE experience—Christmas, Thanksgiving, and Easter. She enjoyed the pageantry of the holidays but not the dogma of religion, as she called it. College had cured her of belief in the limited religious training of her childhood. After losing Lanny, and then Alan, she'd discovered that the real world is cold, harsh, and isolating. To believe in a God who gives a thought for what happens to the humans He created, if He did indeed create them, Liz decided she'd have to check her brain at the door.

It wasn't that her parents hadn't taken her to church as a child. When convenient, like most of her mother's country club friends, the family attended the most respectable church in the community. Each week, immediately upon returning home, they'd change out of their "church" lives into their everyday lives. And though Liz believed in a Supreme Being, she never seriously considered doing anything as illogical as inviting Him into her life. It wasn't that Grandmother Keating didn't try to help Liz make her religion personal. The woman lived her faith as well as talked about the strength she gained from the Good Book.

Liz ran her fingers across the onionskin pages inside the leather-bound volume. She could almost hear Grandma Keating's voice reciting a favorite scripture, Hebrews 13:5. "I will never leave thee, nor forsake thee." Liz didn't know where to find the verse, but the promise brought a temporary calm into her heart. She rested her head against the back of the chair and closed her eyes. The comforting idea of being in God's eternal care would vanish each time the pain of her encounter with Alan returned.

Idly, she flipped through the pages until it fell open to the book of Proverbs. Her gaze rested on a verse her grandmother had underlined in red. "In all thy ways acknowledge him and he shall direct thy paths."

Her eyes misted with tears. "Grandma, if I ever needed direction . . ." Liz read aloud the underlined verse before it. "Trust in the LORD with all thine heart; and lean not to thine own understanding."

*Leave it to Grandma Keating,* she thought, *to reach out to her honey-bunny from a million miles away.* Resting her head against the back of the rocker, Liz closed her eyes and slowly inhaled.

"God?" The heavy braided rag rug covering the wooden floor absorbed much of the sound of her voice. "Oh, God," she began again, "are You really there? After Lanny's death, I begged for Your help, but You remained silent. The same thing happened after Alan left. You didn't say a word! Not one word! I don't know if I expected You to shout aloud or maybe write a message on my bedroom wall, but I received nothing." A tear slid down Liz's face. "Is there a special formula, a secret handshake or code Your people use to get Your attention? I know I've lived my life as though You don't exist, but I'm a good person, aren't I? Is it by harboring doubts about You that I may have forfeited my right to ask for Your help? I don't know how to do it!" She blotted her tears on her sleeve. "Oh, how I wish I could hop a ship for home right now! Forget Alan, forget our marriage—that's what I'd like to do! I can live a good life without having any human love beyond my folks, right?"

She shook her head in frustration. "Oh, who am I kidding? I know what my problem is. I'm totally alone for the first time in my entire life. And I'm scared. Dad's not here; Grandma's not here; Alan doesn't want anything to do with me. I need help! If You are all Grandma Keating claims You to be, please direct my paths because I am at a loss as to what to do next."

Liz sat quietly for several minutes until her eyelids slid shut, and she found herself cuddling with Alan beneath a blue-and-white quilt in their honeymoon cottage in Seattle. She could almost feel his hand caressing her shoulder and sliding down her arm. She smiled when his warm breath tickled her neck, and he nibbled on her earlobe.

"No! No!" The woman started awake to find Miz Mabel's giant tabby cat snuggled in her lap. Startled, the animal leaped to the floor and disappeared under the bed.

Liz gasped. "Where did you come from, big boy? I didn't mean to scare you." She glanced toward the bed. "Why am I sitting here when I could be sleeping in a bed?"

She slipped into her comfy flannel pajamas and slid under the covers. Liz had barely closed her eyes when a knock on the door awakened her. A flame still glowed in the stove. Like a sleepy child on a lazy Sunday morning, she closed her eyes and snuggled deeper under the mountain of downy quilts. *Maybe if I lie perfectly still, whoever is knocking will go away.*

The door opened a crack. A stream of light landed directly across her face.

"Mrs. Ames. Mrs. Ames. Are you awake?" Miz Mabel, swathed in a brown-and-yellow plaid wool robe, filled the doorway.

"I am now," Liz mumbled.

"Good, because Major Judd's driver is waiting downstairs to take you to the office. Mrs. Ames?"

Liz covered her head with a pillow.

"Mrs. Ames. You have to wake up. You need to relieve Major Judd at the station." The woman entered the room. "Nap in the office before the major replaces you in the morning. Come on; wake up, sweetie."

"I'm awake! I'm awake." Liz groaned, sat up, and threw her legs over the side of the bed.

"Good!" A smile creased the woman's face. "While you dress, I'll fix Private Epps a cup of hot cocoa and some toast while he's waiting—such a nice boy. Would you like a thermos of hot cocoa and a loaf of homemade pumpkin bread to take with you?" Miz Mabel answered her own question. "Of course, you would. You dress warmly. You did bring a heavy sweater and a pair of trousers with you, didn't you? While Hollywood movie stars wear trousers to flaunt their independence, we women in the north wear heavy trousers for survival. Those military Quonsets aren't insulated."

Standing before the wall mirror, Liz brushed her shoulder-length hair back and covered it with her black knitted snood. Lines of exhaustion around her mouth and the strain of the day were still evident in her eyes. She straightened her shoulders in defiance. *Since I can't sleep it off, I'll work it off!*

After the death of her son, working long hours for her father had helped. The same means of escape worked after Alan had left. Wearing woolen snow pants and a woolen ski sweater, Liz gave herself one last inspection in the mirror and decided she was as ready as possible to meet the new day—if a new day started in the middle of the night. *But in Alaska, how does one measure winter days and nights?* she wondered as she stuffed her feet into woolen stockings and then into the fur-lined boots Miz Mabel had set on the foot of the bed.

On her way out the front door, Liz glanced at Miz Mabel's grandfather clock—2:30 A.M. In Alaska, night or day during winter, she had discovered—except for a few gloomy hours at midday—everything looked and felt the same. *No wonder the bears around these parts hibernate.*

*Smart beasts. I could handle a six-month-long nap myself. Especially this week,* she thought. A stinging wind threatened to topple Liz into a snowbank as she made her way to Private Epps's waiting vehicle. The young driver smiled as he helped her climb aboard. Liz appreciated that the young man drove her to the Quonset in silence.

Major Judd greeted her at the door. "Boy, am I glad to see you. It has been one long, boring Saturday night. Epps located a fresh pillow and pillowslip for you, along with a couple of extra army blankets to keep you warm. He or his zero five hundred replacement, Corporal Benton, will tend the fire in the stove and do anything else you need done." He glanced greedily at the large woven basket Private Epps placed in the middle of the office desk. "I see Miz Mabel supplied you with sufficient food and beverage for the night."

"Along with a good book," Liz added, tossing a copy of John Steinbeck's *The Grapes of Wrath* onto the radio table. As she unbuttoned her coat, Major Judd leaped to her aid.

"Here, let me help you." As he did, one of the hairpins holding her snood in place caught on the coat's collar. She grabbed for the snood, but not quickly enough as a swirl of flame red curls broke free and tumbled down around her shoulders.

Before she could recover, Will picked up the woolen knitted hairnet and dangled it on one finger. She noted the teasing glint in his eyes. "You look much prettier when that lovely hair of yours isn't trapped inside this thing."

"Thank you for sharing your astute fashion sense!" She snatched the snood from his hands and attempted to recapture the tangle of curls loosed about her shoulders. A grin spread across his face as he crossed the room to the radio station. "Guess I can mark off December 6 from our calendar. Only nineteen days until Christmas and only seventeen days until I fly home to Nebraska for a thirty-day leave."

"Omaha?" She set the thermos of hot cocoa on the radio table. As she turned, her shoulder brushed past his. Startled at the current between them, she jerked away. Acting as if nothing had happened, Will removed his canvas and wool parka from the peg next to where her coat now hung.

"Yep. My mom and dad own a small farm north of town where they grow sugar beets along with field corn for beef cattle. They also run a small herd of milking cows to meet their personal needs and chickens to supply enough eggs to support my mother's compulsion to cook and bake for other people, including the hobos passing by the farm. We didn't know how these men knew to stop—until my dad found a giant X chalked on the rear of the barn, indicating to passersby that ours was a friendly house."

"Sounds like you love your folks very much." Liz's hand trembled slightly at his close proximity. After an instant, she snapped back to become the professional she'd always been. "So nothing worthy of note happening on air tonight?"

"Not a thing, I'm afraid. If the trend continues, you are in for a boring night." Will fastened the buttons on his officer's jacket; threw his heavy parka over one shoulder, and opened the office door. "I guess I'll leave you now to your reading, napping, or whatever. Anything else you need before I go?"

"Nothing I can think of." She seated herself at the radio station and yawned, but not before noting the local time—0310.

"I'll be back to relieve you at the end of your shift. If you need me between eleven hundred hours and noon, I'll be at the Whittier Community Church. Pastor Elwin Gibbs is a great guy, a genuine Christian who practices what he preaches. He delivers a good sermon too."

Liz nodded and smiled. "My grandmother is one of those kinds of Christians as well."

"Like to meet her someday." Will winked and smiled. "Well, gotta go. Have a nice shift." The door closed behind him.

Liz tapped her pencil on the desktop. With the overhead light off, two small green-shaded desk lamps valiantly tried to illuminate the room. When her growling stomach reminded her she hadn't eaten in several hours, she walked over to the main desk and peered into Miz Mabel's basket. As she unwrapped the red-and-white gingham napkin from around the loaf of pumpkin bread, she inhaled the delicious aroma. The fragrance of the spices made her homesick for Gertie and her cooking. Beneath the bread were two apples. At the bottom of the basket was a butter knife, a slice of margarine wrapped in waxed paper, and a small jar of peanut butter.

She cut a slice of the bread and slathered it with margarine. *Maybe it was foolish of me to come to Alaska. Maybe I should have left well enough alone and taken a Mexican holiday. He gave me an out if I wanted it.*

Liz folded her arms as if hugging herself. She ached to be a little girl again, to climb into her daddy's lap, to have him brush her curls from the side of her face and assure her that everything would be all right. *Nothing will ever be right again!* Feeling a sudden chill, she unfastened the lid on the thermos and poured hot cocoa into the cup. As she slowly sipped the steaming liquid, she gazed about the semidarkened room. Her attention rested on the local time clock—0340. *It's only 0340? It's going to be a long night!*

The woman ambled over to the radio desk, sat down, and picked up Miz Mabel's Steinbeck novel. She read a few pages and yawned. The plight of the farmers of the Oklahoma Dust Bowl couldn't hold her attention. Placing the open book on her lap, she leaned her head on her folded arms and closed her eyes. The thud of the book hitting the wooden floor started her awake. She decided the army cot would be more comfortable than the straight-backed desk chair and clicked off the lamp beside the radio console. Sliding the army cot nearer to the cheery flame in the woodstove, she stretched out on the bare canvas. "Oh, Lord, please, whoever You are . . ." Liz pulled the scratchy wool army blanket over her sleepy form. "No nightmares tonight, please."

Her head had barely touched the starched cotton pillowcase before a kaleidoscope of honeymoon vignettes returned: cuddling with Alan before a roaring fireplace in their log cabin hideaway on the shore of the Columbia River; smooching like crazy teenagers near the rushing waters of Multnomah Falls; skinny-dipping in a remote hot springs in Oregon's back country; cavorting in a grassy field speckled with daisies. She lingered in the hazy dreamland until what started as the cries of a high-flying hawk grew into a blast from the radio's emergency horn.

She blinked awake. The red light of the Klaxon lamp pulsated an emergency warning. But it was the dots and the dashes spitting out of the shortwave radio that sent Liz flying to the radio.

The woman grabbed the nearest pencil and slid into the receiver's chair. She recorded the local time on the log—1100 hours. All thought of sleep vanished as she began transcribing the incoming series of dots and dashes into the log. Her mind could barely interpret the horrific message coming over the radio.

"CINPAC—HARBOR CIRCUIT GENERAL PLAIN LANGUAGE MESSAGE QUOTE—AIR RAID ON PEARL HARBOR—

THIS IS NO DRILL—UNQUOTE—HEAVY GUNFIRE—US FLEET SUNK—THOUSANDS DEAD—SK."

"Oh dear God, no!" She gasped as she continued transcribing the incoming code.

The deafening blasts from the emergency horn had also wakened the corporal asleep in the outer office. He burst through the door and bounded across the room to deactivate the Klaxon lamp and to silence the bleating horn.

"Epps! Benton! Whatever your name is! Go get Major Judd immediately!"

"Yes, ma'am. What's happening?" The corporal's fright was obvious.

"Just get Major Judd. Hurry!"

"Yes, yes, yes, sir, er, ma'am," he stuttered, saluted, and fled the office.

Before Corporal Benton's military vehicle tore out of the snowy parking lot, the incoming radio traffic had stopped transmitting from Pearl City, Hawaii, to the chief radio operator at a military headquarters outside Washington, D.C.

"STAND DOWN—ALL MILITARY STATIONS STAND DOWN—ENCRYPTED COMMUNICATION ONLY UNTIL FURTHER NOTICE—USE CIPHER—SK."

Liz sensed the increased tension in the operator's fist. "Cipher?" she shouted at the empty walls. An element of panic tinged her customarily cool demeanor. "Where's the cipher book? Oh, Will, please get here soon." Her hands shook as she rifled through the pile of papers and pamphlets stacked on the floor beside the desk. "Where is it? I can't find it!" When she realized no one could hear her shouts, she paused and took a deep breath. "Of course you can't find it, silly. All the secret military codes would be kept under lock and key!"

Forcing her brain to focus her attention on accurately logging the rapid code coming out of Washington, Liz didn't know how long she'd been transcribing code when the office door slammed against the wall and Will charged into the room. "What's happening?"

She answered his question, while continuing to pencil the ciphers into the logbook. "The Japanese have bombed Pearl Harbor, sinking the U.S. Pacific Fleet. Thousands are dead. The code now coming in is encrypted. We need the military code book to decipher it."

"The book is in the wall safe." Will dashed to the wall safe behind the desk and dialed in the code.

From across the room, Corporal Benton stared in disbelief. "Pearl Harbor? My brother's stationed there. He's in the navy."

"Here! Here it is." Will waved the leather-bound cipher book in the air. "Liz, keep logging the encryptions while I locate today's code." Will riffled through the pages of the book. "Here! Here we are—Sunday, December 7!" Hauling his desk chair beside Liz, he slipped in a fresh logbook and removed the one she'd been using. "Just keep writing. I'll try to make sense out of the mishmash you've already logged. Fortunately, today's code is a simple four-letter offset—*A*s are *E*s and *B*s are *F*s and so forth. Let's see what you have so far."

The room took on a slightly surrealistic air as the radio operators performed their tasks, forcing aside all thoughts of the national tragedy and the thousands of lives lost. Liz recorded with one ear and listened to Will translate what she'd already recorded with the other.

"R—PENDLETON, REPORT RADAR DETECTION OF FOREIGN AIR MOVEMENT OFF CALIFORNIA COAST—SK."

"R—NONE—SK."

"R—FORT CLATSOP?—SK."

"R—NONE—SK."

One by one, the military bases along the Pacific coast reported negative sightings of enemy ships or planes to the military headquarters outside Washington, D.C. Each SK sign-off produced sighs of relief from those huddled together in the small Quonset building in Whittier, Alaska.

"R—DUTCH HARBOR REPORTS NO SIGHTINGS—SK."

"Whew, that one's closer to home." Will wiped his brow with a handkerchief. "Looks like America's at war, ready or not."

The major grabbed a piece of notepaper from his desk drawer and scribbled a quick message. *"Stand down. Pearl Harbor attacked by Japanese. Pacific Fleet sunk. Thousands lost. Be on the alert for sabotage."* He then stuffed the note into a canvas-wrapped tube, clamped it shut, and handed it to his assistant. "Corporal, take this to Colonel Anderson immediately. I don't know if the camp radio is even being manned this morning," he explained. Unnerved by the tragedy, the young soldier grabbed the tube from Will.

"Wait! Deliver Anderson's message first, but on your return to Whittier, give this one to the harbormaster." Major Judd continued speaking as he scribbled another communiqué and stuffed it in a second tube. *"Except for the United States Navy, no merchant ship or fishing boat regardless of nationality is to enter or leave Whittier Port until further notice."*

Liz concentrated on recording the encrypted incoming code while Will resumed deciphering it. "More military installations reporting, no enemy activity sighted, this time along the Gulf of Mexico and eastern Florida coast." He glanced toward Liz. "Looks like you won't be heading for Seattle at the end of the week, Elizabeth. All traffic, radio or sea, has been ordered to stand down until further notice. It looks like the *Sitka Sue* and her crew will be spending the winter in Whittier."

"Oh, no." Liz had been soothing her frayed nerves with the promise of returning home at the end of the week.

"Sorry. All civilian radio traffic and travel is under orders to stand down until further notice. Only authorized military communication will be transmitted."

"But my dad . . ." Liz's hand paused over the logbook. She had never before been beyond the scope of her father's loving hand. Since her first steps, his arms had always been there to catch her when she fell, clearing any obstacles that would complicate her life, including her journey to Alaska to find Alan. And then there was Alan. *What will he say about this turn of events?* She'd really gotten herself in a mess this time. She shivered before she realized her woolen sweater was damp with sweat.

"Believe me, I'm sure your parents already know what has happened. In a couple of hours, the entire world will know." Will cleared the huskiness from his voice. "Fortunately, you have a room at Mabel's. You know, I will be needing your help more than ever now, monitoring and deciphering the daily encryptions." He paused and scowled. "Oh, do you, by any chance, have experience training radio operators? We have to find more bodies to cover the twenty-four-hour shifts. I'm sure the army will more than compensate you for your time and service."

"Of course, I will help in any way I can. As to breaking in new coders, I've been doing that for my dad since high school." Without warning, the enormity of the day's tragedy overcame her composure. When a tear escaped down her cheek, Will impulsively reached out to dry it. She swiped it away. "No, Major! Don't. I've never been a crier, and I don't intend to start now!"

"Sorry." He gave an abrupt nod. "You're right, Elizabeth. It looks like we'll be working together for the next few weeks. Uh, I think we'd be wise to uh, set some boundaries. To make this work, you and I will need to maintain proper office decorum."

Even as she nodded her agreement, Liz knew that working side by side with Major William Judd of Omaha, Nebraska, would not be a good idea. She'd come to Alaska to save her marriage, not destroy it. From Will's speech, she also knew he'd recognized the undeniable tension between the two of them.

"How long will it take to train, say, six men to a proficient level of code?" His question forced her to table her concern for later.

"Two weeks; three maybe, according to their natural aptitude. But until I can get them trained, you'll need help manning the station."

"Er, yes, I guess I will." Color climbed up the major's neck and into his cheeks. Somehow, he'd read her thoughts. Rising from his chair, he strode toward his desk. "Fortunately, with the shortwave operations in the United States on stand-down, the radio chatter should drop off to only an occasional blast out of D.C. But we will need one of us on duty round the clock."

"I can do it if you can."

A grin spread across Will's face. "Good, it may help to have Captain Ames assigned to act as your private attaché, driving you back and forth to the outpost where you can conduct the classes."

Liz rolled her eyes toward the ceiling. *Alan's gonna love that.*

"You'll teach your coding class immediately after breakfast in the mess hall. Emma Dahl is our cook. Her husband maintains the construction rigs for the army while she and their nineteen-year-old daughter, Trudy, operate the mess hall."

*Trudy! Nineteen?* Bells rang and lights flashed like at a carnie show. Liz grimaced. From the sympathetic look in Will's eyes, she knew he knew of the connection between Alan and the girl.

"I'm not so sure . . ."

"Oh, Emma won't mind, really. In the meantime, it's already fourteen hundred hours. You go get some rest and eat a good meal. Let Miz Mabel spoil you while I man the station and choose six recruits for your classes."

Will held her overcoat for her. Relieved that he intended to maintain a proper distance between them, she fastened the buttons and slipped the knitted cloche hat over her tangle of curls. Almost as an afterthought, she asked, "Is it a long walk to Mabel's place? I believe Corporal Benton took the jeep."

The major's otherwise solemn face broke into a wide grin. "So he did. It seems we have a dilemma."

"If you have another vehicle available, I do know how to drive."

"I don't doubt your driving skills. However, in a world of snow, it's easy to get disoriented." The major strode to the office window and peered through the heavy metal blinds. "And the snow is still coming down. I don't want to have to send a dog team out for you. If you'll watch the board for five more minutes, I'll get word to Ralph Lorry. Being it's Sunday, he'll be at home with his wife."

# Chapter 12: Declaration of War

*All wars are civil wars, because all men are brothers.*
*—François Fénelon*

## Base Camp, Maynard Mountain: December 7, 1941

News of the Japanese attack on Pearl Harbor swept through the camp quickly. But the government's official declaration of war was delayed until Monday. Colonel Anton Anderson gathered the men under his command in the mess hall to read the following announcement:

> WAR DECLARED ON JAPAN
>
> "A state of war exists between the Imperial Government of Japan and the Government and the people of the United States and making provision to prosecute the same. . . . The President is hereby authorized and directed to employ the entire naval and military forces of the United States and the resources of the Government to carry on war against the Imperial Government of Japan."

Amarok, along with the one hundred fifty men of the 177th U.S. Army Corps of Engineers and the team of civilian workers, listened to the colonel's announcement. He suppressed his urge to smile.

Standing at the makeshift podium at the front of the mess hall, Colonel Anderson folded the paper from which he'd been reading and put it in his jacket pocket. He gazed at the men assembled before him. "I don't have to tell you men that with the United States at war with Imperial Japan, finishing the tunnel and laying the rails is most vital to our country's defenses. We must put aside our petty differences, whether they be spawned by the military or civilian staff. We must be united. We must work together for the good of our country."

Through the dusty window, Amarok could see the camp flagpole and the Stars and Stripes flapping in the wind off Whittier Glacier. He allowed himself a slight moment of satisfaction. The men standing to his left and to his right were too stunned by the announcement to notice, but Irnig-Kesuk caught Amarok's reaction.

To believe the United States Army and the civilian engineers from Boston would be able to work a day without squabbling was highly unlikely. On that both Aleuts would have bet their monthly paychecks.

Colonel Anderson continued. "Fortunately, the materials we need to protect the snow tent at the mouth of the tunnel have been transferred to a military ship and will dock in Whittier at zero eight hundred hours tomorrow. This project will be top priority. We'll need all hands unloading and transporting the supplies to the outpost. As you've probably already guessed, all holiday leaves are canceled until further notice."

A groan went up from the men.

"Sorry. My holiday to see my family is canceled too," Colonel Anderson continued. "While we will miss one Christmas with those we love, our fallen brothers in Hawaii will never again go home for the holidays. I believe it is appropriate to honor them with a scripture and a prayer." He opened a well-worn Bible. "First, I would like to read from the book of Psalms—Psalm 23. 'The LORD is my shepherd; I shall not want . . .' "

Though Irnig-Kesuk tried, he couldn't understand the significance of the familiar reading. He'd heard it recited at every Christian funeral he'd ever attended. *What do sheep and shepherds have to do with the hard life we live on the frigid Alaskan tundra?* he wondered. *Or, more important, the supposed life hereafter?* Paradise to him would be to own a fleet of fishing boats filled with abundant catches of cod and salmon, not some land containing an abundance of cows' milk and honey.

His adoptive father, the village shaman, preached the importance of maintaining a harmonious relationship between humankind and Mother Earth. That he understood. Irnig-Kesuk's father spoke of the god Ozuno, who walked on water, who flew through the sky each evening on a multicolored cloud. But this passage, which the pale-skinned missionaries loved so dearly, talked about walking through death shadows, of dining in front of and gloating at one's enemies, and then living in some faraway kingdom with their God.

His father, the half-Aleut and half-Japanese shaman, worshiped a god whom Irnig-Kesuk could respect, a god of the earth, wind, and fire, a wise and compassionate god who cared for all his creatures. Whenever the young Aleut held a freshly caught salmon in his hands, he could feel that fish's struggle to escape back to Ozuno, the father god. Each time the moment between life and death came, when the fish grew limp, Irnig-Kesuk considered his own eventual demise.

Again, he glanced sideways at Amarok's expressionless face and wondered if the same comparison between the Aleut's god and the pale skin's God formed in his stepbrother's mind. Amarok had grown up on the same god stories as he. Did he believe his father's stories, or had he accepted those told about the pale skin's God? Or had he abandoned all thoughts of a life beyond the struggles of today? Irnig-Kesuk did not know.

# Chapter 13: A Tug-of-War

*Love is a decision, not an emotion.*

## Whittier, Alaska: December 7, 1941

When Liz finally completed her Sunday morning shift at the radio station and returned to the boardinghouse, Miz Mabel insisted the exhausted young woman eat a hearty breakfast of hot cereal, along with scrambled eggs and freshly squeezed orange juice—liquid gold in Alaska. The juice oranges had come north from California aboard the *Sitka Sue* with Liz.

Miz Mabel's monologue rambled on throughout the meal. "Major Judd says you won't be going home to Seattle any time soon. I'm sorry, but I must confess, I enjoy your company." She barely paused to take a breath. "Can you imagine the thousands of families who are just learning of their sons' deaths at Pearl Harbor? I can't imagine a worse pain than to lose a child. It's so unnatural. Children are supposed to bury parents—not the other way around. My second husband and I buried two babies. I was so mad at God, it took me several years before I would hold another mother's infant in my arms."

At the mention of losing a child, Liz's mouth went dry. A particle of scrambled eggs caught in Liz's throat. She coughed into her napkin several times. Try as she might, she couldn't stop coughing.

"Oh, honey, are you all right? Let me get you a drink of water." Miz Mabel rushed into the kitchen and back again with a tumbler filled with cold water.

Liz thanked her and sipped until the coughing stopped. Red-faced and on the verge of tears, the younger woman excused herself and dashed up the stairs to her room, leaving a bewildered and concerned innkeeper standing alone at the foot of the stairs.

Slamming the bedroom door behind her, Liz flung herself onto the bed and buried her face in the nearest pillow. *What a terrible day—or night—or whatever it is,* she sobbed. She cried over the loss of her son. She cried over the disappointment of not being home in time for Christmas. She cried for the thousands of lives lost at Pearl Harbor. She cried for their families. She cried for her country. She cried for her failed marriage. Liz cried until no more tears would come. At one point, the distraught woman heard a soft knock on the bedroom door, but she ignored it. She wondered if her situation could get any worse. Finally, when her energy was spent, the exhausted young woman drifted into a deep, dreamless sleep. Hours later, she awoke to the sound of someone stoking the stove in the corner of her tiny bedroom. Liz opened her eyes. It was Miz Mabel.

"Sorry," her landlady whispered. "I was hoping I could add a log or two to the fire without waking you. I understand how exhausted you must be, but the temperature outside has dropped. It's going to be a cold night."

Liz sat up and rubbed her eyes. Her eyes stung from all the crying she'd done. "What time is it?"

Miz Mabel turned on the small lamp beside the bed. "Oh, you have plenty of time before you relieve Major Judd. He sent a message a few hours ago and told me to let you sleep a little longer. I fixed him a hot meal to take with him to the office. Are you getting hungry, dearie? You didn't eat much earlier."

"Maybe a little." Her stomach growled. Also, she realized that her willingness to eat something brought purpose and meaning to Miz Mabel's life at this very difficult time. "It was a rough night," Liz admitted.

A shadow crossed the older woman's face. "I know. Did I ever tell you that my first husband died of influenza two weeks before he was to ship out to England?" Her voice dropped to barely above a whisper; tears glistened in her eyes. "I prayed he wouldn't go. I've always wondered if God took him from me for being so selfish."

Liz touched the older woman's arm. "I don't think God acts like that, at least not the way my grandmother tells it."



"I do hope your grandmother is right," Miz Mabel admitted. "I see you have a Bible here. Do you read it?"

"I've read it more in the last few days than I've read it in my entire lifetime."

"Maybe when you get rested, we could read it together. Frankly, the God I learned about in my childhood was not someone I liked very much. It seemed to me that He was always angry at someone. But maybe I had Him wrong. I wish your grandmother were here to set me straight."

Liz laughed. "I wish she were here too—you can't imagine how much. I could use some of her straightening out."

Later, after the two women read several of Grandma Keating's underlined passages together, Liz took the Bible with her to the Quonset. Throughout the long hours of radio silence, she sought out and reread each of the verses Grandma Keating had underlined with red pencil and then decided to memorize the verses.

In the book of Jeremiah, she found verse 3 of chapter 31 underlined. She read the words aloud. "Yea, I have loved thee with an everlasting love: therefore with loving kindness have I drawn thee." Her grandmother had crossed off the two "thees" and penciled Elizabeth's name in the margin, along with another text—Psalm 91. Immediately, Liz searched for the additional text. As she read aloud the treasured promises, a gentle wash of tears fell onto the translucent onionskin paper, lightly puckering the paper. The young woman hugged her Bible to her chest and wept, not tears of sorrow as before, but tears of relief. She could almost feel her grandmother's arms wrapped around her shoulders, holding her, calling her "honey-bunny," and making her feel secure and protected.

★ ★ ★ ★ ★

The next day in the mess hall at base camp, a personal war brewed. When Corporal Benton drove Liz to the outpost and deposited her outside the mess hall tent, the woman braced herself at seeing Alan again and for seeing her rival. She took a deep breath and opened the wooden door. A six-foot-five-inch tall blond giant with a sandy-gray beard and massive arms bulging beneath his plaid flannel shirt greeted her as she stepped out of the cold.

"Welcome. I'm Hans Dahl." His broad smile immediately made Liz feel comfortable.

"Colonel Anderson told my wife you'd be arriving soon after breakfast this morning. Emma and I are so glad to finally meet you, Mrs. Ames. It's Elizabeth, isn't it? May I call you Elizabeth? What a lovely name." He placed her hand in the crook of his arm and escorted her across the dining hall. "Up until a few hours ago, we didn't know you existed, Elizabeth. Somehow old Alan failed to mention he had a wife." A disapproving cloud darkened the man's azure blue eyes. "My wife, Emma, and our daughter Trudy are in the galley. They are eager to meet you as well. I'll go get them."

When Hans freed her hand, Liz gripped the back of the nearest chair to steady herself. Her legs shook. She felt as if she were teetering on the edge of an ice crevasse that was about to crumble. One slight move and she would tumble into an endless abyss from which there would be no escape. Concentrating on maintaining her composure, she didn't notice Alan enter the mess hall and cross to where she stood.

"So you chased me to the ends of the earth! What a dutiful little spouse you are," he hissed. "And now you've ingratiated yourself into my last personal hideaway. How did you get the suave Major Judd to convince the colonel to assign me to you?"

Before she could respond to his venomous charge, he glanced at the Bible she held in her hand. "You becoming religious or something?" He gave a derisive snort. "Doesn't the Good Book say something about the curse of living with a cantankerous wife?"

Every word from her husband seemed to punch Liz in the stomach. "Grandma Keating packed the Bible in my suitcase. It has been a comfort to me since I left home." Silently, she berated herself for sounding like she was apologizing. But that's the direction their disagreements always seemed to take—he accusing and her apologizing, whether or not she'd done anything wrong.

Alan shook his head in disgust. "Well, that would please my saintly mother, wouldn't it? I grew up with that stuff being pumped into my head day after day. Even now, every week she sends me religious pamphlets. Of course, I love her, but . . ."

His revelation thrust a sharp pain into Liz's heart. She could barely breathe. "Your mother has known where you were all this time and didn't tell me?"



Alan gave a sharp snort. "Of course, I wouldn't disappear without telling my mother where I was going."

Liz blinked in surprise. "But she never . . ."

"I got her to promise not to tell you. Do you think I'm stupid?" He shook his head as if dismissing Liz as an inconvenient dragonfly perched on the toe of his boot.

The young woman could barely speak. "Who else knew where to find you?"

"My dad, of course, and my brother and his family."

*I've been such a fool!* She lay the Bible onto the nearest table and turned from him, biting her tongue. She wouldn't give him the satisfaction of being the first to speak. *Not this time,* she thought. *Not this time!*

When he did speak, he spoke to her in the tones that would be appropriate to use when speaking to a subordinate on his crew. "Colonel Anderson ordered me to bring you to his office. He wants to meet you. It goes without saying, I would prefer that you not air our dirty linen in front of my men and my commanding officer. Fortunately, you won't find the colonel quite so malleable as Major Judd. Anderson is about fifty and with a receding hairline."

"I have no intention of airing . . ." Refusing to be beaten down any further, Liz straightened her shoulders and turned to face Alan. "Understood! But in return, I expect you to treat me civilly and with the same respect you would afford any other woman in your presence." She clenched and unclenched her fists several times to reestablish the blood flow through her body. "Be assured, I'm not staying in Alaska for my pleasure; and I am no longer staying here in an effort to reconcile our marriage. The moment the United States government allows civilians to once again travel, I'll be on the first freighter heading south!" She was surprised at the bitterness in her voice. This wasn't the woman she wanted to be. "Don't worry! I will happily leave you to your teenage heartthrob."

"Don't bring Trudy into this!" he hissed, one eye on the closed door between the mess hall and the kitchen. "This is about you and me!"

"Alan, you brought her into our marriage. I didn't." Liz tightened her lips into a pale thin line. "Tell me! Have you slept with her?"

"This is not the time nor the place . . ." Alan trembled as if trying to control the urge to take a swing at her. Finally, he spoke. "No! The girl's as pure as the driven snow."

"Well, there's certainly a lot of that around these parts, isn't there?

Driven snow, that is," she snapped.

"What do you mean by that?"

"You figure it out." She shrugged and brushed past him toward the exit. "And now, if you will direct me to Colonel Anderson's office, I would appreciate it."

In silence, they walked across camp to the Quonset that served as the outpost's headquarters. He paused before opening the door and eyed her for several seconds. "Liz, you've changed. When did you become so bitter?"

"You, you turkey!" She opened the door for herself.

A corporal seated at a small desk in the outer office leaped to his feet and snapped off a salute as they entered the building. The young man immediately announced Liz's arrival to the officer in the next room. As she entered the inner office, the colonel rose to his feet. The military order evident in Colonel Anderson's office was in direct contrast to Major Judd's disorder.

Every available space had been arranged for efficiency and purpose—function before form, as current architects advised. Two file cabinets flanked the colonel's gray metal desk. Every scrap of paper mounted on the wall, from blueprints to maps to memos, was precisely squared off—the corners pinned with black thumbtacks.

"Mrs. Ames!" The colonel extended his right hand toward her. "I am so happy to meet you. So you are the woman who can outkey any man beyond the banks of the Potomac." He released her hand before he continued. "As you know, we have a staff shortage, a crisis, in fact. So we really do need your help. Major Judd tells me that you are an experienced instructor as well."

The colonel picked up a sheet of paper from his inbox. "I've checked over the list of men who will study code with you, as suggested by Major Judd. Obviously, they will be expected to man their posts when they're not in class. I don't need to tell you that we need them trained as quickly as possible. How long do you think it will take for them to become proficient in code?"

Feeling more than a little overwhelmed, Liz swallowed hard. "That will depend on how fast they can absorb the code. While it's a skill to learn, some people are more adept at learning it than others."



"That makes sense. The major suggested they attend classes in the mess hall—saves time transporting them back and forth to Whittier." The colonel snapped his finger toward the corporal still standing in the open doorway. "Corporal, escort Captain Ames into my office, please."

Liz glanced about, surprised that Alan hadn't followed her into the office. "It's the end of the lunch hour," the officer reminded. "By now, the men on the list will be waiting in the mess hall. Mrs. Ames, Major Judd suggested that your husband be assigned to attend to your needs during your time on base. He will also drive you back and forth to Whittier. Consider him your private attaché." A slight smile tipped upward the points of his neat little mustache.

"Sir, I don't think that will be . . ." Flustered, Liz objected.

"Nonsense. This is a national emergency. I need you to have all the assistance possible to train these men quickly."

"But sir," Alan protested, "my unit needs me on the mountain. Just last week I suspected attempted sabotage in the dynamite storage shed."

"And you reported it to me." The colonel waved away Alan's objections. "Don't worry. I've got that covered. Sam, one of the guys from Boston, has stepped up to become temporary crew boss until you return full time. Your primary responsibility until the men are proficient in code is assisting your wife. Your first assignment is to escort her to the mess hall and introduce her to the six trainees." He handed the sheet of names to Alan.

"But, sir . . ."

The colonel turned and gave Liz a slight bow. "Nice meeting you, Mrs. Ames. Thank you for being willing to assist the military in this emergency. Let me know if there is anything you may need. And, Captain," he turned toward Alan, "I expect you to do everything you can to make that happen. You are dismissed."

# Chapter 14: A Stroke of Luck

*He that boasts of his own knowledge proclaims his ignorance.*

## Base Camp, Maynard Mountain: December 1941

"He that boasts of his own knowledge proclaims his ignorance." Amarok silently recited the Aleut axiom as he joined the small group of men gathered at the rear of the mess tent. What a stroke of luck to be assigned to the radio team—a gift from the gods as his father would say. No one would know that he could already send and receive twenty to thirty words per minute. As a student, he would have easy access to the radio room. What could be better for his cause?

Amarok slipped into a chair in the mess hall and crossed his arms. He closed his eyes, trying to focus on the metamorphosis he must make from Amarok to the one he'd carefully nurtured at camp over the last few months. He took a deep breath and held it for several seconds.

A nudge on his arm interrupted his meditative moment. "Say, what's with you? Cat got your tongue?"

Amarok growled. "Didn't sleep well last night. Chip's snoring kept me awake."

"Sorry." The nineteen-year-old seated on Amarok's left groaned. Since his arrival, Private Chip Clark's snoring had become legendary. The young recruit had been shunted from tent to tent until there was no other place to put him.

The door to the mess hall swung open and in stepped a titian-haired young woman followed by the solemn-faced Captain Ames.

"Hey, take a look at that!" one of the men whispered.

One glance toward the door and Amarok sat upright. He gasped at the bevy of golden-red curls tumbling around the woman's shoulders from beneath her woolen cloche. Amarok stared mesmerized, as did the other five men gathered around the wooden table. When she smiled in his direction, the usually bold engineer blushed and dropped his gaze.

The woman's features weren't unusually lovely, quite common really, like many of the coeds he'd met and dated at the University of Washington. It was the hair that stopped him dead. In a world where heavy black braids were the norm, with an occasional Russian or Swedish blonde around to break the monotony, a red-haired beauty was rare indeed. By the looks on the other men's faces, Amarok realized he wasn't alone in his admiration.

When Captain Ames strode over to the long wooden table, the six men stood and snapped to attention. "At ease, men. Be seated," the captain began. "As you know, you have been chosen by Major Judd and the colonel to learn Morse code as quickly as possible to replenish the shortage of qualified radio men on base. Starting tomorrow, your class will begin each morning at zero nine hundred hours and end at twelve hundred hours. For the rest of the day, you will return to your regular assigned tasks. I don't need to tell you how vital it is to the war effort that you learn the code as quickly as possible because the radio is our only link to the world outside Whittier. So no gold-bricking!" Alan's gaze moved slowly across the upturned faces. "Those of you who qualify will be reassigned to Major Judd in Whittier. No more swinging a pickaxe for a while."

The men laughed; the captain smiled. "Colonel Anderson has asked my wife, Elizabeth, to instruct you." The captain gestured toward Liz. The men whistled and clapped until one by one they fell silent as they spotted the heavy frown on the captain's face.

Liz greeted their applause with grace. "If your efforts to learn code are as enthusiastic as your welcome of me today, you are going to be a super class."

Again, the men applauded. She raised her hands to call them to order. "First, gentlemen, we need to get acquainted. One at a time, please stand and give me your name."

A wry smile crossed Amarok's face as he mentally shifted into his adopted persona. *So let the game begin.*

# Chapter 15: Code: SOS

*The years teach much which the days never know.*
*—Ralph Waldo Emerson*

## Base Camp, Maynard Mountain: December 1941

Liz, having spent her adult career operating in a male-dominated workforce, wasn't taken aback by the men's raucous response. Yet having been a woman in a distinctly man's world, she knew that she would need to establish her credentials quickly to maintain control of the class.

As Alan read the list of names, she studied each face to determine which of the men would likely excel at coding and which might be in the class merely to get out of heavy digging on the mountain.

When Alan finished speaking, Liz gave him a polite nod. Slowly, she scanned each man's face a second time, and then pointed to the short, skinny teenager on her left. "Private Trumble? Where are you from?"

"Private Timothy Trumble, from Atlanta, Georgia, ma'am." He looked to be all of sixteen years old, a child in an adult male world.

She nodded and turned toward the burly man standing beside Trumble. "Private First Class Andy Jakes, ma'am. I'm from Newark, New Jersey." And the introductions continued.

"Corporal Richard West, ma'am. I hail from Loveland, Colorado." The corporal cocked his head to one side and with partially closed eyes, shot her a suggestive grin, which she ignored.

A man of average height with black hair and a matching beard rose to his feet. He wore the colorful garb of the local citizenry. "Civilian Moeshe Jones. I'm from Seward, Alaska, ma'am."

"Welcome, Mr. Jones." She smiled and turned her attention to the tall, rangy man beside him.

"Well, how-de-do, ma'am." The man spoke with an obvious Texas drawl. "I'm Private First Class Bobby Ward. And I'm from the great state of Texas—Amarillo, to be more precise."

She nodded and smiled at the last man in the row. He extended his hand. "My name is Lowell Meade, a civilian worker. I was hired out of Anchorage."

Ignoring his extended hand, she nodded. "Good to meet you, Mr. Meade. Welcome to the team. And, gentlemen, we are a team. Being a radio technician demands precision, speed, accuracy, and dependability as well as the ability to work as an efficient unit. When one member of a radio communications force washes out, for whatever reason, another member of the team must pick up the slack. When you miss your shift, the person before you must pull double duty until someone arrives to relieve him. That is even truer now that we are at war. The radio must be manned twenty-four hours a day, seven days a week.

"Captain Ames will hand each of you a typed sheet of the alphabet in Morse code." While the class members studied the sheet, Liz continued. "As you know, Morse code is a type of character encoding that transmits telegraphic information using rhythm. It also uses a standardized sequence of short and long elements to represent letters, numbers, and punctuation of a specific message. The speed is measured in words per minute."

She paused to be certain her class was with her. "The series of dots and dashes were developed in the early 1840s by Samuel Morse. But the use of Morse code didn't come into its own until the 1890s." She tapped out the familiar international emergency code—SOS—on a portable keypad on the table in front of her. "SOS—emergency! Warning! Don't try to memorize the letters by rote. The only way you can learn code is by listening and writing down what you hear. You must memorize the sound, not the written alphabet. And don't try to visualize the dots and dashes. It will only slow you down."

For an instant, she glanced toward the far end of the mess tent and caught a flash of a young woman with blond braids wrapped about her head—Trudy. Forcing herself to focus on the task at hand, Liz keyed a short message.

"Does anyone know what I just said?"

No one raised his hand. "Within two weeks, after daily classes and by putting in four to six hours of practice each evening, you will learn to send and receive Morse code. You will need to do at least thirteen words per minute before you can pass your test to operate the station. Your first assignment is to divide into teams of two and practice sending and receiving simple code. Oh, yes, before you begin—what I keyed earlier, at approximately forty words per minute, was, 'Good morning, gentlemen, are you ready to learn code?' "

The lanky young man from Texas chuckled aloud. "Whooie! Ma'am, you are somethin' else. I ain't never heard anyone code that fast before."

"You're Private Ward, right?" Liz smiled at the giant of a man barely out of his teens.

"Yes, ma'am. I've wanted to learn Morse code since I was a tadpole listening to the radio men send and receive messages to and from company headquarters in Dallas at my pappy's oil rig site. But you, you make those radio guys sound like pikers."

"Thank you, Mr. Ward. Remember, coding is a lot like typing. Some people take to it easily; others struggle. Just the fact that you are accustomed to hearing code should give you a head start on the rest of the class, Mr. Ward."

"Call me Bobby. Everyone does."

Liz flashed him her friendliest smile. "Thank you, Mr. Ward. But in this setting, I will call you Mr. Ward. I'm sure you understand."

"Oh—" The man glanced to his right and then to his left. "Oh, but of course, Mrs. Ames. Swell, I'd better get crackin' on that code. Hey, Tim, ya' got a partner yet?"

Out of the corner of her eye, Liz watched Alan amble toward the kitchen. As a result, she sensed rather than heard Lowell Meade step up behind her. "Aren't you the prettiest little thing north of Vancouver? I want you for my partner, Mrs. Ames. I'd love coding with you or anything else you might like to do together."

Liz had long dealt with overly flirtatious male workers. She'd learned that the direct, wither-them-where-they-stand approach worked best. Pasting on her coldest stare, she and said, "Mr. Meade, if you wish to stay in this class, you will, at all times, maintain a proper decorum around me. Do I make myself clear?"

"Er, yes, ma'am. I didn't mean nothin'."

"Good! In the meantime, you'd better choose your partner and begin practicing." Liz deliberately looked past Meade toward the man seated one over from him. "You're Mr. Jones, right?"

"Yes, ma'am." He avoided her gaze.

She glanced down at Mr. Jones's rough and weathered hands. "I couldn't help but notice that your fingers seemed to move involuntarily to my coding, as if you were eager to get started. I think that you might have a natural bent toward sending and receiving code."

Mr. Jones gave a dismissive shrug and glanced toward the man without a practice partner. "Lowell, I guess you're my partner." Lowell Meade cast a distasteful sneer toward the other man. Immediately, the tension between the two registered with Liz, but she refused to make their problem hers. "All right, men. You're going to begin by listening to me code. I'll start out slowly, but I'll pick up speed as we go. Record what I key on your note pad. For now, you may check your alphabet sheet."

Liz noted that Alan had disappeared into the kitchen. She ached to follow him to find out how he explained her presence to his little paramour, but she realized she couldn't become his guard dog. Returning her attention to the task at hand, she continued with her instruction. "You will note that code is sent and received in clusters of five. Knowing this fact makes it easier to identify the pattern, hence the message. But, let's begin with the universal emergency signal." Slowly she keyed, "DOT/DOT/DOT—DASH/DASH/DASH—DOT/DOT/DOT."

"I got it! Yes, ma'am, I do." Bobby Ward waved his hand in the air like a first-grader discovering he could read real words.

"Good going, Mr. Ward. How about the rest of you? Could you pick up the differences between the dots and the dashes?" When she received a positive reaction from the class members, she keyed the same message at a faster rate. After increasing the speed several times, she suggested the three teams find a quiet place where they could practice undisturbed.

Once they were working in their groups, Liz strode toward the kitchen. She paused and took a deep breath before she pushed open the door. Inside, Alan sat on a stool at one end of a long sheet-metal counter. The girl Liz suspected was Trudy stood at the other end, her cheeks aflame with color. A tall, stocky woman in her midfifties, with braided blond hair crowning the top of her head, her face set in a frown as hard as the metal working surface before her, stood at the center of the counter, vigorously kneading a lump of bread dough.

That Liz had interrupted a tense discussion was evident. She pretended not to notice. "Excuse me, but could I please get a drink of water?"

"You must be Mrs. Ames." The older woman smiled politely. "I'm Emma Dahl, and this is my daughter, Trudy. I'd shake your hand, but . . ." She raised her flour-coated fingers and shrugged. "Making bread for dinner," she explained. "Are you sure you wouldn't like a hot drink of tea or something instead of water? We keep a kettle of hot water available at all times."

Liz shook her head. "No, thank you, cold water will be fine."

"Trudy, don't just stand there." Mrs. Dahl glared at her daughter. "Get Mrs. Ames a glass of water!"

The girl scurried to the back of the kitchen. "Mr. Dahl and I are so pleased to meet you. We hope you'll enjoy your stay in Alaska." The pleasure at meeting Liz didn't reach the older woman's eyes as she pounded the bread dough onto the table with marked determination. When the woman looked up from her task, she cast a sideways glance at Alan. "Imagine how surprised we were to learn that our friend Alan is married, let alone that his wife had arrived here in Alaska."

Alan had the decency to redden. At that moment, Trudy returned with a tumbler of water and handed it to Liz.

"Thank you, Trudy." Acting like she didn't recognize the heightened tension between the Dahls and Alan, Liz took a sip. "*M-m-m,* tastes so good." No one spoke as Liz finished her glass of water and sat the empty tumbler on the counter. "Nice meeting you, Mrs. Dahl and you, too, Trudy. I'm sure I'll be seeing a lot more of you during the next few weeks." She turned and smiled sweetly at Alan. "Alan, I've finished instructing for the day. I would like to head back to Whittier now, so I can rest before starting my evening shift at the station."

Liz paused as the kitchen door swung closed behind her. She could only imagine the conversation that would take place once she was out of hearing range.

★ ★ ★ ★ ★

Between teaching code and filling in at the radio station for Major

Judd, the next few weeks flew by faster than Liz would have imagined possible. Each time she arrived at the station to relieve Will at the end of his shift, she noted that a third person was always present. And at the base camp, Liz also noted that whenever Alan was around, Mrs. Dahl seldom let the girl out of her sight. As for Liz and Trudy, the two women skirted around each another, exchanging little more than a polite smile or a quick "Good morning."

Alan barely spoke to Liz beyond the basic necessities. In the evenings, Liz read alone in her room or chatted with her landlady about the verses they discovered together from her grandmother's Bible.

Liz found a surprising comfort reading and memorizing Psalm 91. Her shift at the station was shortened by a couple of hours when one of the men working on the tunnel admitted he could send and receive code. He was slow, but accurate.

On weekends, Liz and Miz Mabel began attending church. She noted that Will occasionally managed to attend. He purposely sat on the opposite side of the room during the services, and they dined at different tables during the potlucks that followed.

On the nights when she was on duty at the station and all was quiet, Liz's thoughts wandered toward the major—his eyes; his smile; his solid, square jaw; his wacky sense of humor; but most of all, his gentle compassion. Her feelings frightened her.

*Oh, dear God. This is so hard! You know I want to do what is right, but how can You expect me to continue to be loyal to a man who can't stand the sight of me? And how do I stop from caring for a man who obviously cares for—* She didn't know how to complete her prayer.

With no family in Alaska with whom to celebrate the holiday, Liz purposely volunteered to operate the station on Christmas Eve. Along with her grandmother's Bible, she chose a copy of *Gone With the Wind* to read during what would most likely be an endlessly long, quiet evening. Miz Mabel promised to send over dinner that would include a traditional Christmas guinea hen, mashed potatoes and gravy, and squash pie with whipped cream. Anticipating the promised meal, Liz should have had a ravenous appetite. Instead, a lonely Christmas Eve stretched out before her.

When the car arrived to take her to the radio station, she found Alan driving. She attempted to make conversation. "Remember our first Christmas together?"

"Nope!" He shifted the vehicle into gear. The truck lurched forward.

"Sure you do. We attended Christmas Eve services in Portland with your mother and father. I'll never forget the screechy soprano who sang out of tune on the high note in 'O Holy Night.' She held the note for what seemed like forever. I still get cold chills when I think about it."

A smile teased the corners of his lips.

"And remember the deacon who spilled the offering plate? Coins rolled down the aisle to the front of the church during the stately arrival of the three kings."

This time Alan chuckled aloud.

"And who can forget the littlest shepherd falling asleep on his staff?"

"Yeah," Alan said and turned toward her. "We did have some good times, didn't we, Lizzie?"

"Oh, my, yes. Remember feeding popcorn to the seagulls the next morning as we strolled along the Columbia River? They are greedy creatures, aren't they?"

"I think some of my favorite memories were when we packed a picnic lunch and drove to the coast for the day," Alan added.

Liz closed her eyes and sighed. "*Hmm,* me too. Our hideaway cove north of Cannon Beach . . ."

Alan cleared his throat. "But that was a long time ago. A lot of water has flowed under the bridge since then."

"Too much?"

He hesitated before answering. "I don't know. I just don't know." By the time Alan stopped the truck in front of the radio station, his mood had darkened. "Liz, you'd better go in. You can't keep your major waiting."

Her response came out in a whisper. "He isn't my major."

With a shrug, Alan reached across the seat and opened her door. "Have a good evening, Elizabeth."

She hopped out and turned, her gloved hand resting on the seat. "Merry Christmas, Alan."

"Yeah, Merry Christmas." His voice grew husky.

Trudging through the drifted snow toward the Quonset, Liz smiled. She felt that she and Alan had made a bit of progress in communication during the short drive from Miz Mabel's. *Maybe this will be a better Christmas than I thought,* she mused as she opened the door.

Almost instantly, Major Judd appeared. "Hey, Merry Christmas,

Elizabeth." His wide, infectious grin brought a smile to her face. "I appreciate your willingness to split tonight's shift. I'll be back in the morning around zero six hundred hours." He checked his watch as he spoke. "The Dahls have set up a giant Bingo game with Mrs. Dahl's famous pumpkin pies and blueberry pastries as prizes. It should be fun." He glanced down at the books in her hands. "I'll save you some if I win. It should be a quiet shift, so you can get a little reading done. Here's another book you might find interesting." He handed her a copy of Walter D. Edmonds's *Drums Along the Mohawk.*

"Thanks. Hey, maybe if I stay awake, I'll see Santa Claus fly toward the States from the North Pole," she joked.

The smile on his face widened as he put on his overcoat and hat. "I understand Miz Mabel has promised to bring you some holiday fixin's. You know Miz Mabel and her food!"

Liz laughed and patted her stomach. "Oh, do I ever! If she doesn't stop feeding me so well, I'll need an entirely new wardrobe by the time I head back to Seattle."

"Oh, yeah, speaking of Seattle, I almost forgot." He helped her out of her coat and hung it on the hook behind the door. "As my Christmas gift to you, I've arranged for a special military clearance for you to send a holiday message to your family and for them to code a message in return. They'll be on 14.240 MHz at nineteen hundred hours. Remember, only one message each way. Enjoy!"

She gasped in surprise. "Oh, thank you!" Overwhelmed with gratitude, Liz sprang toward him, but caught herself inches before throwing her arms about his neck.

Instinctively, he reached out to receive her and then, surprised by his unintended reaction, quickly stepped back as well. Both reddened at the awkward moment.

Will scratched his day-old beard. "Whoa, if I'd known I'd get that kind of response, I would have arranged permission to exchange messages sooner," he tried to joke. Then, awkwardly, Will left the office. Unnerved by her unintended display of affection, she listened as the major left last-minute instructions with the young corporal in the outer office.

Miz Mabel and her Christmas basket arrived shortly after Will departed for the outpost. The woman burst into the Quonset like a Texas tornado. She set a large willow basket on the major's desk. "I just had to tell you the latest news. I've wanted to tell you before, but you've been so busy with your class and your shifts at the radio station, I, well—" The woman took a deep breath and flashed Liz an ecstatic smile. "I'm getting married again, this time to a Bostonian. Can you imagine? Me?" She giggled like a thirteen-year-old as she spread a red-and-white gingham tablecloth across the major's desktop. "Mr. McGee oversees the civilian workers up at the dig. You've seen him at the boardinghouse, I'm sure." Again, she giggled. "When the tunnel is finished, he says he wants to take me home to meet his Beacon Hill family. Imagine me, acting like a proper Bostonian lady!" Miz Mabel made a graceful pirouette in front of the major's desk.

Liz laughed. "You, my lady, will do just fine in Boston or in any other society in which you find yourself."

"Why, thank you, kind friend." Miz Mabel removed a small pie from the basket. "I feel so silly being in love again. How many times will I be blessed this way?"

Liz swallowed hard. For her, love had resulted only in pain. The loss of her son, the conflicted emotions toward Will, and the desire to save her loveless marriage were hardly blessings to her way of thinking. The only stability in her life came when reading the Word of God, and even much of that confused her at times.

After Miz Mabel left, Liz decided to wait a while before eating. Instead, she covered the food with a napkin and stretched out on the army cot to open the Bible. She had saved the book of Luke to read on Christmas. But when she tried to concentrate on the message, she instead kept glancing at the clocks above the radio every few minutes. Whether London time, Washington, D.C., Singapore, or Pacific, the hands seemed to stand still. At times, she imagined them going backward.

A half-hour before the designated transmission time, Liz penned a brief Christmas message to her family, assuring them all was well and that she hoped to return home soon. Precisely at seven o'clock, the radio came alive. Immediately, she recognized her father's fist.

R—MERRY CHRISTMAS PRINCESS. WE SEND OUR LOVE, MOM, YOUR GRANDMOTHER, ANNE, AND GERTIE. EAGER TO HAVE YOU HOME. TAKE CARE. GIVE OUR LOVE TO ALAN—SK.

Her father had barely signed off when Liz returned with her Christmas greeting, including the part about thanking Grandma Keating for the best Christmas gift of all—the Bible.

R—GRANDMA, HOW DID I LIVE SO LONG WITHOUT PSALM 91? TELL YOU MORE LATER. KISSES AND HUGS—SK.

The radio went silent. For a brief moment, she'd felt her loved ones' presence, but in an instant, they were gone, and she was once again alone. She sniffed back a tear and bowed her head. "Oh dear God, You promised never to leave me and never to forsake me. I want to believe You, I do. Somehow that promise isn't enough tonight."

Curling up on the cot, she pulled an army blanket over her legs and closed her eyes. Liz didn't know how long she'd slept when a deafening explosion brought her to her feet. She ran out of the building and stared in the direction of the tunnel. The corporal on desk duty charged out of the building behind her. Flames of red, orange, and white shot high into the night sky. Like fireworks on the Fourth of July, a shower of fiery red embers rained back down onto the frozen earth.

*What in the world? Of course, it's Christmas Eve. Holiday fireworks. But,* she thought, *the explosion came from halfway up the mountain. No one would be working in the tunnels tonight,* she reasoned. Her next thought took her breath away. *Could it be a Japanese attack?*

"I'd better tell Major Judd," the young man stammered.

"I'm sure he already knows. He planned to go to the camp tonight. Besides, everyone in a fifty-mile radius heard it, I'm sure, maybe farther." She gestured over her shoulder toward Whittier. Throughout the tiny town, doors flew open. The town's residents burst out of their homes. The light spilled out beyond the snow-covered doorsteps. All stared at the unexpected fireworks display filling the sky.

Shards of granite and ice chunks tumbled down onto the town and the surrounding area. Before the flames subsided, a jeep roared into the lot. Will leaped out, lifted Liz off her feet, and carried her into the protection of the Quonset. Likewise, the holiday revelers ran for cover, some into their homes and others under the bodies of nearby trucks, cars, and sheds. No one knew where the fiery shrapnel might land.

"I thought you were going out to the mess hall."

"I was, at least, that's what I'd planned to do." He held her close.

Liz had barely regained her equilibrium when the lights throughout town blinked and went out. Instantly, from the clearing behind the

Quonset, the whirr of the emergency generator came to life. It wasn't until the lighted dials on the radio flashed on that she realized Will was still holding her in his arms. Shaken by his close proximity as much as by the explosion, she looked up at him. He titled his head forward. As his lips threatened to claim hers, she stepped back.

His face reddened. "Sorry. Did I misread . . . ?"

She shook her head. "No, but I almost forgot that I'm married."

Staring at her lips, he exhaled slowly and released her from his grasp.

# Chapter 16: No Holiday for Sabotage

*Demoralize the enemy from within by surprise, terror, sabotage, assassination. This is the war of the future.*
*—Adolf Hitler*

## Base Camp, Maynard Mountain: Christmas Eve 1941

Nursing a cup of cinnamon-flavored eggnog, Captain Alan Ames retired to a quiet corner of the mess hall to escape the celebrating throng. Seated at long rows of wooden tables, the majority of service men as well as several civilian workers labored over homemade Bingo cards. Each hoped to win a pumpkin pie piled high with mounds of whipped cream or, at the least, a blueberry tart.

Twisted swags of red and green crepe paper streamers hung from the ceiling light fixtures along the length of the mess hall. At the front of the room, surrounding the snack tables, a constant line of men waited to wolf down homemade Christmas sugar cookies. Others hovered over the two large metal kettles filled with eggnog. Giant red satin bows and pinecones punctuated the massive evergreen wreaths dotting the walls. A large fir tree decorated with homemade stars, paper chains, and cellophane-wrapped candy canes stood to the left of a large stove.

Vocalists of every tone and texture gathered around a wind-up phonograph and sang "Jingle Bells" with Bing Crosby. By the volume and the off-key notes filling the room, Alan suspected someone might have spiked the eggnog.

A movement in the back row of the singers caused Alan to stiffen. He watched the Texan, Corporal Richard West, slip his arm around Trudy Dahl's slim waist. It took all his self-control not to dash across the room and punch the arrogant guy in the nose. But then, Alan remembered he no longer had a right to the apple-cheeked, nineteen-year-old blonde's attention.

Since the day Mrs. Dahl met Liz, Alan had been denied contact with the girl. Besides missing Trudy's company, he also missed the good-natured acceptance into the Dahl family that he'd enjoyed before they'd learned of Liz's existence. The loss had left him morose and lonely on this Christmas Eve.

The outside door swung open and Colonel Anderson stepped into the mess hall. Since being assigned as Liz's attaché, Alan had felt alienated from the man. One of the junior officers greeted the base commander with a mug of eggnog and a plate of cookies. Alan glanced at his wristwatch—7:05 P.M. It would be a long night.

By the time the revelers had switched from "Jingle Bells" to "God Rest Ye Merry, Gentlemen," Alan had had enough. He stomped out of the mess hall and into the midwinter darkness. A brisk breeze forced him to burrow into his coat collar. Snow crunched beneath his boots as he trudged toward his sleeping quarters.

Alan wallowed in self-pity as he pictured his mom and dad attending Christmas Eve services with his brother, Sam, and his family in Portland. He imagined Liz's parents gathered around a giant Noble fir in their perfectly appointed parlor in Seattle, opening presents. He could almost hear Grandma Keating regaling the family with her latest madcap escapade. Despite his loneliness, Alan smiled until his thoughts turned toward Liz.

*Ba-boom!* The ear-splitting explosion shook the camp, followed by a second explosion and a third. Angry flames burst from the tunnel entrance and into the icy night. The ground shook. Alan stared in disbelief as the partiers rushed out of the mess hall to discover what had happened. Lethal shards of ice and rock flew high into the air and then rained down around them.

*Accident? Earthquake? Volcanic eruption? Espionage!* A mishmash of possibilities bombarded Alan's mind as he joined the others running toward the tunnel entrance. He knew, whatever the cause, that there was a good chance someone had been hurt in the blast.

"No! Wait!" Colonel Anderson shouted and grabbed at the captain's arm as Alan passed him on the trail.

Alan tried to yank himself free from the colonel's grasp. "Gunter, the night watchman!" the captain shouted.

"Wait! There could be another explosion." As if on cue, a fourth detonation shook the night air. The two officers dived for the protection of a nearby equipment storage shed. After several seconds of silence, the colonel rose to his feet. "Grab a head lantern from the shack before you try to assess the damage."

Once equipped with a source of light, Alan charged up the rugged supply trail. Colonel Anderson matched him step for step. As the two officers reached the clearing where the snowshed had been protecting the entrance to the tunnel, Moeshe Jones staggered toward them. Over his left shoulder, he carried the injured night watchman. Both men's faces were coated with soot and grime. Blood poured from Gunter's forehead.

"Here, let me help!" Alan shifted the unconscious man from Moeshe's shoulder to his own. "What happened? Is he alive?"

"Yes, sir." Moeshe leaned his hands on his knees to catch his breath. "We need to stop the bleeding. There's so much blood."

"Right!" Alan lowered Gunter to the ground, ripped off his own shirt from under his parka, and tied it as a bandage around the injured man's head. "We need to get him to the infirmary. Moeshe, grab his other arm." With the unconscious man suspended between the two men, the procession moved gingerly over the slippery ice and splinters of wood.

They hadn't gone far when the colonel asked, "What were you doing at the tunnel, Moeshe? You weren't on duty!"

"No, sir. I wasn't." Moeshe's lips formed a thin, grim line.

Colonel Anderson was far from finished talking. "Too cold for a moonlit walk! You'd better have a good reason for being up at the tunnel at this hour," the colonel continued. "You're specialty is demolition, right?"

Moeshe paled. "Yes, sir!"

Alan didn't like the way the conversation was going. He'd worked closely with Moeshe and believed he knew him well. "Let's not jump to conclusions, Colonel. I'm sure there's a logical explanation for the accident, which we will discover during our investigation." Alan knew with nerves still rattled by the Pearl Harbor attack, it wouldn't take much to set off a lynching of sorts. "Nothing can be gained by jumping to conclusions, sir."

*"Humph!"* By the tone of the colonel's voice, Alan suspected that Anderson had assumed that the explosion was no accident.

Two medics with stretcher in hand charged up the slope. Two military police officers followed. As the medics placed the injured night watchman on the stretcher, the colonel turned to the two police. "Take Jones to the brig and stay with him until I get there! Just as a precaution."

Alan trailed behind the medics as the onlookers parted to make way for the stretcher. At the infirmary, he shot a quick glance at the prisoner. The two men's eyes met for an instant before Moeshe dropped his gaze.

As the military police led away the prisoner, Alan turned to the colonel. "Aren't we getting a little ahead of ourselves, sir? Moeshe is a hard worker and I consider him to be loyal as well."

By the hard set of the colonel's jaw, Alan knew this wasn't the time to defend his colleague. *What happened?* Alan wondered as he trudged back to his quarters. *It has to have been an accident. Surely, it was just chance that Moeshe happened to be in the tunnel when the explosion occurred. He's a good man. He must have had a good reason for being first on the scene.*

Then he remembered how Liz had marveled at the speed with which the man had learned code. "He's ready," she'd confided to Alan. "I'm arranging for him to take his first shift the day after Christmas." *Did Moeshe seem to learn so quickly only because he was already proficient in sending code?* Alan asked himself.

*If the explosion is due to sabotage and Moeshe is responsible, is this demolition expert also responsible for all the slowdowns and equipment breakdowns we've had during the past few months?* Alan wondered. *Has the guilty culprit been right under my nose all along, and I didn't suspect it?*

Alan's mind replayed possible scenarios for hours. He'd barely fallen asleep when the off-tune notes of reveille stirred him awake. Before heading to the mess hall for breakfast, he climbed to the tunnel entrance to survey the damage. He had no doubt, as he surveyed the damage, that the dynamite had been precisely arranged to cause the most damage. He knew of no one other than Moeshe with the skills to cause such destruction.



Christmas morning or not, the mess hall buzzed with the whispers of both military and civilian personnel discussing the previous night's tragedy. As Alan filled his plate with a large serving of scrambled eggs, a junior officer who also worked in the tunnel sidled up to him. "So what's the scuttlebutt, Captain? They're saying that the explosion wasn't an accident. I hear they're holding Moeshe Jones in the brig." The junior officer continued. "I've always suspected that guy of something—too quiet for my taste. Like he has something to hide! The guy comes and goes like a shadow."

Alan topped his stack of pancakes with a dipper of hot canned peaches. Grabbing a handful of Christmas cookies, he placed them on the corner of his tray. "The man is innocent until proven otherwise! That's the American way, remember?"

"But, Captain, we're at war. Peacetime rules don't apply. Desperate times call for desperate measures."

Alan shook his head. "Keep your suspicions to yourself, Lieutenant." Finding an empty table in a corner of the room, Alan ate his eggs and hot cakes in silence. It irked him to think that he might have been wrong about Moeshe. He'd drunk the last of his cup of hot chocolate before the colonel's aide sought him out.

"The colonel wants to see you immediately, sir."

Alan dropped the Christmas cookies into his jacket pocket and made his way across the compound to Colonel Anderson's office.

"Sit down, Ames!" The colonel gestured toward the straight-backed chair in front of the desk. "He's not talking! Moeshe refuses to explain or to defend himself!" Like a caged lion, Colonel Anderson paced back and forth across the office. "I don't understand. If Jones would just explain to me why he was in the tunnel at that time of night! If it wasn't sabotage, he must have had a good reason for being up there. He may have seen something that would help our investigation." The colonel paused midstride and stroked his clean-shaven jaw. "Captain, you and he worked so closely together. Maybe he'll talk to you."

Alan straightened. "What is Gunter saying?"

"Nothing. The man's still in a coma."

Alan hated to think that Moeshe might be guilty of sabotage and treason. Yet, if innocent, why wouldn't Moeshe defend himself? A short explanation could clear his name. "Of course, sir. I would be glad to talk with Moeshe—immediately if you wish."

Anderson raised one hand. "No, not yet. Wait until after lunch, after the man has had several hours to think about his situation." Colonel Anderson wearily lowered himself onto the chair behind his desk. "I want some kind of statement from him before the army sends one of their investigators from Anchorage," the colonel admitted. "I don't trust those guys from headquarters."

Alan pursed his lips and frowned. "Have you considered asking Lowell Meade to talk with Moeshe? I believe the two men grew up in the same Inuit village. They also attended Washington State University at nearly the same time as well."

Colonel Anderson leaped to his feet. "Good idea, Ames. Go find Meade and get him to the brig. He might be able to get through to the guy where you and I can't." He pounded his fist into the palm of his hand. "I'll get to the bottom of this one way or another. Oh, and before you go, tell me, have you been to the tunnel this morning? How would you assess the damage?"

"Yes, sir. From where I sit, it will take us two weeks or more to clear out the debris before we can determine the integrity of the mountain. Whoever set those dynamite sticks knew what he was doing."

The colonel shook his head. "Again, the finger points to Moeshe, eh?"

Reluctantly, Alan nodded. "Perhaps. In the meantime, we need every tunneler available to help clear the debris from the entrance. Fortunately, we have enough lumber on hand to construct a new snowshed, hopefully before the next storm hits."

Colonel Anderson nodded. "That's the first good news I've heard today. The D.C. brass is on my back to complete this tunnel and have it operable by spring. It seems they already have another project for us even before we finish this one. But right now, we can deal with only one problem at a time. Go ahead. Find this Meade fellow."

"Yes, sir." As an afterthought, Alan added, "Don't worry, Colonel. We'll get through this crisis and back on schedule with or without Moeshe Jones's assistance."

"I wish I shared your confidence." The deepened furrows on Anderson's face appeared to have aged him ten years overnight.

Alan strode from the office and climbed the rugged hillside to the entrance to the tunnel. The Boston firm's front loaders and bulldozers had already moved several of the larger rocks from the entrance, leaving the smaller debris to the tunnelers manning the shovels.

"How's it going, men?" Alan asked the foreman of the team.

"Fine, Captain. We've made a lot of progress since dawn."

"Good! Any idea what happened here? An accident perhaps?"

The foreman shrugged. "Looks like sabotage to me, sir." Alan peered into the mouth of the tunnel. The deafening sounds of jackhammers and pickaxes made further conversation impossible. Heavy dust clouds billowed from the opening, sending the two men coughing for cover.

Once they rounded the corner from the opening, Alan asked the foreman, "Anybody see Lowell Meade this morning?"

"Yes, sir. I saw Meade in the dynamite shed checking inventory."

Captain Ames nodded and climbed across the rubble to the lean-to where the explosives had been stored. "So much for security," he muttered as he brushed past the gnarled remains of the chain-link fence that had surrounded the small enclosure.

In the middle of the shed, he spied Meade talking with a coworker. They appeared to be inventorying what was left of the supply of dynamite sticks.

"Captain." Meade waved toward Alan. "What a mess, huh? Have they figured out how this could happen? The rumor around camp is sabotage. But I doubt that. Who would do such a thing?"

Not wanting to encourage camp gossip, Alan's face remained expressionless. "It's too soon to know."

The civilian worker looked up from his clipboard. "How is Gunter? I heard he was hurt real bad in the explosion."

"Gunter's still unconscious. He has a head wound and a broken leg. After he wakes up, I'm sure he'll be able to clear up a few of our questions."

"Yeah, I suppose. I kind of liked the guy. Sometimes we played cards in the barracks after hours." The man paused. "When Gunter wakes up, ya think they'd let me visit him? See how he's doing?"

"Can't say. You'll have to ask Colonel Anderson. Speaking of the colonel, he wants to see you, Lowell, in his office ASAP."

Meade's face paled. "Me? Why? I don't know anything about the explosion."

Alan kicked at a small chunk of ice with his boot. "But you do know Moeshe better than anyone else in the camp. Personally, I believe the guy is innocent, but he refuses to defend himself. The colonel is hoping you can convince him to tell why he was at the tunnel at that hour and what he might have seen."

The man shrugged. "I can try, I guess, but I really don't know him that well. We were both orphaned as babies and adopted into Aleut families. True, we were both sent to the University of Washington on scholarships. His adoptive father is part Japanese, I believe."

Alan detected a note of bitterness in Lowell Meade's voice. "Moeshe's adoptive father is part Japanese?" Alan frowned.

"Yes, he is. As my people say, 'The wolf and the shaman are of one nest.' "

# Chapter 17: The Prisoner

*Jesus Christ came into my prison cell last night,*
*and every stone flashed like a ruby.*
*—Samuel Rutherford*

## Base Camp, Maynard Mountain: December 1941

Surrounded by the gray walls of the six-by-six-foot cell, Moeshe Jones lay curled in a fetal position on the wooden cot. He closed his eyes and remembered the world of his childhood. In his memory, he sailed past a series of rugged icebergs in the bay and into the protected cove where his father moored one lone fishing boat. The prisoner imagined the water's swirls of cobalt blue and emerald green, the shimmering jades cascading down off the icy cliffs, and the royal purples set deep in the incandescent pillars of ice.

He could almost hear the snow crunching beneath his caribou-skin *kamiks* as he trudged up the shoreline to his father's whalebone-framed fishing hut. The one-roomed structure, draped with furs and animal skins, was tucked back in an alcove, protected from the tearing Arctic wind.

In the dim twilight of winter coming through the dusty window of his cell, the prisoner eyed the army-issued boots on his feet and shivered. What he would give for a pair of homemade *kamiks*. Moeshe tugged the army-issued woolen blanket up under his chin. He would rise above this discomfort. He would soar above his pain like an eagle on a strong wind.

The metal door to his cell swung open, bringing him back to the cold reality of his situation. Moeshe immediately recognized his visitor. The visitor began to taunt, "Imagine Irnig-Kesuk, the number-one son of the great shaman of the north, becoming a hero and a villain in one fell swoop."

The empty expression on Moeshe's face remained impassive. "My name is Moeshe Jones—C7-121."

"To the pale skins, yes. But, then, Irnig-Kesuk is also a pale skin, isn't he? Always has been, at least on the inside! They almost accept you as one of their own, don't they? *Almost* is the key word. But they will never fully accept you, you know. To them, you will always be a second-class citizen. And when you are found guilty of treason and espionage, where will you be then? Shipped to Washington, D.C.? Or merely to Anchorage, where your revered father can see you on trial for betraying your beloved code? Regardless, you will always be Irnig-Kesuk, a man without a people!"

The prisoner stared past his visitor as if the man were invisible. "My name is Moeshe Jones—C7-121."

"Yeah, yeah. And I'm Emperor Hirohito." The other man snorted. "So tell me, why were you up at the tunnel entrance on Christmas Eve? What were you looking for? The colonel wants to know."

Moeshe continued to stare through unseeing eyes. "My name is Moeshe Jones—C7-121."

"Face it, Irnig-Kesuk, you know you're not one of them, no matter how much you cozy up to the army brass. Guilty or not, you will be blamed for the explosion."

"My name is Moeshe Jones—C7-121."

"Personally, I don't believe you sabotaged the tunnel. You're too weak. It takes a strong man, a man of action, to pull off such a coup." The visitor strode to the dusty window, peered out at the snow-covered world beyond, and then turned to face the prisoner. "Just out of curiosity, what did you see before you became the hero who saved Gunter's life—not that anyone will believe you anyway?"

The prisoner fingered the dog tag on the metal chain about his neck. "My name is Moeshe Jones—C7-121."

The visitor snorted again. "You wear the pale skin's ID tag like a whipped pup!" Both the visitor and prisoner hated the tagging done by the *gussak,* or outsiders', government.

"My name is Moeshe—"

"You are hopeless! I came here to help you fight the pale skins and their accusations, but you won't even help yourself!"

"My name is Moeshe—"

"By the way, I know why you were at the tunnel site. I know more about you than you might think."

"My name is . . ."

The visitor gave a dismissive wave and called to the guard. "Sergeant! Let me out of here. This man disgusts me!"

Moeshe stared into the darkening shadows of the cell as the metal door clanged shut once again. He'd always expected this moment would come when he would have no one and nothing with which to defend himself. He closed his eyes and took a deep breath, mentally returning to his father's sanctuary, a place at one with the sea and sky. In his father's world, even when caught between the cold grip of ice, wind, and pounding seas, life became so simple—no problems, no guilt, no regrets, no fear.

"A cup of hot tea?" Captain Ames stood in the open doorway holding a teakettle and two mugs.

Moeshe started in surprise. He hadn't heard the cell door open.

"Thought you could use a bit of warmth about now." The officer set one of the mugs on the floor, filled the other with hot, steaming liquid and handed it to the prisoner. "Sugar?" The captain removed a napkin from his jacket pocket, opened it, and handed Moeshe several cubes of sugar. "Sorry, but I couldn't bring any cream." He sat down on the far end of the cot. "How are they treating you?"

Still silent, Moeshe accepted the cup from his supervisor and took a sip. The tea warmed his mouth and throat. A second sip warmed his heart as well.

Captain Ames added three cubes of sugar to his own cup and stirred it with a pinkie finger. "I like mine dark and sweet. Poor Gunter is still unconscious in the infirmary, but doc expects him to waken soon."

At the mention of the injured man, a heavy silence like an icy-cold sheet hung in the air between them. Moeshe ached to remove it, but his survival demanded he keep silent. Finally, Alan broke the silence. "I understand you aren't talking to anyone, that you won't defend yourself or tell your side of the story. I don't understand, Moeshe. Why? I know you didn't sabotage the tunnel, not after all the long hours you spent working on the project. But why in the world were you up there at that hour on Christmas Eve? If you saw anything that will help in our investigation, anything that might clear your name, please tell me."

Moeshe took a sip. "My name is Moeshe Jones—C7-121."

"What? What are you talking about?" Alan ran his hand over his short, cropped hair. "I don't understand."

Moeshe continued to stare at the closed metal door behind Alan.

"Please, Moeshe, I don't think you set off the charges in the tunnel. Please help me prove your innocence. You must defend yourself." Several minutes passed, but Moeshe remained silent. Reluctantly, Alan admitted defeat and left Moeshe's cell.

Over the next few days, several buddies came and went from the six-by-six-foot cell, but Moeshe's response was always the same. "My name is Moeshe Jones—C7-121."

For the prisoner, life on the military base beyond the small barred window faded to insignificance as he mentally plodded through deep snow to his father's warm and inviting home. Fearing he might forget, Moeshe drove himself to recall every detail of tribal life he'd learned since infancy. He willed himself to relive his childhood. But regarding his birth parents and his rescue at sea by a Russian sea captain, he had only the tales of his shaman father. His memories of the Aleut woman who raised him past infancy but died giving birth to a son were equally blurred with time.

His memories of the rollicking aurora borealis' displays he'd witnessed over the years brought the most joy to his heart. His father had claimed the northern lights were the gods dancing. His studies at the university had given him a more scientific explanation. In between flights of the heart, Moeshe practiced sending Morse code.

On the fifth morning of his imprisonment, Moeshe tapped out a twenty-five-word message to his father on his cot's wooden frame. He started in surprise when he heard a reply message tapping on his cell door. The door squeaked open and Mrs. Ames, the red-haired code instructor appeared. She breezed into his cell like the first warm breeze of spring after a long cold winter. He smiled in spite of his stoic resolve.

During the time he'd studied code with her, he'd come to admire her spirit and intellect, but even more, her intense compassion for others. Aware of the friction between her and her husband, he wondered why the captain would risk losing a woman like her.

On her arm she carried a basket, along with a stack of books. The woman glanced about the cell and clicked her tongue. "Moeshe! You can't read in this light. You'll hurt your eyes." She knocked on the door. "Guard! Will you please see that Moeshe is given a lantern and a small table as soon as I'm gone?"

She turned back toward the speechless prisoner. "*Tsk!* I can't imagine why Colonel Anderson didn't realize you might need a table and light by which to read. Personally, I can't go a day without reading something! I suspect you have the same problem." She set the food basket on the floor and the stack of books beside the basket. Curious, he glanced toward the books. Immediately, he recognized the book on top as the pale skins' Holy Book.

With a flourish, the woman removed the cover from the basket and then spread out a small yellow-and-white calico cloth on the cot. "Miz Mabel, from the boardinghouse in town, packed fresh-from-the-oven corn bread, a jar of peanut butter, and her homemade blackberry jam, along with dried salmon, caribou jerky, a pint jar of stewed tomatoes, and a few of her famous oatmeal-raisin cookies. I just love her cookies. Here, try one."

Overwhelmed, Moeshe accepted the cookie from the woman and took a bite. The morsel was sweet and chewy. Liz sat down on the far end of the cot.

"Seriously, how are they treating you, Moeshe? Are you getting enough to eat?"

"Yes, ma'am. I receive hot meals three times a day."

"That's good. It's fortunate Miz Mabel lives in Whittier. I fear the two cooks would vie for feeding rights." The woman chuckled at her own joke. "I told Miz Mabel you liked to read, so she sent along these books as well. Let's see, *The Good Earth* by Pearl S. Buck, a biography of Andrew Jackson, *Cimarron* by Edna Ferber, a William Faulkner novel—I've never been much of a Faulkner fan, myself—and an unused Bible she found on the top shelf of her library." Mrs. Ames blew a layer of dust off the cover. "Since being stranded in Alaska, my copy of this Book has been my savior. It seems like there's a verse or a story included to get me through every situation. Have you ever spent much time reading the Bible?"

Moeshe's eyes watered as he shook his head. He blamed it on the nip in the air. Instinctively, he wiped his nose on the cuff of his sleeve.

"As I'm sure you already know, the Bible is a collection of books, sort of a spiritual anthology, if you will. If you decided to read it, I'd recommend you begin by reading the book of John. Somehow, John helps the rest of the Bible make sense."

Mrs. Ames chatted about the classes he'd missed and how happy she was to learn he was practicing his code in his cell. "It's a case of use it or lose it, I'm afraid." It didn't seem to bother her that Moeshe had said only a couple of sentences.

All too soon the guard announced the end of Mrs. Ames's half-hour visit. As the woman rose to leave, she took Moeshe's hand in hers and closed her eyes. "Dear Father God, Creator of the universe. Be with my student Moeshe as he faces this very difficult time in his life. Grant him peace and wisdom, strength and grace. Remind him that You love him more than he can imagine and that we, his friends, are praying for him. Amen."

Mrs. Ames picked up the basket and breezed past the prisoner into the corridor outside his cell door. "Now, don't forget!" She shook her finger in the face of the bemused guard. "My student needs a lantern and a small table as soon as possible. Also, a chair would be nice."

And she was gone, and, with her, the tantalizing breath of spring; her radiant smile, a dancing ray of sunlight in his dark, cold world. Moeshe felt devastated by his loss.

# Chapter 18: A Daring Challenge

*Women, like men, should try to do the impossible. And when they fail, their failure should be a challenge to others.*
*—Amelia Earhart*

## Alaskan Wilderness: January 1942

With the arrival of the New Year, mail delivery from the States for military personnel had been resumed. This included letters from Liz's parents. While each letter took more than a week to process through the military protocol, the messages boosted the woman's spirits. Her dad's short notes kept her apprised of the changes at the office. She was surprised to learn that following Pearl Harbor, her radio buddy Brad had joined the navy. She kept hoping to hear his "fist" on the wire, but as yet that hadn't happened.

Her mother's and her sister's flowery letters were filled with tales of shopping trips to bridal shops, bakeries for wedding cake design, and a print shop to order the invitations. Her sister Anne's fiancé had enlisted in the army, thus giving them a month to pull off their wedding, the event of the country club's social season. Liz felt bad that she would miss the wedding, but, under the circumstances, she knew it couldn't be helped.

And then there were Grandma Keating's letters. Liz dreaded their arrival, yet she hungered for the wise woman's counsel. Grandma was the only person with whom Liz had shared news of her angry confrontations with Alan and of her concern over her growing affection for Major William Judd.

As poetic and whimsical as Grandma's humorous tales could be, her advice regarding Major William Judd was direct. "I won't mince words, my dear. From what you've told me, I suspect your friendship with your major could be straying into dangerous territory. No good can come from the scars you will inflict upon your heart as the result of breaking your marriage vows. What seems to be a source of solace and comfort, and a distraction from your temporary heartbreak, will become a cancer on your conscience for years to come. Read Matthew 5:28. Also read the story of David and his dalliance with the lovely Bathsheba. Nothing but pain came out of their tryst. Imagine the agony that would have been avoided if they'd not strayed over that invisible line into sin."

In her heart, Liz knew her grandmother was right. Each day, upon returning to her room at the boardinghouse, she contemplated where to draw the invisible line her grandmother had mentioned. Alone at night, she argued that Will was just a good friend and a good Christian man—a friend. Everyone needs a friend, right? That he was God's man was part of what she admired in him.

And though she refused to admit it to herself, she eagerly anticipated seeing Will at the beginning and end of her evening shifts. He didn't need to check in with her, but he always did. Instead of keeping their relationship totally professional as planned in the beginning, both Liz and Will found excuses to stay a while and chat. Sometimes these chats lasted for hours.

Since coming to Alaska, Liz was increasingly frustrated by Alan's monosyllabic replies to her attempts to reestablish communication increasingly. Sooner or later, she knew they'd need to "have it out," as her father would say. As a result, other than the pleasant conversations she had with Miz Mabel discussing wild game recipes and the widow's newest sweetheart, Liz's primary human contact was with Will and her frequent visits with Moeshe.

Liz and Will had much in common. She relished discussing politics and religion with him. It reminded her of the late-night debates she'd enjoyed with her father during her teen years. Way into the night, they would discuss the moral issues on building an arsenal of bigger and more destructive bombs; the flaws in the philosophy of Descartes; even which automobile—a Chevy or a Ford—was better built.



With Will, her brain cells came alive; he challenged her on every turn, yet the man didn't slink away like an injured puppy or huff like a steam engine whenever she adequately proved her point.

That was Alan's pattern. Whenever he lost a philosophical or political battle, he would go off in a pout. And religion? It seemed that Alan had his mind set against the existence of a caring God. And he refused to discuss the subject with her.

Logic told Liz where her friendship with Will would lead. But she brushed away the thought of any real danger. One subject they didn't discuss was their growing relationship. She rationalized that as long as she maintained Grandma Keating's invisible line, she would be safe.

One night, an hour before the end of her shift, Will popped into the office with a pack of letters for her and a batch of Miz Mabel's walnut-topped brownies. Instead of his usual light banter, he sat down behind his desk and studied his hands while she reported on the radio activity of the evening.

When she finished giving the official report, she waited as he took a deep breath and began, "We need to talk. Colonel Anderson and I had a long conversation this evening regarding—everything. Actually, he talked; I listened."

"I don't understand."

"He's unhappy with, uh, our growing friendship. And while he admits it's not his business, he felt the need to warn me against possible entanglements. But that's neither here nor there." Will continued, "Come spring, the Army Corps of Engineers is going to construct a road from Fairbanks, through Canada, to the States. They're calling it the Al-Can Highway. The colonel is sending your husband on an air-reconnaissance mission to recommend a route where the northern portion of the road should run across the mountains of eastern Alaska."

Baffled, Liz couldn't imagine where this conversation was going.

"As you know, to get the tunnel project back on schedule has involved all able-bodied men, and I still need your help staffing the station. Yet, the colonel intends to send you with Alan to chart possible routes for the proposed road. It seems the colonel believes Alan needs you along to transmit daily radio reports back to base. Obviously, the colonel can't order you to go, but he strongly advises it for both of our sakes. Also, I need to point out that the flight could be dangerous."

He eyed her from across the desk. "I'm not crazy about having you go, but the colonel believes it would give you and Alan the opportunity to work on your problems." Will stared down at his hands folded before him on the desktop. "Of course, there will be a third person along—the pilot. You know him—Lowell Meade. He's one of the guys in your class who couldn't get his code up to speed, remember?"

Painfully aware that her first thought had been how much she'd miss Will, Liz heaved a heavy sigh. "Some people grasp code immediately. Others just can't quite process it in their minds," she mumbled. "Lowell was certainly one of the latter. I hope his piloting abilities surpass his radio skills."

"The colonel assures me it will only be for a night or two," Will explained. "You'll be spending a couple of nights in a cabin the army maintains along the north-south military flyway. It's the primary air route for transporting war materials from the States to Fairbanks. I've been to the cabin. It's primitive, but not too uncomfortable, if you don't mind camping." Will spun a pencil lying on his desktop. "You'll check in with me at twenty hundred hours each evening with the day's coordinates and with Alan's recommendations for the proposed route." Liz followed the spin of the pencil for several moments and then gazed at the worry lines settled in Will's forehead.

"I'll do it, of course, but there's more you're not telling me. What is it?"

He hesitated before answering. "This is a little awkward, but our, er, friendship seems to be attracting unwanted attention. Colonel Anderson chewed me out royally. He's afraid I'm risking my career over a dalliance with a married woman."

A wave of red suffused Liz's cheeks. She stared down at her hands. "I'm sorry." An unexpected resentment welled up inside of her. She'd always liked the colonel; now she wasn't so sure. "But we've never acted improperly."

"No, thank God. But I must confess, at least on my side, Anderson's right. Frankly, I do care much too much for you, Liz—definitely more than I should. You've been the one bright spot in my Alaskan experience." He cleared his throat and glanced away. "I've thought about it, and I know how torn you've been. I think having you go on this two- or three-day mission may help you to clarify your thinking as far as Alan is concerned; that is, if you think you're up to roughing it." He raised an eyebrow.

Picking up on his light challenge, Liz sniffed. "Of course, I'm up to roughing it for a night or two. While I'd definitely prefer a luxury hotel suite in downtown Seattle, Alan and I backpacked into the Cascades several times. Besides, sleeping in a cabin beats roughing it in a canvas pup tent any night."

The office door swung open and her shift replacement strode into the room. Will rose from behind the desk. "Good. I'll tell the colonel you're willing."

Liz paused before asking, "Just out of curiosity, what does Alan think about this plan? He has been told, right?"

"Oh, yes, he's been told." Will rolled his tongue around inside his cheek. "He wasn't exactly happy about it, but, as you know, an order is an order."

Liz rolled her eyes toward the ceiling. "This is sounding like more and more fun by the minute! By the way, when do I leave for this great Alaskan adventure?"

Again, Will cleared his throat. "Tomorrow morning at zero eight hundred hours."

"Tomorrow morning?" She blinked in surprise.

He chuckled in spite of the situation. "And pack light—one small case. Three adults, the necessary surveying tools, and the weight of the radio equipment will be about all the reconnaissance plane can carry."

True to form, the next morning Miz Mabel had a large basket of food prepared for the flight. "Most of the food is preserved so it can last a long time should you need it. Flying any time of year in Alaska is risky, but in early January? Well . . ." The woman grimaced. "I'm not happy you are going on this foolhardy mission."

Liz shuddered as she tugged on the mukluks Ralph Lorry had insisted she use during her stay. Whatever the season, she much preferred traveling by ship to flying. And she prayed Lowell was a better pilot than he was a radio operator.

Before leaving for the airstrip, Liz slipped her grandmother's Bible in her overnight case. Overnight or not, having the Bible to read could fill in any awkward moments between her and Alan when Lowell was around, she decided. As she closed the door to her room, Liz decided before they left for the Alaskan wilderness, she would stop to see Moeshe.

★ ★ ★ ★ ★

Liz peered out the side window of the four-passenger plane Lowell had dubbed the *Minna.* The multiple grays and blues spread across the landscape captivated her. She wondered what the six months of summer must be like so close to the Arctic Circle. She thought about how upset Moeshe had become when she told him about her planned foray with Alan and Lowell into the Alaskan wilderness.

"Don't go," the prisoner warned. "It's not safe! Tell Colonel Anderson you won't go. He can't make you go, you being a civilian."

Liz and Moeshe had become fast friends over the few weeks since his arrest. Daily she'd visit him in his cramped cell with a basket of homemade food from Miz Mabel and a new stack of books for him to read. With her every visit, Moeshe became more relaxed around her. They spent a few minutes practicing code, and then chatted about everything from the daily gossip circulating through camp to the reality of a spiritual universe.

Since the truths of the Bible were almost as new and fresh to Liz as they were to Moeshe, they saved time at the end of each visit to share their latest scriptural discoveries. For the Aleut, accepting the white man's God as the Creator of the universe was a difficult issue. Elizabeth's point of doubt was in believing that a God, any God, could watch over and care about her personal problems.

Whenever they came across a difficult passage in their personal study, they would discuss the possible meanings and how it could apply to people in the twentieth century. And yet, for Liz, there was a difference in their friendship from that of the one she shared with Will Judd.

"I really wish you wouldn't go," Moeshe insisted. "I have a very bad feeling about this flight."

"Why, Moeshe, you must have a reason for feeling as you do," she insisted.

"Lowell isn't what—" He started to reply, and then tightly clamped his lips shut. "I'm sorry. I can't say anything more. I just advise you not to go."

As the small plane lifted off at the base's airfield, Elizabeth couldn't shake her apprehension. Moeshe's advice had set her nerves on edge. Her neck and shoulder muscles cramped as she clutched the leather loop above her window, the loop she'd secretly nicknamed her glory handle since every time the plane jounced, bumped, or swayed, she'd grab the strap and whisper, "Oh, glory!"

Up front in the cockpit beside Lowell, Alan pressed a pair of binoculars to his eyes. Spread out across his lap was a topographical map, circa 1900. "Fly over that ridge. I suspect there's a river down there we might be able to follow. Having the proposed road go around the mountain would be a whole lot simpler than trying to scale it or tunnel through it."

"Yes, sir." Lowell Meade banked the plane sharply to the right. Again, Liz grabbed the strap to maintain her balance. The plane slowly circled to the north side of a massive snow-covered mountain peak and then dropped into a hidden valley. Boulders shaped by eons of glaciers appeared less than an arm's span from the left wingtip.

"Looks good. I'll record our position, and this evening Liz can radio in our report if the static isn't too much of a problem." Both Alan and Liz knew when flying so far north the weather conditions could play havoc with radio transmissions.

"We'll need to refuel within the hour." Lowell tapped the glass on the odometer. The *Minna* carved a direct path through the sky like a war-horse returning from battle. "I'm heading toward the refueling station and the cabin where we'll spend the night. Keep an eye portside for an orange windsock."

Occasional tiny villages, clinging to the edge of frozen rivers, had long since been replaced by a world of dazzling white mountain slopes and peaks.

"To your left!" Liz pointed toward a cabin visible in the pale light. A mile-long, snow-covered valley containing a landing strip stretched between two mountains.

"Good eyes, Mrs. Ames!" Lowell turned his face just enough for her to appreciate his strong profile. As the plane dropped closer to land, they could see that the airstrip, which had appeared smooth from higher in the sky, was pocked with windswept waves of ice and snow. From the looks of the terrain, Liz knew it would be a rough landing.

"Hang on," Lowell called over his shoulder as the plane dropped like a hungry eagle toward the earth and the landing gear dropped into place. The *Minna* struck the ground with a couple of bounces before tobogganing down the icy airstrip and coming to a stop less than ten yards from the weathered log cabin and two outbuildings. Identifying the smaller of the outbuildings as an old-fashioned outhouse, Liz groaned. The other structure appeared to be a lean-to where firewood was stacked. Fifty feet east of the cabin stood a lone fueling pump like a faded red painted sentinel of civility against the surrounding primitive elements.

"Whew! Sorry about the rough landing." Lowell relaxed his grip on the wheel and unbuckled his seatbelt. "Welcome to our new home away from home, at least for one night."

Alan released his seatbelt. "Hey, I'd say that looked like some pretty skilled flying. How are you doing back there, Liz?" As he opened his door, a blast of frigid air smacked him in the face.

Liz glanced toward the leather encased radio equipment by her side. "I think I'm OK. I just hope the radio wasn't damaged."

Alan laughed. "What about the plane? We do have to fly out of here tomorrow."

With the wind whipping snow off the mountain, the perilous terrain had put out no welcome mat for the human intruders. Having exited through the pilot's door, Lowell Meade disappeared under the plane, checking for structural damage.

"Thanks to the wind, the snow is barely ankle deep." Alan spoke to her through a thin veneer of politeness.

Liz hopped out of the plane, arched her back and stretched, hoping to flex her cramped muscles. She threw back her head and inhaled the bitterly cold air. Her gaze drifted from the mountain peak across the snowfield to the rough-hewn cabin. The log cabin had a narrow porch across the front and a boarded-up window that faced the wind. Here and there, moss peeked through the ten inches of snow on the shingled roof. A pair of snowshoes, a pickaxe, and a wide snow shovel hung on S-hooks along the edge of the porch.

*No place like home.* The woman groaned and grabbed her overnight case. "It's going to be tricky establishing a clear radio signal from here," she shouted to Alan. Hugging herself against the incessant wind, she hoped against hope that the best position for radio transmission would be from inside the cabin next to a warm and cozy fireplace. Intent on her analysis of the conditions, Liz didn't hear Lowell come up behind her.

"The lean-to on the south side of the shack is where radio operators usually set up their station. From there, they can send and receive clear cipher to Whittier, Seward, and Anchorage." In each hand, Lowell carried an army brown leather duffel bag full of equipment. "Don't worry, ma'am. I may be lousy at coding, but I do know how to erect a radio station and an antenna." Meade winked and laughed as he fell into step beside her. "You just get yourself inside that cabin and get settled while I set up the radio."

Liz glanced back at the aircraft. "Please tell me our plane is in good working order."

"Oh, yes, ma'am. The *Minna* is a tough li'l gal, I assure you." Meade turned and whistled the first bars of "Over the Rainbow" as he trudged across the snowy landing strip toward the lean-to.

A strange knot settled in the pit of Liz's stomach as she watched the man disappear around the corner of the cabin. She wondered whether she should go with him to be certain he set up the station properly. He did seem to know his way around electronics, and Alan told her earlier that the man had a degree in engineering along with his pilot's license. Deciding that Moeshe's warnings had set her nerves on edge, Liz shook away the doubts and made her way carefully to the cabin porch.

By the time she scraped the snow from her boots and entered the one-room structure, Alan had opened the shutters on the cabin's only window and was stuffing kindling into a woodstove. Her eyes quickly adjusted to the interior's semidarkness. Pushed against the wall to her right was a three-tier wooden bunk bed. At the foot of the rough-hewn bed frame were rolled-up mattresses swathed in waterproofed canvas. By the number of droppings on the wooden floor, she guessed that more than one family of vermin was homesteading there for the winter. A wooden table and three mismatched, straight-backed kitchen chairs occupied the center of the room. And in the middle of the table sat an unlit kerosene lamp.

To her left, a topsy-turvy kitchen of sorts had grown around a make-shift cupboard created out of six wooden crates turned on their sides and nailed to the wall. The crates held serving dishes, military-issued canned goods, and several cooking utensils. A metal first-aid kit painted red and white occupied the top shelf.

A metal pail, a floor mop, and an aging broom, along with a pile of rags, which Liz instinctively knew was a nest for birthing batches of the resident rodents, completed the supplies available. The only space upon which to prepare food was a thirty-by-thirty-inch metal counter beside a cast-iron wet sink. She sighed with relief when she spotted a hand pump mounted to the sink. "It could be worse," she mumbled. "At least there's fresh water if the pipes haven't frozen and burst."

"Pretty rugged, eh, especially for a woman of your tastes." Alan straightened and latched the door to the stove. A flame glowed from behind the glass in the door. "I still don't see why Colonel Anderson insisted that you come along. Any one of the men you trained could have done the job as well, producing less inconvenience." He emphasized the word *men*.

"I agree. But, as you know, there's the wrong way, the right way, and the army's way to do a job." Liz grabbed the broom and began to sweep up the mouse droppings on the dark wooden floor.

"Why don't you boil a kettle of water while I bring in our luggage? We could all use a hot drink by now." Alan headed toward the open door. "By the way, where is Lowell?"

"Setting up the radio station, I imagine."

"Oh, of course. In the meantime, I'll bring in our stuff from the plane. I'll be right back."

Liz swept a pile of mouse droppings into the dustpan and tossed everything out the open door into the nearest snowbank.

"There!" Feeling an exhilaration a pioneer farm wife must have felt when settling into her newly constructed cabin in the North woods, Liz inspected her work. "I better check out our food supply," she announced to the empty cabin.

Instead, she grabbed a rag, which had once been a military-issued undershirt, and a sliver of a bar of lye soap from one of the wooden boxes and began by scrubbing the tabletop along with each of the straight-backed chairs. By the time Alan returned from the plane with a stack of blankets and Miz Mabel's basket of food, Liz had unrolled the mattresses on the bunks. "Just put the blankets over here." She pointed toward the scarred wooden table. "With a lace tablecloth on the table, a coat of wax on the floor, and a pair of gingham curtains on the window, a woman could turn this place into a charming honeymoon haven in no time."

Without a word, Alan set the blankets on the lowest bunk. Her eyes misted as he added, "You always could turn a house into a home, Lizzie." This was one of the few kind things he'd said to her since she'd first arrived in Alaska. Liz swallowed the sudden lump in her throat.



"Thank you, kind sir. I thought I'd use some of the army food to stretch out Miz Mabel's yummy treats." She held up one of the tin cans off the shelf. "Would it be so difficult for the army to label the contents of each can? What an adventure this is going to be! Inside this tin can could be anything from peaches to asparagus spears to motor oil."

Alan's laughter surprised her. Being out here in the wilderness seemed to have soothed up his petulant attitude. He placed the large basket of food on the table. "By the weight and the size of this basket, I'd say we have enough of your landlady's good cookin' to last a month of Sundays."

Liz chuckled aloud. "I surely hope so, considering my vast culinary skills. Did I ever tell you about the summer Gertie tried to teach Anna and me to cook? Ugh! Whenever we protested, she warned us that there'd be days like today. You do remember Gertie's cooking, don't you?"

"Do I! Especially her melt-in-your-mouth pie crusts! My favorite was her cherry pies."

"Nothing better!" A wave of homesickness washed over Liz as she searched in a small metal tray of kitchen tools for a can opener. Choosing one of the unlabeled cans from the shelf, she removed the lid. "And so begins the adventure. What will we dine on tonight? Ah, peas. OK, good start. Which tin can should I open next?"

Alan's arm brushed against Liz's shoulder as he reached past her to one of the larger cans on the shelf. "How about this one? I'm mighty hungry."

She turned her head in time to find her lips inches from his. Resisting the urge to close the gap between them, she took the can from his hand and fumbled with the can opener.

"Here, let me open that for you." His hand brushed over hers as he gently claimed the can opener and proceeded to open the can. Removing the serrated lid, he peered inside. "*Hmm,* looks like baked beans to me. Beans and peas, what a delightful meal!"

Liz grabbed an iron frying pan from a nail on the wall beside the sink. "Hey, I'll add a few strips of Miz Mabel's caribou jerky to the griddle and we just might have a true Alaskan gourmet meal." She glanced toward a small shelf of spices on the nearby wall. "How about some minced garlic, powdered onion, and chili pepper? Voilà! We will have a dish to set before a king!"

Her face reddened when she remembered that she had always referred to Alan as the king of their castle. By the dismayed expression on his face, she surmised that he recalled the memory as well. For an instant, their gaze held. Instinctively, he took a step forward as if to gather her in his arms.

Behind them the door swung open and slammed against the wall, breaking the spell. Lowell entered the cabin. "*Brr!* It's cold out there. You're all set up to send and receive messages tonight, Mrs. Ames. Fortunately for us, the lean-to is on the leeward side of the cabin. And so is the outhouse, I might add." He removed his bulky parka and hung it on a hook behind the door.

Unsettled by the emotionally charged reaction she'd felt toward Alan, Liz couldn't decide whether she was happy or sad for Lowell's interruption. She poured the beans and peas into the frying pan and sprinkled on several herbs and spices, hoping to make the mixture palatable, and placed the pan on the stove's cooking grate. A third can of sweetened pears, a small tin of soda crackers, a few of Miz Mabel's gingersnaps, and a pot of hot tea completed the evening's menu.

The conversation around the table focused on home. Liz told about life in Seattle, tagging after her father at the local farmers' market. "The apples. I loved the smell of freshly picked apples piled high on wooden crates."

Alan talked about Portland. "I especially loved going down to the Willamette River when the big ships were in port. I'm sure my parents thought I'd more than likely join the navy. But instead, I joined the Army Corps of Engineers." He laughed. "How about you, Lowell, where do you call home?"

"A tiny fishing village. Life was tough—full of disappointments. One had to be strong to survive. I soon learned that trust is a weakness. It's quite simple really—the strong live and the weak die." The man's ruddy face narrowed into a frown as he glanced down at his plate of food. When he looked up, the man's eyes had softened. "I grew up in a small Aleut community outside Dutch Harbor, one of the islands in the Aleutian Archipelago."

"Sure, I've heard of it," Liz volunteered. "Isn't Moeshe from the same area? You must have known him before coming to the base."

Lowell slumped in his chair. "Sort of. Our paths have crossed a few times over the years."

A look of surprise crossed Alan's face. "How'd you know that? Moeshe doesn't talk much about his personal life."

"I've visited him a few times since his incarceration. As a result, we've become friends. We talk a lot about God and politics and literature and life in general. Did you know that when he was only a tiny baby, the village's shaman adopted him? Isn't that right, Lowell?"

Lowell toyed with the peas on his plate. "That's how the tale is told."

"Speaking of Moeshe, Liz," Alan interrupted. "Before we flew out this morning, the colonel told me he's been cleared of all charges. They're hot on the trail of identifying the traitor who did set off the dynamite."

"Really?" Liz's face brightened. "That's fantastic! So he's been freed? I never believed for a moment the man was capable of such a dastardly act. He has too much gentleness in his eyes."

Lowell's face darkened.

Alan continued. "Yeah, someone further up the army chain of command sent down the word to free him immediately."

"No surprise! Moeshe always seems to land on his feet—that one." Lowell stabbed a bean with his fork as if the legume might flee his plate on its own power.

"Well, I, for one, am relieved. I never could figure out why he wouldn't defend himself against the charges. Want seconds?" Liz passed the pan of beans to Lowell. He accepted them without a word. They ate in silence for several minutes before Lowell slammed his silverware on the table beside his plate. "The man's real name isn't Moeshe. It's Irnig-Kesuk—or at least that's what his shaman father calls him. In Inuit, the name means 'drawn from the deep.' " The bitterness in Lowell's voice startled Alan and Liz.

"Irnig-Kesuk?" Liz blinked in surprise.

"Irnig-Kesuk adopted the name Moeshe after he entered the pale skins' world. As you know, Eskimo tribesmen often assume any number of names during their lifetimes. One of the results of this custom is that it drives European and American officials crazy." Lowell chuckled aloud but quickly sobered. "At one point, government agents assigned numbers to individuals, since they couldn't follow the changing of their names. Many of the older folk in my village still go by their assigned numbers." He pushed back his chair, rose from the table, and adjusted the damper on the stove.

After a minute, he turned to face the couple. His eyes had hardened. "Forgive me, but Irnig-Kesuk and I would be considered brothers in your pale skins' world, but we have never been friends."

"Brothers?" Liz blinked in surprise.

Lowell continued. "Irnig-Kesuk has always had it easy. He attended the University of Washington on a generous scholarship from a shipping magnet, while I had to wash dishes in a greasy diner to pay for my room and board. But it's fine. Adversity made me stronger!"

"Brothers?" Liz glanced questioningly at Alan.

"Not by birth, Mrs. Ames, but by circumstance," Lowell explained. "Our father adopted both of us. When my mother died in childbirth, my father took off to the Northwest Territory and was never seen again. As for Irnig-Kesuk, no one knows who his parents were."

Sensing Lowell's increasing irritation, Liz glanced at her watch and rose to her feet. "Oh my! It's going on seven o'clock. I want to clean up the kitchen before twenty hundred hours. In the meantime, Alan, if you could please write out the message you wish me to send to Major Judd, I would appreciate it. Thanks."

With the mood broken, the men carried their dinnerware to the sink. Lowell muttered something about checking the plane's landing gear while Alan quickly wrote out the message he wished her to send and then exited the cabin as well. Liz poured the hot water into a porcelain enamel basin from under the sink, and before picking up the bar of lye soap, she helped herself to a second gingersnap—her reward for not complaining about being stuck with cleanup. In a very short time, she stacked the last of the clean dinner plates to dry on the wooden rack beside the sink. Her thoughts drifted to Will, so steady, so predictable. It would be nice to hear from him, if only via Morse code.

Liz took advantage of her few minutes of privacy to sponge bathe before the men returned to the cabin. Brilliant red curls tumbled down around her shoulders as she unfastened the pins that had held her hair in a bun at the nape of her neck. Quickly readjusting her clothing and fastening her hair in place, she felt refreshed and once more presentable.

She fastened her watch back onto her wrist. It was nineteen fifty-five hours! Grabbing Alan's message to transmit, she slipped into her heavy jacket and dashed from the cabin. Slipping and sliding, she inched her way to the lean-to. A stack of seasoned firewood filled half of the structure. An ax had been embedded in a large cutting log at the front of the stack.

As she stepped over a few scattered pieces of kindling, Liz ducked to avoid decapitating herself on the wire antenna Lowell had strung between the roof and a nearby tree branch. Short of breath due to the biting cold air, and more than a little excited to make contact with Will, she dropped onto the three-legged wooden stool behind the metal radio table and removed the protective canvas tarp from the radio equipment. Satisfied she was ready to transmit, she checked her watch once more—nineteen fifty-eight hours.

Liz had barely checked in with Will when she sensed someone leaning over her shoulder. If the woman had one irrational pet peeve when operating the radio, it was having someone hover over her as she transmitted. Impatient, she glanced up to find Lowell within inches of her left shoulder.

"Please, Lowell, step back. I don't mind if you watch at a distance, but I need elbow room."

"Sorry, Mrs. Ames." A wisp of irritation crossed the man's face as he stepped back.

She signaled her arrival on the frequency. Immediately, Will replied. R—WHITTIER RECEIVING—SK.

A warm sense of well-being filled her heart. She smiled and keyed in Alan's written message. *Good old Will,* she mused. *He's the kind of man a woman can always count on to be there for her.* Recognizing her thoughts had once again strayed into dangerous territory, Liz shook her head and focused her attention on the piece of paper on the table before her. Her nerves tightened when, behind her left ear, she felt Lowell breathing heavily. Finishing her transmission, she turned and glared. "Lowell! Please."

"Yes, ma'am. Sorry."

"Thank you." With Will's reply coming in, she quickly scribbled down his cipher.

R—INFORMATION RECEIVED—STOP. HOPE YOU HAD A GREAT FLIGHT—STOP. UNTIL TOMORROW—STOP. SAME TIME, SAME FREQUENCY—STOP. SEE YOU SOO—

Without warning, a surge of static overrode Will's message. The unusual atmospheric change in the night air caused her spine and fingers to tingle.

By the time the woman made her notations in the logbook, shut down the station, and covered the equipment with the canvas tarp, Lowell was nowhere to be seen. To keep it safe, she momentarily considered transporting the radio equipment into the cabin until morning, but the sky was clear and the south-facing lean-to was protected from the wind, so she dismissed the idea.

Liz closed her eyes. It felt good just to sit alone for a few minutes to still her troubled heart. She dreaded the night. Sleeping in a cabin with two men, one she barely knew and the other whom she knew all too well, went beyond being awkward.

"What was Colonel Anderson thinking when he sent me out here?" she mumbled. For several minutes, she stared into the southern sky and thought of her cozy Craftsman cottage in Seattle. She had to admit it would be fun to help her mother and her sister finalize the plans for Anne's spring wedding. "Will I be home by then?" she asked the night air. Chances were improving, since the army would need supplies shipped, which could involve her father's merchant marine ships, but she didn't know for sure. A smile crossed her face as she imagined her homecoming. But when she remembered leaving Alaska also meant leaving Will, she frowned.

Liz dreaded heading into the cabin. She hoped the two men would retire quickly and she could silently slip into her bunk without drawing their attention. But as she neared the front of the cabin, Alan called to her. "Lizzie, come here. Come quickly! Ya gotta see this! Hurry!"

Thinking something terrible must have happened, Liz dashed around the corner of the cabin and froze in her tracks. Aurora borealis—the northern lights! She gasped in delight. Vibrant flashes of emerald green gyrated above the horizon in a primitive dance of color and light. Static crackled in the crisp, night air. Transfixed by nature's phenomenal display, she could barely catch her breath. Liz raced to the front of the cabin to get a broader view, where she found Alan and Lowell mesmerized by the incredible display. The aurora danced and twirled across the sky like brightly clad partiers at a Brazilian festival.

"Oh, Lizzie, isn't it glorious?" Alan pulled her into his arms. Captivated by the show of lights, she didn't resist. "What are the chances of seeing a northern lights display this early in the evening?" He whispered in her ear. "They usually are visible closer to midnight when the sky is its darkest."

"It's magical," Liz gasped. Regardless of how often she'd viewed nature's spectacle in the skies north of Seattle, seeing them again was always a thrill. "Fox fire, that's what the Finns call the lights." She paused. "Now

I understand why Will's signal broke up tonight."

At the mention of Major Judd's name, Alan abruptly released her and stuffed his hands in his pockets. If Lowell observed the couple's sudden mood change, he ignored it. Instead, he shared a piece of his native folklore. "My people believe that the sky is a giant dome arching over the earth—like an upside-down porcelain teacup. At the top, there is a hole where spirits pass through to the heavens. The sky-dwellers who live in the outer heaven carry torches to guide new arrivals to their ranks. The whistling crackling noise is the voice of the spirits communicating with those of us who remain. We must answer them in whispering voices." Transfixed, Lowell stared at the heavenly display as he spoke. "However, some Inuit tribes believe the aurora borealis are the dancing souls of deer, whales, and salmon. Many shamans teach that viewing the northern lights will heal diseases. These tribal leaders look to them for medical advice—my father for one."

"That's right, your father is a shaman." Alan sidled closer to the man.

"Er, yes, he is."

"What an experience it must be growing up in such an environment. And your adoptive mother?" Alan bored into Lowell's explanation.

"She died when Irnig-Kesuk and I were toddlers, leaving our father to raise us alone. He never remarried."

A new blaze of emerald swirled across the sky. Lost in the wonder, Liz caught her breath. "I think they look like the skirts of Spanish dancers twirling on a giant stage."

"That's a female fantasy for you," Alan taunted. "About your father . . ." He addressed Lowell again.

Piqued over Alan's put-down, Liz interrupted, "I am glad my heart is young enough to still find a touch of magic in this world. I don't, as yet, reduce every gift from nature to scientific reason and logic."

Whatever tenderness she'd earlier felt toward Alan had vanished. "Of course, I understand the technical causes for the aurora, how the solar winds circle the earth's magnetic field; how the electrically charged particles from the sun get sucked into that magnetic field and then race toward the magnetic poles. But nothing can explain away the spontaneous joy in response to the raw beauty seen."

Without responding, Alan turned, stalked into the cabin, and slammed the door behind him.

# Chapter 19: A Day of Revelation

*The revelation of thought takes men out of servitude into freedom.*
*—Ralph Waldo Emerson*

## Alaskan Wilderness: January 1942

Liz stood outside for several more minutes, hoping the aurora borealis would give an encore. It didn't. Somewhere in the darkness, a wolf howled. Finally, there was nothing left for her to do but go inside the cabin.

After what she hoped would be her last trek to the outhouse, Liz pressed the metal latch on the cabin door. The hinges squeaked in protest. Sensing both men were still awake, she tiptoed into the cabin. Flames flickered behind the tiny glass window on the stove. In the semidarkness, her right hip collided against the edge of the table.

"Ouch! Sorry," she whispered. No one replied. She felt her way along the length of the beds, slipped off her mukluks and parka, stretched out fully dressed on the lumpy mattress, and pulled the woolen blanket she'd earlier placed at the foot of the bed over her.

As her eyes adjusted to the darkness, Liz could make out Lowell's supine form on the floor in front of the stove. Above her head, she heard Alan mumble as he turned over. Liz closed her eyes. As her thoughts raced through the events of the day, the words, *"Lo, I am with you alway, even unto the end of the world,"* popped into her mind. *This place surely qualifies as the end of the earth, doesn't it, Lord?* she prayed.

She'd intended to read before going to bed, but the fantastic light display had superseded her plans. *Was that a special gift from You, God, to remind me that You are with me?* she prayed silently. *If so, thank You for reminding me You are still in control of the universe.*

Liz turned from her side to her back and stared at the bottom of the bunk above her head. *And what about Alan? One minute he's flirting with me, and the next he's belittling me. It's going to be a long couple of days, Lord.*

One of the promises Grandma Keating had underlined in the Bible surfaced in Liz's mind. *"My grace is sufficient for thee: for my strength is made per—"*

While she didn't know how long she'd been asleep, Liz heard a series of dots and dashes. Automatically, her mind translated the message, though she was dreaming she was in her father's radio room. DOT-DOT-DASH-DASH. In the mystical land between semiconsciousness and sleep, she paused to listen, expecting the code to disappear along with her dream.

At first the message was nothing more than a series of random letters. But when the coding stopped, the unexpected silence inside the cabin set her ears to ringing. *Must have been a tree branch scratching the side of the cabin,* Liz thought. Rolling onto her left side, she attempted to fall asleep again.

As she drifted off, the tapping resumed once more. DOT-DOT-DASH-DASH-DASH-DOT. Her eyes popped open. This couldn't be part of her dream! She slipped her stocking feet over the edge of the bunk, sat up, and listened. DOT-DASH-DOT-DOT.

*It has to be a branch scratching against the cabin,* she told herself a second time. Mentally, she retraced the area around the outside of the building. There were no trees close enough to the cabin. *Mice? Perhaps the mice are back to reclaim their squatters' rights,* she decided. And when the tapping stopped, she lay back down and burrowed beneath her blanket.

She groaned, hating to move. But like it or not, she realized she had to make a trip to the outhouse, or she'd never fall back to sleep. Above her head, she heard Alan's familiar snore. Again she sat up, tugged on her mukluks, and rose to her feet. Putting on her heavy parka, she slipped out of the cabin as silently as possible, despite the door's noisy protest.

"This is so frustrating! All I want to do is sleep!" she mumbled into the darkness. She'd barely finished her business, when she heard the staccato pattern of code once again. This time she knew no animal, no branch, and no breeze could be making merely random noises. And now, Liz was wide awake. From the lean-to next to the outhouse, the coder tapped a mishmash of letters ending with "SK." She paused to listen for a coded reply. Who could be using the radio equipment at such an hour? Alan was asleep, and it certainly couldn't be Lowell. The man had failed miserably at sending and receiving code while in her class.

Liz adjusted her clothing and quietly opened the door to the outhouse. She peered around the open door in the direction of the lean-to. Red, green, and white lights on the radio console blinked and flashed in the darkness. She could see the silhouette of the man hunched over the desk.

"What do you think you're doing?" The outhouse door slammed shut behind her. Startled, Lowell jumped to his feet.

"Lowell, get away from that radio!" She started toward the lean-to. "What frequency are you on? You have no clearance to operate this rig."

Liz sensed a flood of resentment and confusion emanating from him, like a wolf backed into a corner. He stood poised, a pencil in one hand and what appeared to be a hunting knife in the other. "Mrs. Ames, I don't want to hurt you, but I have a job to do. Go back to bed and forget you saw me."

Liz blinked in surprise. And then, the bewilderment cleared from her brain. "You're the spy!" A note of hysteria edged her tone. "Who were you coding—a Japanese submarine?"

An ominous growl emerged from Lowell's throat. "You're leaving me little choice, Mrs. Ames. Please go back to bed."

The woman vigorously shook her head. "I can't do that. I'm responsible for this radio station and all cipher being transmitted and received from it!"

Everything seemed surreal, almost as if she were trapped in a scene from an Alfred Hitchcock nightmare.

Lowell charged toward the startled woman. As she tried to back away, she slid on the ice and fell. Her knees shook like gelatin as she scrambled to her feet. Her brain ordered her legs to run, but her body refused to move. *Scream! Scream for Alan!* her mind ordered. But when she tried to scream, no sound came out of her mouth.

With the speed of a striking sidewinder, Lowell grabbed her tousled hair. She struggled to break free, but he held on with a viselike grip, pulling her tight against his body. She recoiled from the heat of his breath on her neck.

"You couldn't leave well enough alone, could you? You had to stick your nose in where it didn't belong," he hissed.

In what felt like slow motion, the man lifted the knife. Suddenly, her sense of survival exploded with a surge of adrenaline. Wriggling against his restraint, she doubled her fist and plunged it hard into his nose. The blow was clumsy, but it stunned him enough to loosen his grip. She broke free from his grasp, dashed into the outhouse, and slid the wooden bar across the door.

*Scream,* she told herself, *scream!* If Liz had one unusually powerful gift, it was her loud voice. Her grammar school teachers were always shushing her. In the junior high glee club, the director always told her to sing more softly. Taking a deep breath, the woman let go with a scream loud enough to awaken an entire community. "Alan! Help! Help!" she shouted.

Lowell let go of a string of curses, some in English and some in Aleut. He slammed his shoulder against the door. The rickety outhouse shuddered with each blow. Dust clouds billowed about her face. She coughed and screamed again.

"You're cornered. Give up! You have nowhere to go, Mrs. Ames," Lowell ordered

"Help! Help!" Her teeth chattered as she slid to the floor and pressed her back against the door. The traitor was right. She had no place to go. Sooner or later, the rusty hinges would give, or the wooden door would splinter. And Alan, a heavy sleeper, probably would never hear her cries. *Oh, dear God, I need those angels You promised to send when I'm in trouble. I need them to encircle this outhouse!*

Despite her predicament, the idea of having a half dozen angels dispensed from heaven to surround an outhouse in the wilds of Alaska brought a smile to her lips and she giggled.

Outside the door, the man ranted about the futility of resisting. He switched from beating the door with his shoulder to kicking it with his boot. With each strike, she could feel the wooden door crack against her back.

*"If any of you lack wisdom"— I certainly lack wisdom, Father God. You said to ask and it shall be given you. Well, I'm asking. Actually, I'm pleading! Help me!* Promise after promise tumbled from her lips, promises she'd been memorizing since arriving in Alaska.

Just as the wooden door threatened to splinter into kindling, the barrage stopped. She pressed her ear against the door, hoping Lowell had retreated.

"Liz! Where are you?" It was Alan's voice.

"He's got a knife!" she shouted. "Lowell's your spy, Alan!"

"I'm coming," Alan shouted. "Stay put."

She obeyed for several seconds. Finally, her curiosity got the best of her. Cautiously, she lifted the bar on the door and peered outside to find a barefoot Alan and the enraged Lowell hunched over, face-to-face, circling one another in the snow.

"Lowell, think about what you're doing. We can work something out." Alan's voice held a strange calm. "Liz, go back to the cabin and lock yourself inside." Alan circled to the right, then ordered, "Elizabeth, go inside the cabin!"

"Listen to your hubby, Mrs. Ames. You don't want to see me gut him." The traitor's voice had taken on a guttural tone that sounded demonic. "In case you haven't guessed by now, I am your saboteur. I not only dynamited the shed, but I cut the fuel lines on several of the big rigs as well. I poisoned the oatmeal one morning, causing everyone to get sick. And all the while, I was sending and receiving messages to a Japanese submarine off the coast of Seward. Pretty good, huh?" Over his left shoulder, he added, "And you, Mrs. Ames, I fooled you into thinking I was incapable of passing your foolish little code test. I've been ciphering from a fishing boat in the Bering Sea since I was eleven!"

Alan and Lowell continued to circle each other. "Are you still here, Liz? I told you to go to the cabin!" Suddenly, the very real threat of personal bodily harm broke through to her terrified brain. She dashed to the front of the cabin, as Alan soothed, "Lowell, you don't want to hurt anyone. I'm your friend. Put down the knife."

The cold night air amplified the sound of the men's voices. "Don't call me Lowell! Lowell Meade is the English name I adopted to fit into the pale skins' world. My name is Amarok! *Amarok* means 'gray wolf' to my people. And you, Captain Ames, are anything but a friend."

A feral shriek followed by the sound of a struggle filled the air. Fearful for Alan's safety, she rushed around the corner of the house in time to see Alan holding Lowell's wrist, both men gripping the hunting knife. Though Alan towered over Lowell by more than four inches, the shorter man was all muscle.

Without warning, Alan's bare feet slipped from under him. He struggled to maintain his balance but fell backward, hitting his head against the corner of the radio table. The rickety table holding the radio equipment crashed to the ground. As her husband fell, the knife over which they'd been wrestling flew into the woodpile.

When the spy sprang to retrieve the knife, she bounded into the cabin. But before she could lower the wooden bar across the door, her attacker pressed his bulk against it. The door bowed under his weight. Liz scrambled across the floor and scooted under the peeled log bunk bed. She curled into a ball in the rear corner and prayed he couldn't reach her in the darkness of the cabin.

The door slammed against the wall. "You can't hide from me, Mrs. Ames. Face it, you have nowhere to go and no one to help you now."

Purposefully, he crossed the room and dropped to his knees beside the log bed frame. She scooted farther into the back corner. When he thrust his left arm under the bed frame, she caught the glint of the knife in his fist. Lowell probed the dark space with the knife, barely missing her toes on one pass. To keep from crying, she bit the side of her hand and silently prayed like she'd never before prayed.

When the man failed to reach her with his hand, he tried to crawl under the bed, but the bulk of his upper body couldn't fit beneath the low bed frame.

"Come out, Mrs. Ames. Look, I like you. You always treated me as an equal, not like most of the other *gussaks* around camp." The tone of Lowell's voice had changed. "If you come out right now, I promise I won't hurt you. Besides, your husband needs you. When he fell, he hit his head and broke his leg. I need you to help me carry him into the cabin."

Despite the plea to help Alan, Liz sensed the evil in Lowell's words. A wiser voice inside her head warned her to stay where she was.

Changing tactics, Lowell again tried to wedge himself under the bed far enough to reach her, but couldn't. When he tried to back out, he banged his head against the heavy log frame. Spewing out a stream of angry epithets, the man clambered to his feet, tromped across the room, and grabbed his duffel bag.

"Have it your way, Mrs. Ames. You're just like the others—all those haughty coeds at the University of Washington. They thought they were better than me. Well, I showed 'em!"

She didn't respond. The man continued. "When my logistics professor, Professor Yamakari, recruited me to spy for Japan, I knew this moment would come. It's my chance to even the score. If only Irnig-Kesuk hadn't blown my cover. He was always the cooperative, compliant one, running to Daddy, trying to get me in trouble."

While stuffing his items into a duffel bag, Lowell continued to talk as if he couldn't stop himself. "He did fool me. I never imagined Irnig-Kesuk was a government agent. That's what last night's cipher from my contact was about—that my cover had been compromised. Thanks to my dear stepbrother, I am now a fugitive from the U.S. Army Military Police. So you see, I can't go back to Whittier. But don't worry, I have an escape plan."

Lowell continued babbling as if she were not present. "Alaska is a wild and wonderful land. One can easily hide where no one will ever find him." The man snatched Miz Mabel's food basket from the table, slung his duffel bag over his shoulder, and headed toward the open door. "Sorry, but when your husband fell, he broke the table and destroyed the radio. Believe me, there's nothing left to repair. But just in case you're too crafty for your own good, Mrs. Ames, when I leave, I'm taking the antenna wire with me. Sure glad I refueled the plane last night."

From the doorway, he squatted and peered under the bed one last time. "How long do you think you two stranded greenhorns will last with only a few cans of army rations and one pair of snowshoes between you?" he taunted. Then with an evil chuckle, Lowell stood to his feet and slammed the cabin door behind him.

It seemed like hours before Liz heard the plane engine start. She wiggled out from under the bed and reached the cabin window to see the *Minna* lift off and climb into the sky. The plane circled once and disappeared over the top of the mountains to the east.

Grabbing the blanket off the bottom bunk and the first-aid kit from the cupboard, Liz ran to find Alan shivering in the snow. From the strange angle of his left leg, she knew it was broken in at least two places.

A wave of panic rose in her throat. For the first time, neither of them could walk away from the situation. For the first time in their marriage, she knew she needed to remain calm. She couldn't turn to her dad for help. And Alan couldn't run away to the U.S. Army Corps of Engineers for solace. They needed one another's cooperation to survive.

"Oh, dear God! What do I do?" As she uttered her prayer, her mind began to clear. Later, she would recall that it was like a cloud of witnesses as described in Hebrews 12 directing her step-by-step. She knelt down in the snow beside her spouse.

Alan uttered a painful groan as he regained consciousness. "What happened? Where am I?"

"Stay still! You've been hurt. I'm going to try to get you inside." She placed the first-aid kit on the snow beside him and covered him with the blanket. "Your leg is broken. If you try to walk on it, you may be crippled for life."

"You can't move me by yourself. Go get Lowell to help you." When Alan tried to sit up, he winced with pain.

"He's gone. Lowell's gone."

"Gone? Where?"

"Lowell, or Amarok, as he prefers to be called, flew out of here a few minutes ago. Don't try to move. Let me find some wood and put your leg in a splint."

"Are you all right, Liz? Did he hurt you?" Tears welled in Alan's eyes. Even at their son's funeral, Liz had never seen her husband show any emotion other than frustration and anger. "Where's Lowell? You need his help."

Liz repeated, "Lowell took the plane and left. We're on our own." She sorted through the woodpile until she found two flat boards. She strapped the boards to both sides of his leg with a roll of adhesive tape from the first-aid kit, while Alan gritted his teeth against the pain. Finished, she stood up. "Next, I'm going to roll you onto this slab of wood and use it as toboggan to get you inside the cabin."

Alan grimaced with pain as she slid the board under his body. She tied the strap from the first-aid kit to the end of the six-foot-long board. Inch by inch, she pulled Alan on the makeshift toboggan to the front door. Once there, Alan tried to help her shift his body from the board onto a blanket.

"Let me do it. Don't try to move," she ordered. Hauling him inside the cabin, she closed the door. She felt chilled despite the sweat she'd worked up moving her husband. With the fire no longer burning in the stove, a tingly cold had seeped into the cabin. "I'm not going to try to lift you onto the bed. Instead, I'm going to roll you onto Lowell's mattress in front of the stove to help you stay warmer."

Once she got Alan in place, a fire going again, and water boiling in the teakettle, Liz glanced about the tiny shack and realized that though it was hardly a second honeymoon haven, they were alone for the first time in almost a year. She gazed down at her husband. Alan's eyes were closed, his brow furrowed with pain. She studied his motionless form on the floor in front of her. "Are you sleeping?" she asked, measuring his pulse on his neck with her fingers. "Good, you're still alive."

She straightened when a new thought niggled her brain, *What if he dies out here?* "No room for panic," she scolded aloud. Her words seemed hollow. "When I don't check in with Will tonight, the army will begin looking for us. Perhaps the next thing to do is to stomp out an SOS in the snow on the landing strip."

Leaving a glass of water beside Alan's sleeping form, she went outside and eyed the pair of snowshoes hanging from the eaves. Though she'd never worn snowshoes, Liz had watched the camp workers snowshoe across deep snow as if they were gliding on a dance floor. *How hard can it be?* She fastened the leather straps of the snowshoes onto her boots and tried to straighten up. "Whoa! Whoa!" Her feet slipped. She grabbed the snow shovel for balance.

Once stabilized, Liz tried to lift her foot. It felt glued to the ground. After a few tries, she learned to lift her heel first. Slowly, she mastered the skill.

Liz worked throughout the morning. Damp with sweat, she paused to examine the handiwork she and the snow shovel had created. Her stomach growled; her hair hung in frozen icicles around her face; her arm and back muscles ached. But the SOS she had scraped on the landing strip stood out in dramatic relief against the surrounding terrain. "There! Any pilot worth his salt will spot that!" she spoke into the silence. But in her mind, Liz had to admit, *This is the Alaskan wilderness. What plane or pilot is going to accidentally fly over the field and read my message, at least before tomorrow, morning since the army won't know we're missing until nightfall?*

★★★★★

"Don't move, Alan. You've broken your leg." Those were the last words he recalled hearing before he lost consciousness. When he awakened, his throat was parched. His tongue stuck to the roof of his mouth. His leg throbbed with pain. He opened his eyes to a hazy blur. He heard the door open and a human form hovered over him.

"I'm thirsty," he gasped, struggling to lift his upper body from the floor. "I need a drink of water."

The rim of a cup was pressed to his lips. Cool water dribbled onto his bristled chin. He tried to wipe it off his face and chest.

"Try not to move." Alan recognized his wife's voice, the same tone of voice she'd once used to soothe their colicky son.

"I need to get up." He tried to shift his body, but an excruciating pain shot through him.

"You can't. You broke your leg. You must lie still." She lifted the blanket and studied his injury. "Your leg is swelling. I'm going to wrap it in snow to bring down the swelling." She spoke as if he could understand her. "Later, I'll make a poultice of Epsom salt from the first-aid kit and rehydrated powdered eggs in the food storage. It's Grandma Keating's remedy for sprained ankles, so I figure it should be good for broken bones too."

Bewildered from his head injury, Alan strove to make sense of what had happened. In the back recesses of his mind, he remembered getting into a fight with Lowell, but he couldn't remember why they had fought.

Liz left the cabin to fill the dishpan with snow. Minutes later, she returned to the cabin and packed the snow around his leg. Alan shivered before a wave of soothing darkness flooded over him. From somewhere outside him, he heard a man groan, "I–I–I'm cold."

One by one, he felt the weight of blankets being placed on top of him. He heard a woman speak, "There! That should keep you warm. I need to fetch some wood for the stove, and then I'll make us something to eat. Don't worry; I'll leave the cabin door open. Call if you need me." And she was gone.

He glanced around the cabin, the desperation of their situation partially sinking in. For a moment, he regretted the wall he'd built around his life.

He'd heard the rumors around camp about his wife and Major Judd. In his quarters at night, Alan would lie awake imagining the two of them together, laughing, sharing their deepest thoughts, making love on the floor of the radio room.

His thoughts returned to his predicament when Liz returned carrying an armload of wood. She looked exhausted and yet beautifully disheveled. A dark bruise marred her right cheek. Lowell! Alan shut his eyes; the head injury and pain made it difficult to think clearly.

He listened as Liz put firewood in the stove. He felt her kneel beside him and check his leg again. "The swelling is going down, I think. Let me get a few towels to sop up the melting snow. When you need to, uh, relieve yourself, don't try to do it alone. I am here for you."

A wave of humiliation washed over him. It hurt worse than any physical pain in his leg. "Elizabeth, I'm sorry."

"Sorry? Why? It's not your fault. No one planned for this to happen."

"True, but I'm the reason Colonel Anderson sent you out here."

"What?" Liz brushed a tangle of curls from her sweaty neck.

Alan continued. "I thought if you and I could recapture some of the romance of our honeymoon, we might . . ." He reached out to touch her forearm.

She pushed him away. "Are you out of your mind? Tell me how your romantic interlude would have happened with what's-his-name along?" Irritation filled her voice.

"I don't know. I would have figured something out, I guess." He covered his eyes with his forearm.

Indignation forced her to her feet. "Well, I hope you're still in a figuring mood because you obviously got your wish. We are certainly alone now!"

"You don't know how lonely it's been for me here in Alaska, with no one to talk to," he whined.

"You mean you've been lonely since the Dahls barred you from dallying with their daughter, Trudy." Now Liz was snarling. "Before they learned you were married, you were far from lonely, or so I hear tell."

He started to speak, but stopped. Liz was right—and not in a conciliatory mood.

She held his gaze for a moment, shook her head, and heaved an exhausted sigh. Her shoulders slumped as if all the fury had washed the last vestiges of strength from her body. "Look, we're going to be fine. When I don't make contact with Will tonight, he will alert Colonel Anderson, and they'll send out a search party for us, right?"

Alan frowned. "What about the radio?"

"It's smashed to smithereens, as Grandma Keating would say."

"I'm sorry . . ."

She averted her gaze as she adjusted the blanket around his shoulders. "Look, let's just make the best of our situation. Don't worry. As soon as the army gives me the OK to leave Alaska, I'll go to Reno or Mexico, wherever you like. I'll give you the divorce you requested and—" Her voice broke. "We'll never need to see one another again."

"Is that what you want?"

"A divorce was your suggestion, remember?" She shrugged and stood up.

"But I . . ."

Liz turned away and changed the subject, closing the door to further discussion. "Are you hungry enough for another surprise meal? Let's see." She crossed the room, chose a twelve-ounce can from the shelves and opened it. "For your dining pleasure, Captain Ames, we have, uh, green beans." She opened a second can. "With a side of stewed tomatoes. Not a bad combination. And for dessert . . ." She opened a third can. "Asparagus spears."

Alan laughed at her imitation of a French waiter.

While the food was heating, Liz refilled the kerosene lamp and placed it in the center of the table, ready for use.

Liz dished up the food, and the couple ate their meal in silence.

* * * * *

By midafternoon, dark, heavy clouds had filled the sky. Alan watched helplessly as Liz lugged several more armloads of wood into the cabin to keep the fire burning throughout the night. On her last trip, she brushed several flakes of snow from her shoulders.

"It's snowing?" he asked.

"It has been for the last hour. I think we're in for a big storm." Once the logs were piled behind the stove, she dropped into the nearest chair. "The SOS I shoveled on the airstrip will be all for nothing, I'm afraid. Fresh snow already hides the message. I'll have to do it all over again tomorrow." Her eyes swam with tears of fatigue and frustration.

A lump rose in his throat. He swallowed hard. "I'm sorry."

Too tired to reply, a sob escaped her exhausted body.

"I am sorry."

"Stop saying you're sorry, Alan! It doesn't help!" She crossed the cabin and leaned over the empty sink. Her shoulders heaved.

"I'm just . . ."

"Just stop it, OK?" She grabbed a can of food from the shelf and stabbed the can opener blade into the lid. "It's time to make your dinner!"

"Aren't you going to eat?" he asked.

"I don't know. Right now I'm too tired and too upset to try."

Silenced, he watched her dump a can of apricots onto a plate and then drop the empty can on the floor. It rolled toward him, stopping short of his shoulder. She didn't bother to retrieve it. After rehydrating a measure of dried eggs and powdered milk with water, she dumped the unsavory mixture into a frying pan on the stovetop.

Minutes later, she scooped the scrambled eggs onto the plate with the apricots and handed it to him. "Here! Eat!" The grayish egg mixture swam in the sweetened apricot juice. Ever since he was a child, Alan had never been able to tolerate having one food touch another on his plate. Nauseated but too tired to do battle with the woman he realized he still cared for, Alan turned his face away.

Liz grabbed her coat from the wall hook and opened the door. "I need to make a trip to the outhouse before it gets dark."

# Chapter 20: Stranded in a Blizzard

*Security is not the absence of danger,*
*but the presence of God, no matter what the danger.*
*—Anonymous*

## Alaskan Wilderness: January 1942

Liz knew that sooner or later, she'd have to return to the cabin. The snowstorm that began with big, lazy flakes quickly intensified to sharp, icy pellets. Despite the storm, she stayed inside the outhouse until the cold seemed to have seeped into her bones. Recalling all the times she'd sought refuge in her porcelain hideaway at her father's company in Seattle, the woman laughed aloud. "I guess some things never change."

Finally, after adjusting her clothing, Liz trudged through the layer of new snow to the cabin door. Her earlier footprints had already been obliterated.

At the squeak of the door's hinges, Alan jerked awake. His bedding was wet with sweat, and he'd thrown off his covers. His broken leg looked fiery red and twice its normal size.

"Are you all right?" she asked, hanging her coat on the wall hook.

"I had a bad dream," he mumbled.

She washed her hands in the sink. "Can I do anything for you?" Her eyes rested on the empty dinner plate. Either he'd licked the platter clean, or he'd found another way of disposing of his meal.

"I am thirsty." The metal tumbler she'd placed beside his bed lay empty on its side.

"I'll get you more water. Or I could fix you a cup of warm powdered milk."

She bent to retrieve the tumbler and touched his forehead. It was hot. As she straightened, he caught her hand. "I truly am sorry for how this has turned out."

"I know. Me too." She gazed down at the emotionally vulnerable expression on his face. The love she read in his eyes startled her. "All we can do now is make the best of our situation, I guess."

"I'm sorry to have to ask, but could you empty this can for me?"

She glanced at the tin can beside him. "I managed to, uh, take care of my needs without spilling a drop." His ravaged face broke into a boyish smile despite his obvious embarrassment.

She blushed. "Oh, I'm sorry I wasn't here to help you. Of course, I'll be glad to empty it."

"No more apologies, right? Besides I can't have you waiting on me hand and foot. I need to do what I can without your help."

She shook her head to dislodge the image of the proud and self-sufficient, first-year engineering student with whom she'd fallen in love, now humbled and incapable of meeting his most basic needs. She reapplied the poultice to his leg and settled him for the night. After dividing a tin of soda crackers between them, she sat at the table to read a few chapters from her Bible. As she flipped through the gilt-edge pages to Psalm 139, she felt his gaze.

Remembering that God knew her comings and goings even out here at the ends of the earth brought her comfort. That He knew and forgave her sins didn't escape her either. Silently, Liz read the words, "O Lord, thou hast searched me, and known me." Her eyelids drooped from exhaustion. "We'll keep it short tonight, Lord," she whispered and returned to her reading. "Thou knowest my downsitting and mine uprising, thou understandest my thought afar off."

"What are you reading?" Alan's voice startled her.

She yawned and rubbed the back of her neck. "Grandma Keating's Bible. When things get tough, it helps me to stay focused. I try to read a chapter or two every night before going to bed."

"You've really found it helpful?"

Expecting derision from him, she blinked in surprise. "Oh my, yes. I don't think I could have survived the last few weeks without it."

"Would you mind reading a few verses out loud? I could use a bit of encouragement tonight." Again, he surprised her. Alan had always mocked people whom he claimed used religion as a crutch, instead of using logic when dealing with their problems.

"I'd be glad to." Liz began reading verse 3. "Thou compassest my path and my lying down, and art acquainted with all my ways." She read verses 4, 5, and 6. Before beginning verse 7, she glanced over at Alan. He'd burrowed beneath his blankets. His eyes were closed. She couldn't tell whether he was awake or asleep.

When she gently closed the book, Alan asked, "Is that all you plan to read? Please go on; I'm listening."

Exhausted as she felt, Liz shrugged and continued. "Whither shall I go from thy spirit? or whither shall I flee from thy presence? If I ascend up into heaven, thou art there; if I make my bed in hell, behold, thou art there. If I take the wings of the morning, and dwell in the uttermost parts of the sea; even there shall thy hand lead me, and thy right hand shall hold me." She paused to nibble on a soda cracker.

"I can see why you like that chapter. I guess I didn't think about how alone you must have felt, stranded up here. Maybe that's been the problem all along—I was thinking only of how miserable I felt and not being concerned about anyone else." He turned his face toward her. "Please read some more."

From underlined verse to underlined verse, she read until she was too exhausted to continue. For several minutes, silence filled the cabin. Then Alan spoke, "You've had a harrowing day. Why don't you try to get some sleep."

"I really am exhausted," Liz admitted. She pushed her chair back from the table, walked across to the door, and peered outside. A flurry of snowflakes swirled past her into the cabin. "If you'd like, I'll read more tomorrow. Obviously, we'll have all the time in the world since we're going to be snowbound until this storm quits. They can't send a search plane to find us while it is snowing."

"I hope you've strung a rope between the outhouse and the cabin. If, God forbid, you head to the outhouse and turn the wrong direction, you would get lost in minutes in this storm."

"Yes, I did," she assured him. After filling the teakettle with water, she shed her heavy wool shirt and trousers and laid them on the back of one of the chairs. That's when she realized Alan was watching her every move. *Why am I feeling ill at ease standing before him wearing only my woolen underwear?* she wondered. *He's my husband, for pity's sake. Besides, my long johns cover me from my neck to my ankles.*

When the teakettle whistled, she poured the boiling water into the porcelain-coated washbasin, added some cold water and attempted to take what her grandmother called a "spit bath."

Recognizing the look of envy in her husband's eyes, she asked, "I'm sorry. I never thought that you might feel grimy after today. Can I fix you a basin of warm water?"

He eagerly nodded.

She prepared the water and then set it on the floor by his side. "There. I think you can manage from here."

"I don't know. I could sure use your help." A teasing grin spread across his face. He reached for her hand, but she successfully eluded his grasp.

"Uh, I don't think that's a good idea," she demurred. "Besides, I wouldn't want you to grow accustomed to having me do what you can do for yourself."

He caught the sudden twinkle in her eyes. Alan had barely washed and rinsed the soap from his body when Liz emptied the soiled water outside the cabin and turned down the flame on the kerosene lamp.

For some reason, the mattress on the lower bunk seemed lumpier than it had on the first night. She tossed and turned, trying to find a spot where her body wasn't too bruised. She'd barely closed her eyes when Alan broke the silence. "If we get out of here alive, is there any possible future for us, I mean, for our marriage?"

"I don't know, Alan." Liz was too tired to think.

"Surely, we can go back to who we were when we first fell in love. You're still you and I'm still me." His eyes pleaded for her to agree.

She heaved a deep sigh. "Not really. We've both changed. One can't recapture the blush of innocence."

"Is it because of Major Judd?"

At the mention of Will, her lips tightened into a tight frown. "I don't know how to answer that. All I know is things are different now. I'm a much different person from the person I was when I arrived in Whittier.

Frankly, I'm not sure I still love you after you told me that you may never have loved me."

Alan sighed. "I was angry when I said that."

"Perhaps, but many times, feelings expressed in anger are more reliable than those spoken otherwise." Liz paused to control her emotions. "When you walked out on me, I thought I'd die. No, I'm definitely not the same naïve little wife you abandoned in Seattle. You can't sashay back into my life and expect me to fall into your arms as if nothing has happened."

"I'm sorry."

"Personally, I don't think our real problem is either Trudy Dahl or Major Judd. Our real problem—the one at the core of your anger—is Lanny. You still blame me for Lanny's death, don't you?"

"I don't know." Alan's voice was barely audible.

Liz swallowed hard. "I appreciate your honesty, Alan. Sooner or later, we will have to deal with it. As Grandma Keating says, 'Babies die and no one knows why.' I refuse to believe either you or I could have saved his life if we'd been there. Our son's death was not my fault. It wasn't your fault either. It's not even God's fault. Like it or not, we live in a world of sin, disease, and death. Maybe someday—" Her voice broke. She blinked back a wave of tears.

An uncomfortable silence followed. Finally, Alan spoke. "In my mind, Lanny's a closed chapter. Can't we just move on from here?"

"Run away, you mean? Like you did when you walked out on me?" Before turning her face to the wall, she added, "We both know how well that worked out for us."

She'd almost drifted off to sleep before he spoke again. "We could buy one of the smaller San Juan Islands like we talked about, remember? We could build that little cottage I designed. We'd raise our own chickens, along with a goat, maybe a cow or two." His voice grew dreamy. It was as if he hadn't heard a word she'd said, as if he believed he could snap his fingers and she'd leap back into his arms. "With red shutters, it would have to have red shutters, and a picket fence to protect your herb garden from foraging deer and rabbits." He paused for a moment. "Liz? Are you awake?"

She punched the flannel shirt she'd been using for a pillow and turned her face to the wall.

She'd been asleep for a few hours when Alan moaned, "I'm cold. I'm so cold."

Climbing out from under her warm blanket, she found his body and his bedding damp with sweat. "Hold me," he muttered. "I'm so cold."

At a loss to know what else to do, she draped his blankets over a chair beside the stove to dry, covered him with her own blanket, and then lay beside him and snuggled up against his back. Her body felt so right pressed against his, like a hand in a well-worn leather glove. He'd been the only man she'd ever loved or with whom she'd ever made love. She was surprised at the flame of passion reignited within her.

So many times when alone in their marital bed in Seattle, Liz had craved the feel of Alan's body next to hers. She fell asleep humming the song Alan had whispered to her on the night he proposed, "I'll be loving you, always."

Sensing rather than seeing the first rays of morning light seeping through the cracks around the door, Liz awakened surprised to find Alan asleep beside her. His fever had dropped. He looked as peaceful as an innocent child despite the three-day stubble of a beard growing on his face. He groaned as she quietly crawled out from under the blanket. After a trip to the outhouse, she started breakfast. The aroma awakened him. Her combination of dehydrated eggs, milk, and a can of creamed corn, along with a little chili powder, almost smelled appealing.

After helping Alan perform his morning needs, she put on her coat, mukluks, and snowshoes. This time, a layer of freshly fallen snow made stomping out an SOS easier. By the time she returned to the cabin, she found Alan's face flushed with fever again. Sweat beaded on his forehead.

"Is there any aspirin in that first-aid kit?" he asked. "My leg is killing me."

"I'll look." She found a small packet of pain medicine in the bottom of the box, filled a glass with water, and gave him two of the pills. Then she checked his leg. It had swollen again and was discolored. "Time for another Epsom salt poultice," she announced as she stirred the egg white–Epson salts mixture in the only mixing bowl she had. "The snow stopped but the sky is still overcast. When I was on the airstrip, I think I heard a reconnaissance plane flying above the clouds, but there's no way the pilot could see me or my SOS from that altitude." She packed the poultice around his leg and wrapped it with a towel. "Alan, your leg is getting worse. I'm afraid we can't risk waiting for help to arrive. If we wait another day or two for the skies to clear, you might lose your leg."

His silent, pain-filled gaze followed her to the sink. Determined, she rinsed out the compress cloths and hung them over the edge of the sink.

"Do you recall the coordinates of the small Inuit village we flew over on our way here, the one in the canyon? If I remember right, it's not more than two or three miles from here." When Alan failed to answer, she continued. "I could go for help and be back before nightfall." She hurried on with her plan. "I could set out enough food and water for you to last until I get back with help."

"That's ludicrous!" He shook his head. "You can't go out there alone, woman. You'd be lost in no time."

She smiled and held up a compass. "Not so. I found this in the bottom of the first-aid kit. And I do know how to use it. Remember, you taught me how to use it when we went hiking."

"And if another snowstorm moves in, what will you do then? Curl up in a snow cave and die?"

"From what I can tell, the clouds to the west and south are not threatening." Liz hauled her duffel bag out from under the bunk bed and unzipped it. If she kept busy, she hoped the fear building in her stomach would subside. "I'm going to leave my Bible here for you in case you get bored and want to read something. The book of John is my favorite. I have it marked."

Alan lifted himself onto one elbow. "Elizabeth! You can't go out there alone. I forbid it!"

"You forbid it?" She chuckled. "Alan, you and what army battalion will stop me?"

His face paled. He lifted one arm toward her. "Elizabeth! Please! Surely by now, Colonel Anderson has sent out a dog team or something."

"Maybe, maybe not." She continued packing the bag. "If our evil friend returns to camp and tells them we fell into a crevasse and died or something, no one will search for us until spring." She shivered at the thought.

"That would be murder. As bad as Lowell is, he wouldn't do that."

"The man is desperate. But he won't go back to Whittier. His cover's blown."

Alan frowned and pursed his lips thoughtfully. "Stop and think for a moment. All of my wilderness training tells me it would be better for us to stay here than to go wandering off in the vast unknown."

She glanced down at him. "I'd agree with you if your leg wasn't turning purple. Time is running out if you want to keep from having your leg amputated."

Realizing he couldn't deter her with logic, Alan shot her his best pleading look. "I'm going to worry about you all day."

Her voice grew husky. "Probably so. And I will be praying for you as well." After putting food and water within easy reach for Alan, she dressed in as many layers of clothing she could wear and still walk comfortably. Liz slipped the compass in an outer pocket of her parka and planted a kiss on Alan's forehead. "Before I go, let's pray for both of our safety."

She knelt beside him and cradled his hand in hers. If she considered changing her mind about leaving, the unmasked pain on his face overrode that possibility.

"Dear heavenly Father." *So far, so good,* she thought. She'd never before prayed out loud, even in front of Miz Mabel or Moeshe. "Thou hast promised to— Oh, I can't pray in churchese, God. I'm just going to tell You what's on my mind. You know our situation. You knew before we left the outpost camp what would be the outcome of this expedition. With You there are no surprises. And You already know how our story will end." Gently, she rubbed the back of Alan's hand as she spoke.

"You said we should ask for what we need, so I'm asking. Please send a platoon of angels to watch over Alan while I'm gone. Also, You are the Great Physician, ease his pain and stop the infection from spreading." Liz let out a heavy sigh. "Also, I would appreciate it if You would send a couple of Your stronger angels to lead me through this wilderness to where I can find the help we need. Amen."

After the amen, Alan held on to her hand a minute longer. A tear slid down the side of his face and onto his pillow. She, again, was tempted to scrap her plan. But one glance at his leg, and she knew she had to try to get help.

"Be safe," he whispered, lifting her fingers to his lips.

Liz resisted the urge to gather him into her arms and comfort him. Instead, she gently removed her hand from his and rose to her feet. "Don't worry, I won't do anything crazy. I'm not that brave." Picking up the duffel bag packed with a few first-aid supplies and a stash of soda crackers, she slung the strap over her shoulder, along with the woven strap on the water-filled army canteen. "I think I have everything I need. How about you? I think everything you'll need is within your reach."

He nodded, his eyes dark with concern. "You're really going to do this, aren't you? I can't talk you out of it?"

"Afraid not." She blew him a kiss and hurried out the door. "Good-bye," she called.

Liz's first goal was ascending the pass over the mountains to the west of the valley. The route of the trail was obvious even though it was covered with snow.

When she crested the pass, she rejoiced. The clouds in the west had broken, revealing the hazy winter sun. Liz took a short rest break, ate a few crackers, and drank some water. Excited with her progress, she remembered to thank God. "You helped me make it this far, Father," she prayed aloud. "Together we can make it the rest of the way."

It was clear that the next part of her trek would be more difficult. Instead of another valley on this side of the mountain, a deep canyon with a river at the bottom followed the mountain range. A narrow trail ran along the mountainside with a steep slope on one side and a sheer drop off into the canyon on the other. Liz would have to inch her way along the narrow icy trail, slowing her progress and preventing her from reaching the village before darkness fell in the late afternoon.

At one point, Liz lost her footing and slid eight or ten feet along the steep trail, stopping just inches from the canyon rim. Liz sat on the ground, shivering uncontrollably as the sun disappeared behind a giant rock formation. She'd been so intent on each step she needed to take that she'd failed to notice a bank of storm clouds gathering overhead. Accompanying the clouds, a strong wind shrieked through the canyon, now forcing her to follow the trail on her hands and knees in some places.

"I will not panic. I will not panic!" She chanted aloud, knowing her chances of surviving until morning grew less the lower the temperature dipped. To force all thought of doom from her mind, she repeated aloud, "I can do all things through Christ! I can do all things!"

Aware that the icy wind was lowering her body temperature as well, she forced herself to keep moving. Inch by inch, with her back against the rock wall, she proceeded until she found a cave in the rock beside the trail just big enough for her to crawl into to be out of the wind. Here she ate the last of her crackers, her last source of energy.

As the hours dragged by, and she grew sleepy. It would be so easy to forget everything—to fall asleep. But Alan needed her.

While her thoughts grew more jumbled, she continued to quote her grandmother's favorite scriptures. Between verses, she prayed aloud,

"Daddy, You said You'd be with me to the ends of the earth. Does this place qualify?" Her laugh echoed off the opposite canyon wall. It comforted her to address God in such a personal manner. If there was any human she trusted on planet Earth, it was her father.

" 'I can do all things through Christ who strengtheneth me.' In all things give thanks. Give thanks?" When a new burst of laughter erupted unbidden from her throat, she wondered whether she was losing it. No, she vowed to never give up and never give in. "OK, give thanks! Let's see, just what can I be thankful for tonight? I'm thankful for this cave that protects me from the wind."

One by one she listed her blessings. She declared she was grateful for each family member and each friend she'd accumulated during her lifetime. She gave thanks for herself, who she was, and for her fiery red hair and sprinkling of freckles—something she'd despised as a child. In spite of her best effort to stay alert, at some point Liz fell asleep. She awakened in daylight to discover a bank of snow had formed around her little alcove, insulating her from the worst of the subzero temperature. Her stomach growled. That's when she remembered she'd eaten the last of her stash of crackers. "Now what, Daddy? I guess it's time to begin that diet I'm always talking about, right?"

She crawled out of her tiny cave and stretched. "Can't stay here forever!" She tried to recall landmarks she might have seen during the flight from the base camp. Remembering she'd seen a footbridge suspended across a deep ravine, she checked her compass. If her calculations were correct and this was the correct canyon, the bridge couldn't be far from her current location.

Liz walked until the trail divided; the one to the left continued to parallel the mountain range, and the one to the right headed into the canyon. She'd have to choose. Logic told her to follow the trail leading into the canyon, where she thought the Inuit village might be.

The cold and her increasing hunger had sapped her strength. As she leaned against a giant boulder to rest, Liz swiped at a tear freezing on her cheek. "I won't cry! I won't cry! I can do this! 'I can do all things through Christ who strengtheneth me.' "

After a rest, she forced her feet to continue. To encourage herself, she began shouting into the ravine, "Though I walk through the valley of the shadow of death, I will fear no evil, for thou art with me." Her voice echoed off the rocks and ice, bouncing the words of encouragement back to her own ears. At some point along the way, where, she wasn't sure, Liz had acquired a walking stick. Swinging the stick revived her spirits.

"Did You hear me, Lord? 'Thy rod and thy staff will comfort me'! As to the banquet You promise to prepare for me, a bowl of corn chowder would certainly taste good about now. I'm hungry enough to chew on my caribou-skin mukluks for nourishment."

The idea struck her funny bone. Liz threw back her head and shrieked. Her laughter rang up and down the canyon. Out of breath, she stopped. "You silly goose. You'll laugh yourself off the trail and into the canyon if you're not careful."

Her moment of hilarity shifted to the possibility she might not find either the bridge or the Inuit village they'd flown over two days before. The voice of doubt scolded, *You are a fool, Elizabeth. You knew better than to leave the protection of the cabin. You thought you were so wise, a real Florence Nightingale setting out into no man's land to save your husband's life.* The voice continued. *You had to prove yourself as capable as any man in a man's world. Isn't that what Alan said after Lanny died? Well, this time you've done it. You are so alone! No one will find your body until spring, if then. Too bad you won't survive to learn a lesson from your hardheadedness.*

Liz shook her head, as if to rid herself of the negative thoughts. *No! No! I am not alone. My God is with me. He promised! "Though I walk through the valley of the shadow of death, I will fear no evil."* Determined to drown out the negative voice in her head, she again shouted the promises of Psalm 23. "Though I walk through the valley of the shadow of death, I will fear no evil!" The sound of her own voice gave her courage as she continued to inch her way along the narrow pathway.

"Though I walk through the val—" She stopped midsentence and listened. She thought she'd heard another human voice. When silence followed, she decided it was the howl of the wind. "Though I walk—" She began the verse again, only this time much louder. Hoarse, she persisted. Again, she stopped, thinking she'd heard her name being called. Puzzled, she decided she must have been imagining things. *Oh God, am I beginning to hallucinate? Am I going crazy?*

Immediately, the answer came from the opposite side of the ravine. "Hello! Mrs. Ames!" It was a man's voice.

"Hello! Mrs. Ames, can you hear me?" The faceless voice called again.

Uncertain, she called back, "Hello?"

"Mrs. Ames, can you see me? I'm on the south side of the canyon; you're on the north."

Liz blinked in disbelief to see a man on a dogsled pulled by eight huskies on the opposite side of the canyon. The driver was Moeshe, and he was waving his arms. Relief bubbled up from within her. She jumped up and down, waving both of her arms in the air. "I'm over here!"

Suddenly, her foot slipped, sending ice and snow from the edge of the canyon tumbling down the steep cliff. The walking stick in her right hand prevented her from following.

"I can see you," he replied. "Are you all right? Where is Captain Ames? Is he all right?"

"I'm fine, but Alan broke his leg. He needs medical attention badly."

"What are you doing out here alone?"

"Getting medical help for my husband."

"Where's Lowell Meade?"

"He took the plane and left us stranded at the cabin."

Moeshe paused a moment. "I was afraid something like this might happen."

"How do I get to you? I thought there was a wooden bridge somewhere along here."

"There is, several miles farther up the canyon." He pointed in the opposite direction from where she was headed.

"Oh no!" she wailed. "What do I do now? How do I get to you?"

"You don't. You need to continue walking in the direction you're going. You're not far from an Inuit village. They will take care of you while I find Captain Ames and get him the medical help he needs."

"How far to the village?" Exhausted beyond reason, Liz felt she couldn't take one more step.

"Another mile, but don't worry! I am sure that by now, the villagers have heard your shouts and have sent scouts out to help you. I have portable radio equipment in my gear. When I reach your husband, I will contact both Whittier and the village where you will stay. God be with you, my friend." Moeshe hopped onto his sled and shouted. His eager dog team charged up the opposite side of the canyon.

Liz watched until the dog team was out of sight. As she turned back in the direction of the Inuit village, she spotted someone approaching on her side of the canyon.

# Chapter 21: A Time for Contemplation

*"I know the plans I have for you," declares the* LORD, *"plans to prosper you and not to harm you, plans to give you hope and a future."*
*—Jeremiah 29:11 (NIV)*

## Alaskan Wilderness: January 1942

With the slam of the heavy door, Alan prepared his mind for the worst. Liz was gone, probably forever. His head ached, his leg throbbed, and his heart trembled with fear. He had known from the start that Trudy Dahl was but a tantalizing diversion, a toy with which to while away his lonely off-hours during the Alaskan assignment. Her giggles and upturned nose were alluring, but her naïveté only reminded him of the enchanting woman with whom he'd fallen in love. To be honest, Alan had been relieved when the Dahls put an end to the blossoming relationship before he did something stupid and irreversible.

"Why didn't I tell Elizabeth the truth? Why didn't I tell her that, except for a stolen kiss or two, there was nothing between Trudy and me?" Alan cried aloud to the imagined or real forest critters with which he shared the cabin. When his thoughts drifted to Major William Judd, he wondered how far that little flirtation went. Had Judd kissed his wife? If so, had she returned his kiss? Did they continue beyond where he and Trudy stopped? His mood darkened from self-recrimination to self-pity.

Knowing he'd goaded her into the major's arms didn't ease his frustration.

An unexpected prayer, the first since childhood, formed on his lips. "Oh, God, I've so loused up my life. I denied You in my youth. I thought I didn't need You. I believed I could live my life just fine without You—up until yesterday, that is. Quitting my job; joining the army; abandoning my wife, even asking for a divorce—I determined my own destiny. I've really messed things up. And now, as an encore to my litany of poor choices, I might lose my leg, perhaps even die in this lonely wilderness. If You are really in the forgiving business, as my mother claims, can You forgive me for being such a knucklehead?"

All the plans he'd dreamed had disintegrated when Liz walked out the cabin door. Alan tried to blink away a fresh bout of tears running down the sides of his face. He'd shed more tears in one day than he had since he was a child of five. Even while standing over Lanny's baby-blue, satin-lined casket viewing the face of his tiny son, Alan had remained stone-faced.

Alan's father, a stern disciplinarian, had believed in the Word of God, especially the verse that says, "Spare the rod and spoil the child." If the Word were true, the boy believed he must have been the most unspoiled child in the Pacific Northwest. It was during one of the all-too-frequent beatings for breaking one of his father's ironclad rules that five-year-old Alan vowed never again to satisfy his father's wrath by shedding tears.

Throughout his childhood and teens, the boy had avoided trouble whenever he could by staying out of his dad's sight. After school and during the summer months, he'd ride his bike along the Willamette River trails until suppertime, eat, and head for his room. On days when the weather was bad, he'd hide out in his room doing homework or reading, perhaps a science book or the latest edition of *Popular Mechanics*. But, sooner or later, his father's wrath would once more fall on the boy's head, or more accurately, his back.

Years later when Liz gave birth to a son, Alan decided he'd been given the chance to be the perfect father. But as the infant's needs and disruptive cries demanded Alan's participation, the new father began to resent the infant. He'd enjoyed Elizabeth's loving attention. But once the baby arrived, it seemed she took the time to care for Lanny and time working at her father's shipping company, leaving little time and energy to meet his needs.

Recalling his resentment, Alan realized how silly and immature he sounded, but knowing that didn't lessen his pent-up anger. Outwardly, he blamed his wife for not staying home with the boy; inwardly, he blamed himself for the times Alan wished the child had never been born. As he lay helpless and alone, the man wondered if this was God's punishment for thinking such thoughts. A God of punishment and vengeance was the Supreme Being his father worshiped and the only father Alan knew.

Lost in his musings, Alan didn't sense the drop in temperature inside the cabin until a swarm of goose bumps covered his arms. Propped on one elbow, he eased a small log into the stove; then he lay back and closed his eyes. Perhaps if he slept, when he awoke, Liz would have returned. Sleep was how he'd handled his loneliness as a child.

It worked. Alan had barely closed his eyes when he sensed Liz leaning over him. But instead of being stranded in the rustic cabin, he dreamed he was in the bedroom of their Craftsman cottage in Seattle. He smiled up at her.

"You are so lovely," he murmured, gently curling a long strand of her fiery red hair around one finger. "I don't tell you that enough, do I?" He opened his eye and found he was still alone, and his mattress was damp with sweat. His tongue stuck to the roof of his mouth. Incredibly thirsty, Alan realized his fever had soared again. Propping himself up on his elbow, he lifted the edge of the blanket from his leg and recoiled from what he saw.

"Liz! Liz, I need your help." His voice rang off the rafters. An eerie silence followed. He swallowed two pain pills and tried to apply a poultice as Liz had instructed. Fumbling, he exchanged the wet blanket for a dry one and fell back against the mattress exhausted. When he heard a scratching on the cabin door, he shouted, "Who's there? Elizabeth, is that you? Lowell, did you come back?" When no reply came, he realized it must have been a rat or another forest creature hoping to escape the cold. He admitted to himself, "The company would have been nice."

Darkness fell. From what he could see beyond the window, the clouds looked threatening. He tried to remember what Elizabeth told him before she left. *Did she say she'd be back before nightfall? How long has she been gone, one day, two days, a week?* Drifting in and out of consciousness, he'd lost track of time.

Slowly, his pain eased. As he nibbled on soda crackers, he imagined his wife lost in a blizzard, stranded on a glacier, or having fallen into a crevasse, unable to escape and dying alone.

"Where are you, Liz?" Alan cried out. "I shouldn't have let you go out there alone. You can be such a stubborn woman!"

He groaned as he rolled onto his side and picked up the Bible she'd left within his reach. Turning up the flame on the kerosene lamp, he leaned on one elbow as best he could, and opened the Book.

"In the beginning God created . . ."

*Hmmph,* he grunted, crunching on another soda cracker. The professors in college and graduate school had successfully debunked that theory. He flipped through the pages, stopping long enough to skim underlined passages. He remembered Elizabeth's suggestion that he begin with the book of John. A frown creased his forehead as he scanned through Deuteronomy, Job, and the Psalms.

"All right, here it is—The Gospel According to John." Alan began reading. "In the beginning was the Word." He mumbled the rest of the first and second verse. " 'All things were made by him; and without him was not anything made that was made.' Isn't that what I just read in Genesis?" he asked himself. Frustrated, he threw the Book down and rolled onto his back. Staring at the massive log rafters above his head, he wondered who designed and built this primitive cabin. Who raised its walls? Who plastered its ceiling? Who leveled the floor?

Logic told him that a tree hadn't just fallen during a storm and a cabin grown up around it. Someone had to plan where the door, the window, and the woodstove would be most efficiently placed. Someone had to cut down the trees, saw them into logs, stack them, and plaster the chinks in the walls. Wherever he gazed, he saw evidence of some man's handiwork. A new thought grew in his mind. If this simple structure out here in the wilds of Alaska needed a builder, a creator, surely the natural world and its complexity would need a Master Designer as well.

Humbled by this new idea, he opened the Bible, found John once more, and began to read. He read the entire book of John, and then Matthew, Luke, and Mark. He studied the four accounts of the life of the Man, Jesus. He analyzed the variations as told by the four different authors. And though the miracles he found in the book of Acts exploded his carefully constructed logic, Alan knew from history that Christianity had to have had an inexplicable force behind it to infiltrate the entire then-known world.

The apostle Paul's letters captivated him. Hungry for more, Alan read into the night, stopping long enough to feed the stove with wood and open a can of "mystery food," which turned out to be sweetened peaches, to sustain him.

Alan fought against a growing desire to believe in the Christ and His sacrifice for humankind's sins. Finally, in the darkest predawn moments, his resistance broke. He could no longer deny his need for a personal Savior God. A God who could love him so much as to willingly die for his sins baffled him. He'd never loved anyone that much. And better yet, that the same God could forgive his most terrible behavior and remember it no more blew his carefully constructed paradigms to smithereens.

As for Alan, he remembered every single beating his father had given him as well as those his dad gave his mom. He felt every scar left on his body from the whippings he'd received. He relived the day when, after a particularly fierce beating, the fifteen-year-old grabbed the strap from his father's hand and snarled, "You will not hit me again—ever! If you do, I will leave, and you will never see me again!"

For the first time, Alan understood why his mother held on to her Savior so tightly during the worst of her husband's rages. While Alan had never struck Elizabeth, he realized he'd beaten her down emotionally, especially after the death of their son.

Alan stared at the hefty beams above his head through misty eyes, noting each scar inflicted by the builder's ax—all visible long after the creator had gone. In his mind, like a scratched phonograph record on a record player, the phrase, *"God will remember their sins no more,"* played and replayed.

For the first time ever, Alan felt overcome with raw remorse. He gasped to catch his breath. "Forgive me, Father, for injuring my precious wife so deeply. Can she ever forgive me? Can You forgive me?" And then, one after another, the faces of people he'd injured paraded through his consciousness. One after another, Alan asked for forgiveness.

Exhausted but filled with a strange and exhilarating emotion he could only describe as peace, he laid the Bible aside and swallowed two more pain pills with a swig of water from the pitcher Elizabeth had left within his reach. He laid back and closed his eyes, hoping to sleep.

The sound of dogs yipping outside the cabin started him awake. A flicker of hope sprung up in his heart. The cabin door flew open and banged against the wall. The shadow of a human figure loomed over him.

"Elizabeth?" Alan called.

The intruder chuckled. "Afraid not." The intruder placed a canteen of water to Alan's lips. Much of the water spilled as the injured man struggled to take a drink.

"Elizabeth?" Alan asked again.

"No, my friend. It's me, Moeshe."

"Oh, no! Elizabeth!" He shuddered as his surroundings came into focus. His wife had gone for help and had not returned. The injured man's eyes filled with terror as he tried to rise to a sitting position. "Moeshe, my wife is somewhere out there in the snowstorm! Hurry! Go find her. Oh, please, you must find her."

Moeshe pushed Alan back against the mattress. "Don't worry about your beautiful wife, my friend. My people are caring for her until I can get you to safety. Now that the storm has abated, Colonel Anderson will be sending a plane to airlift you to a hospital in Anchorage." Moeshe checked Alan's leg. He clicked his tongue. "Mrs. Ames was right. That leg of yours needs medical attention far beyond simple first aid. How did it happen?"

Alan told Moeshe as much as he could remember about the fight and about Lowell's betrayal. "Lowell or Amarok, as he insisted we call him, left us to die. Who knows where he is by now?"

"You don't need to worry. The army took him into custody when he landed in Anchorage to refuel the stolen plane. I'd been on his trail for weeks. It was my job to report his traitorous radio transmissions to enemy agents back to army headquarters in Washington, D.C. I was waiting for orders on to how to proceed with his arrest when the tunnel blew, and I became the prime suspect. By the time Washington cleared things up, you and your wife had already left camp with him. When he realized his disguise had been uncovered, he used this assignment as his escape, though I never thought he'd risk anyone's life to do so."

"He said your name isn't Moeshe, but Irnig—something." Alan squinted up at the man.

"Did he tell you he is my adopted brother as well? The same shaman father adopted both of us." Moeshe removed the dried Epsom salt plaster from Alan's leg, and replaced it with a fresh poultice. "Irnig-Kesuk is my

Aleut name. It means 'drawn from the deep.' I have since chosen to go by the Russian form of my name, a name given to me by the Russian fishing boat captain who rescued me as an infant. Mouzeza means 'drawn from the water' too, like Moses the great Jewish leader in the Bible. The captain knew he couldn't raise a boy at sea, so he gave me to my half-Japanese shaman father. All my life I've been told that a Divine Being rescued me from drowning for a specific purpose. As a result, I've tried to live my life that way." Moeshe wrapped Alan's leg with a clean dish towel. "When I moved to Washington for an education, I changed Mouzeza to Moeshe."

"What a heritage. Personally, I'm glad you lived to rescue me. Moeshe fits you. But I never would have made the biblical connection."

"I recently came to appreciate the name more after your wife left a Bible in my jail cell. Captain Petrov, the man who first rescued me, believed voices of the sea directed him to me. My adoptive father believed the sea god saved me. But I've since learned that a greater God watched over me and still does."

"Really?"

Moeshe gathered the soiled poultice towels and dumped them into the sink. "Shamanism and Christianity have many beliefs in common. For instance, my father believes in many gods. You Christians say you believe in one God. Yet the Bible speaks of worshiping three Gods—a Father God, a Son God, and a Being called the Holy Spirit. I'm not sure how this works, but I have an open mind."

Alan frowned, and after a few seconds, offered a silent prayer for wisdom. Perhaps it was a thought his mother had planted years earlier. Perhaps it was God-inspired. Maybe it came because of his scientific training, but a new illustration entered his head.

"You're right. What Christians call the Trinity is a mystery because the Trinity is, and yet isn't, Three separate Beings." He paused for a moment. "Let me describe it this way: the Trinity is like $H_2O$. We call it water when it's a liquid. Yet $H_2O$ can also be steam, or a solid as in ice. That's kind of the way I think I can understand the Almighty God to be. He's the same basic substance, but in three different forms, each of the forms serving a different purpose. Does that illustration make any sense?" The engineer listened in amazement to his own words as the concept tumbled from his lips.

"I'll have to think about that one," Moeshe responded. "There is one important difference between my father's multiple gods and the God you call Jesus. None of my father's deities willingly died for me or can forgive my sins. They speak of eternity as being a privilege mortals must earn, while the Bible's Deity offers it as a gift of love."

"You came to this discovery on your own?"

"When everyone else shunned me as a saboteur, your wife came to visit me every day. She brought goodies to eat and books to read. The remarkable thing was that she never once asked me if I blew up the tunnel. It was as if that information wasn't important to her. When we studied the Bible together, she never pressured me into seeing things her way. Instead, we discovered the truths together." Moeshe smiled to himself. "It wasn't until she left with you and Amarok on this mission that I realized how much she'd influenced my life. That's when I decided that if she's an example of what a Christian is, I wanted to be one. As to the Trinity idea, I may never understand it, but I can certainly understand the kind of godly love she demonstrated toward me."

Moeshe rinsed out the soiled cloths in the sink and sat down on the floor beside Alan. "The way I see it, in the story of the jailbreak, the apostle Paul's jailer couldn't have understood all the ins and outs of Christian theology, yet, when he gave his heart to God, he was considered saved. So why can't I be the same, but without the earthquake, I might add?" Moeshe laughed aloud.

Alan chuckled. Moeshe continued. "Mentally, I escaped from that tiny cubical many times a day before Colonel Anderson actually released me. The story I didn't like during my incarceration was the story of Joseph. He was jailed much too long for my liking. And he was innocent as well!" The Inuit's enthusiasm for his newly discovered storehouse of information was contagious. "How about you, Alan? Is there any one Bible story you've found you enjoyed more than another?"

"Definitely! And you already mentioned it. The forgiveness of the Cross—bar none. I cannot comprehend being that selfless and loving to be willing to die such a cruel death that two thousand years later, I might live."

For the next few hours, the two men shared their exciting discoveries from God's Word. Laughter filled the cabin when Alan said, "How about the story of the demons being sent into a herd of pigs? Can you imagine hundreds of pigs committing suicide off a cliff into the sea? And the logistical problems that must have caused for the villagers! I can imagine hundreds of bloated bodies bobbing up and down in the waves for days."

Moeshe threw his head back and laughed aloud. "Only a member of the U.S. Army Corps of Engineers would think about the cleanup!"

Toward the end of the afternoon, the roar of a plane engine overhead ended their conversation. Moeshe ran to the door and flung it open. "Yep! Looks like the cavalry is here." He turned and grabbed Alan's heavy parka from the hook behind the door. "Here. Let's get you bundled for the flight to Anchorage. The interior of those little puddle jumpers can be anything but warm."

"Before we leave, will you do me one more favor? You're going back to the camp by land, aren't you?" Alan asked.

"Yes."

"I'd like to write a short note to my wife. Will you deliver it for me?"

"Absolutely."

Within five minutes, Alan was loaded onboard the plane. Before Moeshe closed the door, Alan grabbed his arm. "You are going to help my wife, right? Promise me she'll be safe."

"I promise you, my brother," Moeshe assured Alan. "The dogs and I will not rest until Mrs. Ames is seated at Miz Mabel's dining room table."

# Chapter 22: A Time of Peace

*Peace and friendship with all mankind is our wisest policy,*
*and I wish we may be permitted to pursue it.*
*—Thomas Jefferson*

## Inuit Village, Alaskan Wilderness: January 1942

A juxtaposition of fear and comfort tussled within Liz's heart. She tried to open her eyes, but they felt glued shut. Believing herself to be crouched in the ice cave, she sensed rather than saw a female gray wolf and two cubs gently licking her face until the wolf called out her name. The face of the mother wolf dissolved into the wrinkled face of an older woman, a stranger with a comforting smile. She was gently dabbing a cooling salve onto Liz's face with a washcloth.

"Mrs. Ames, Mrs. Ames," the stranger coaxed. "You must wake up."

Liz moistened her lips with her tongue and tried to speak.

"Here, sip some hot tea."

Liz took a sip of a hot liquid.

"That's good." The stranger sat back, removed a kettle from a small, iron stove in the middle of the room, and poured a second cup of tea.

Cosseted in a blanket of silver fox fur, Liz gazed about the dimly lit hut. The log walls had been chinked with plaster. To her left, canned goods and iron cooking kettles stacked the four shelves on the wall. Liz looked up at the face of her benefactor. "Where? Where am I? Who are you?"

"My name is Talini, or Snow Angel, in English. Welcome to my home." A green plaid wool shirt and an ankle-length skirt swathed the slight, bony woman. One long, thick braid swooshed down her back. She turned toward a rough-hewn wooden door and called out.

A cheer went up from outside the hut. Talini glanced back to Liz. "I just told them you had awakened. The entire village has been concerned for Moeshe's friend."

"Moeshe?" Liz thought for a moment. She wasn't sure if she'd actually seen Moeshe on the south side of the ravine or had only hallucinated. Even now, she questioned whether she were awake or trapped in the warm, tranquil stage before one dies of hypothermia.

Gently, Talini lifted Liz's head and shoulders to give her another sip of tea. "Yes, dear. Moeshe asked us to care for you until he returns."

"Returns?" A series of vignettes rolled in slow motion through her mind—the cabin, the fight, Alan— At the thought of Alan, she started. "Oh no! My husband? Where is my husband?" Liz struggled to sit up. "He's hurt. He needs my help."

*"Sh, sh, sh."* The woman gently pushed Liz back into the fur cocoon. "Rest. Your husband is in good hands with Moeshe, I promise."

"And Lowell?" Liz shivered. "He left us at the cabin to die."

"Lowell? Oh, you mean Amarok. He's a bad apple, he is." The older woman clicked her tongue and shook her head sadly. "A stake to his poor father's heart! He loved and cared for Amarok in the same way he cared for Moeshe. And look at the difference between the two men. Reminds me of the Cain and Abel story in the Bible."

Liz enjoyed listening to the lilting cadence of her hostess' voice. "You speak beautiful English, Talini."

"Thank you. I am a teacher. I studied at the University of Idaho. I enjoy using my English occasionally, outside the classroom that is." Talini's dark eyes twinkled; her face broke into a broad grin. "After obtaining my teaching credentials, I returned to my village and have been teaching here ever since—more than thirty-five years. But wait, I'm being selfish. The entire town is eager to welcome you, especially the two boys who rescued you. Are you feeling strong enough to be engulfed in love?"

Apprehensively, Liz glanced toward the closed door. "Yes, I think so."

"First, I will introduce you to Papa Ludi. Papa Ludi is our village elder. Ludi is too old to hunt and trap. The rest of the men in our community are out trapping. And the boys here in camp are too young to go with them."

Like a doting mother, Talini adjusted the fur robe about Liz's shoulders and smoothed her tousled red curls back from her face. "Ludi was the town's shaman, a holy man, before an itinerant preacher and his wife came to town and spent a winter with us. Their love and compassion made us want to know more about the God they served. After Elder and Mrs. Brown moved on to another village farther north, Papa Ludi took their place." Talini rose gracefully and opened the door.

A sea of curious smiling faces filled the doorway. With one soft command from the woman, the faces and bodies retreated to make room for a tiny, gnomelike man with shoulder-length white hair. The man stepped over the threshold, bowed in front of Liz, and held out his hand toward her. In it he held a slab of bark with the sketch of a wolf. Every detail of the wolf and the surrounding area had been burned into it.

"Thank you. It's beautiful." Liz examined the intricate detail in the artwork. "Did you draw this?"

When Talini translated, the man's face broke into a boyish grin. He nodded.

"It is truly lovely. What beautiful work." When Liz attempted to return the sketch to the man, Talini shook her head. "It is a gift for you."

Liz smiled at the old man. "Why, thank you. I will treasure it always."

When Talini translated Liz's words, the man returned her smile. But his smile quickly turned to a frown when he spoke a few words in his native tongue. Talini translated it for Liz.

"Ludi apologizes to you for Amarok's despicable behavior." She paused to listen to the old man speak and then continued. "Amarok brings shame to all the native people."

Liz frowned. "I don't understand. Lowell, or Amarok, isn't from your town. He is Aleut; you are Inuit. How did you know him?"

Talini translated Liz's question and waited for the man's reply. "Both Amarok and Irnig-Kesuk have visited our community many times since the army came to Whittier. The Inuit are a naturally kindhearted and generous people. We accept strangers as guests, and guests as family. We housed the two young men and fed them as we would our own, and Amarok rewarded our kindness with betrayal." The old man paused. "Unlike his brother Irnig-Kesuk, who brought only good to our village,

Amarok has forgotten a wise saying of his people. 'A selfish person dies young.' "

While Talini finished translating his words, Ludi dropped his head to his chest and closed his eyes. He sat silently for what seemed like five minutes to Liz. She wondered if the man had fallen asleep or was ill. Suddenly, he lifted his head; his face broke into a broad smile and he spoke. Talini again translated. "But today, we will not dwell on the bad wind of evil, but the good wind that brought you to our village!"

The tribal elder lifted one hand. Talini opened the door and signaled for the villagers to enter. One by one, Talini introduced the other members of the community, from the eldest to the youngest. Each bowed, squatted on the floor in front of Liz, and handed her a homemade gift—a baby rattle, a small rabbit-fur piece, an Inuit doll, envelopes filled with dried berries, caches of herbal tea, and slabs of fish jerky—and then made room for the next to present his gift. Liz admired each object and thanked them profusely.

When his turn came, Bjork, a ten-year-old boy, inched shyly toward Liz and handed her an exquisitely carved soapstone eagle perched on a small tree branch. Each of the bird's feathers was intricately detailed. "This is beautiful. Did you carve it?"

The boy shifted nervously and looked at the floor. "Yes, ma'am."

"You are very talented, Bjork. And you speak English?"

The boy looked questioningly at her and then at his teacher. When Talini repeated Liz's compliment in Bjork's language, he beamed with pride. "A little."

"Very good. Your gift will always occupy a special place in my home and in my heart." Tears sprang into Liz's eyes when the youngest villager, a five-year-old girl named Nukka, climbed into Liz's lap. The girl's ebony bangs fringed her eyebrows. "Sorry. I couldn't make you anything special, so this is my gift to you—a hug." She wrapped her tiny arms about Liz's waist.

"Thank you, Nukka. What a very special gift you've given me. I will never forget your precious gift either."

Nukka smiled happily.

A nod from Talini, and the women and young girls squatted on the floor circling Liz, while the boys lined the walls of the cabin.



"My people love to sing," her hostess explained. "They sing for celebrations like weddings and birthdays or for no reason at all. Any excuse will do. If you wish, join in; if not, it is good manners in our society to just listen in silence." At a gesture from Talini, the women began singing an old favorite of Grandma Keating's, "At the Cross." The familiar melody took on deeper meaning when sung in an Inuit dialect.

The tempo shifted to a military tempo with "We're Marching to Zion." As Liz listened, she tried to imagine the visiting missionary couple teaching the words to the villagers.

After the group sang several hymns, Talini stood. "It is time that we break bread together." Several of the women hurried from Talini's hut and quickly returned with pots of hot tea. Two returned with several whole raw fish and cut them into small pieces with sharp, curved knives. Talini laughed when one of the women offered Liz a raw fish head and Liz involuntarily wrinkled her nose.

"Wait." Talini spoke to the woman in Inuit and then handed Liz a strip of dried fish. "Here, you may find this more to your liking, but first a blessing." Talini bowed her head and offered a short prayer in her native tongue before handing Liz several hard dry crackers.

Liz nibbled slowly on her crackers and dried fish. Friendly chatter filled the small hut as the others devoured the chunks of raw fish with gusto. No one seemed disturbed by Liz's silence. When Liz finished eating, five-year-old Nukka climbed back into the woman's lap.

At the end of the evening, each person blessed Liz before they departed. After the last guest left, she blinked back her tears and thanked Talini. "It has been an unforgettable evening I will always cherish. I've never experienced such hospitality."

Talini smiled and touched Liz's fingertips to her own lips. "It has been an honor, dear sister. For native people, hospitality is a sacred joy."

The two women talked late into the night, as if they'd know each other for years. Liz shared her heart regarding Alan and her lost son.

"And you love your husband still?"

"I don't know," Liz admitted.

"Is there another man also in your heart?" the woman asked.

"No! Yes. Not really. I mean Major Judd is a good friend—that's all. We've never—" Liz stopped abruptly. Her face reddened. "I am so confused. I think I might love Will, and I suspect he feels the same toward me." A groan escaped her lips. "Oh, I don't know. My heart tells me one thing; my head tells me another."

There was neither judgment nor condemnation in the Inuit teacher's manner. She merely nodded and listened silently as Liz explained her complicated feelings for Will, Alan's fling with Trudy Dahl, and her husband's declaration of love for her at the cabin. "I don't know what I want most anymore," Liz wailed. "And now that I'm going back to Whittier, I will again see Will. I am so confused."

"Remember, dear sister, whatever choice you make, you will live with it for a very long time. So before you make an irrevocable decision, seek the truth," Talini replied. "The Master said, 'Ye shall know the truth and the truth will set you free.' He's the One to ask for advice on matters of the heart, not me." She pointed upward.

"What about you, Talini? Why did you return to this remote village after experiencing the outside world?"

Slowly, hesitantly, the woman shared her grief over losing her fiancé in an accident the year before she left for college. "With Nattig gone, I lost my will to live. If it hadn't been for my missionary friends, I don't know if I could have kept going. They arranged for me to attend the university with the understanding that after I graduated, I would return to teach my people."

"And there have been no other men in your life since?" Afraid she'd gotten too personal, Liz's face reddened.

Talini patted Liz's hand and grinned. "The truth for me is, I'm afraid I'm a one-man woman."

"I always thought I was too, but now I'm not so sure."

"Don't worry, my sister." Talini rose to her feet. "You are a wise woman. You'll know what you should do when the right time comes. But for now, you need to get a few hours' sleep before Moeshe returns for you."

It seemed that Liz had barely closed her eyes when a knock sounded on the door. "Miss Elizabeth! Miss Elizabeth!" It was five-year-old Nukka. "Brother Moeshe is here to take you back to the army post."

Liz ate a quick breakfast of dried fish and oatmeal while Talini wrapped Liz's gifts with burlap and secured the package with twine.

When the two women emerged from the hut into the solemn gray of a winter morning, the entire community waited to say farewell. Liz glanced around the group expecting to see Moeshe and his dog team, but he was nowhere in sight. "Where is he? Where is Moeshe?"

Talini pointed toward the far side of the canyon.

"Hello!" Moeshe shouted and waved.

"He is waiting to take you to Whittier."

"But, how?"

"Look to your left. See that basket?" Talini pointed toward a large woven basket on the ground near the edge of the canyon. Strung across the canyon to the other side was a thick hemp rope connected to a pulley system. The handle of the basket appeared to be looped over the rope.

Liz blanched. "A basket? Where's the bridge?"

Talini chuckled. "That is our bridge. Don't worry. The rope is stronger than you may think. And that basket can hold at least three of the likes of you. The women of the village, including me, wove it."

Horrified, Liz backed away from the canyon rim and from her hostess. "Oh, dear God, I can't do this. I'm terrified of heights. I don't want to seem ungrateful, Talini, but can't Moeshe rescue me some other way?"

"I suppose he could, but if Moeshe and his dog team had to go back to the bridge, return to the village; pick you up, and go back to the bridge and then down to Whittier, it would take many extra hours. And with those storm clouds rolling in from the northwest . . ." Talini pointed toward the sky. "Moeshe must get you down to the outpost camp as quickly as possible, or you both will end up stranded on the mountain, possibly for the next three days."

Liz could barely breathe as she studied the basket and rope for several more seconds. "Not that anxious."

"Please ask Moeshe to bring a new supply of medical supplies when he returns next week." Talini took Liz by the hand. "Come. It really isn't as scary as it looks, my sister. The ride will be over in no time." The woman placed the large bundle of gifts from the community into the basket and helped Liz climb aboard.

"Now what?" Liz asked.

"Just sit down and fold your hands into your lap. You can bury your face in your lap if it helps." Talini placed a silver fox blanket on Liz's shoulders. "A gift to remember me by."

"As if I could ever forget you." Liz kissed the back of the woman's hands. "Thank you again, for everything." With all the adventures she'd endured since leaving Seattle—Lowell's attack, Alan's broken leg, and the night alone in the blizzard on the mountain—nothing compared to the abject terror she felt as three young boys pushed the basket off the side of the cliff. Her breath caught in her throat at the sudden drop. The rope held. For a moment, the basket swayed in the breeze.

"No! No! Please!" Liz cried as she dangled high above the crevasse. "No! No! I can't!" She grabbed for Talini's hand.

"Sit still!" Talini stepped back. "Close your eyes. Think happy thoughts."

"Happy thoughts," Liz mumbled. "What happy thoughts?" Instead, violent images raced through her brain: the rope above her head unraveling and breaking, the basket plummeting to the canyon floor, wolves and ravens feasting on her broken body. "Yeah, happy thoughts!"

As the wind swayed the tightly woven basket in the breeze, Liz cowered in the bottom of the basket, her face buried in the silver fox blanket on her lap. The basket zipped along the rope at a steady clip, and then stopped abruptly. Liz tensed, fearful the basket had gotten stuck on a knot in the middle of the canyon.

"Mrs. Ames, Mrs. Ames." It was Moeshe's familiar voice. He touched her shoulder. "Let me help you out of the basket."

Reluctantly, Liz opened her eyes. Tears welled in her eyes and then cascaded down her cheeks. She'd made it safely to the other side of the gorge. Her legs wobbled like Miz Mabel's homemade jelly as she struggled to her feet. As Moeshe lifted her from the basket onto the ground, she almost fell into his arms. From across the ravine, her new friends waved and cheered her safe crossing.

Moeshe seated her on his dog sled behind eight muscular huskies and wrapped her in caribou skins before placing the bundle of gifts on the front of the sled. A shout from their driver, and the dogs leaped forward. She buried her face against the biting wind as the dogs charged down the narrow mountain trail toward the military camp.

# Chapter 23: Choices of the Heart

*Our choices show who we truly are.*

## Base Camp, Maynard Mountain: January 1942

The dog team had barely slowed to a walk in front of the mess hall when Will burst from the headquarters building. He ran, slipping and sliding on the icy walkway, toward Liz. "You're safe! Oh, thank God. We were so worried. I've been praying like I've never prayed before. How are you, Elizabeth? You poor sweetheart! Are you all right?"

That his questions were jumbled mattered little to either of them. All pretenses that theirs was a casual friendship vanished when he lifted her from the sled and wrapped his arms possessively about her, holding her close. Taking her face in his hands, he studied it as if he were about to kiss her but thought better of it. Half of the camp followed, including Colonel Anderson, when Will scooped her into his arms and carried her into the mess hall.

"I'm fine, Will. I'm fine."

Reluctantly, he released her and set her carefully on her feet. "I've been so worried about you. I thought I'd lost you forever."

At his declaration, both froze. The growing audience leaned forward not wanting to miss her response.

Flushed, she pushed a moist curl away from her left cheek. She had to admit she'd never before felt so alive. "Where is Moeshe? I need to thank him."

Someone in the crowd called out, "He's caring for his dog team."

She touched Will's face and took a step back. "Moeshe and the villagers took good care of me, though I wouldn't want to relive the basket ride across the canyon anytime soon." She'd barely sat down when Mrs. Dahl brought her a cup of hot chocolate. Trudy placed a napkin and a massive, freshly baked bear claw on the table before her. Will slipped into the seat across from her.

"We've been so worried, Mrs. Ames," Trudy admitted. "You are a very brave woman."

"Not really." Liz clutched the warm cup between her hands before taking a sip of the hot drink. "If I've learned anything about survival in Alaska, it's that you do whatever you have to do when you have to do it."

"On the contrary, Mrs. Ames." Colonel Anderson shook his head in disagreement. "Some women would have curled up in a fetal ball or dissolved into hysteria when confronting the situations you did. I commend you for keeping your head about you." He sat down on the bench next to Will.

"Thank you, Colonel." Liz took a sip of the hot drink to cover her feelings of awkwardness at his praise.

The colonel glanced toward Major Judd and then back at Liz. "As Moeshe probably told you, we have Lowell in custody in Anchorage."

"Yes, he did say that. What will happen to him?"

The colonel's bushy eyebrows narrowed. "Lowell will be tried for treason, probably in Anchorage. And I imagine, with all the mounting evidence we have of his activities, he'll be convicted. After that, I don't know."

"Do you think he'll be executed?"

"Maybe yes, maybe no. I think he'll more likely get life, probably in a stateside prison."

She frowned. "And Alan? How is he doing? I've been so worried about his head injury and his leg."

"We airlifted him to Anchorage for treatment. But due complications caused by the delay in treatment, they flew him on to the military hospital in Seattle. I've arranged for you to meet him there."

Despite her conflicted emotions, Liz smiled. "Thank you, Colonel. Did they save his leg?"

"Last I heard, they were treating the infection with a newly developed antibiotic. But the man is going to have a long healing process before he's back to normal."

"Oh, thank God. I don't know what Alan would do if he were left permanently disabled." She paused and glanced away before adding, "It will be good to be home again." And as an afterthought, she added, "And in time for my sister's wedding."

"Your parents are eager to have you home as well, especially your father. I think he's contacted me at least once a day every day since the communication ban was lifted. He's certainly kept Major Judd busy delivering messages."

Liz's eyes misted. "That's my dad. When he gets his mind set on something, he's like a bulldog with a bone."

"No bother. If you were my daughter, I'd do the same." The colonel arose from the table. "I would like to meet him someday—seems like a good man."

"The best!" Liz nodded. "The best."

The colonel leaned his hands on the back of his chair. "If the weather holds, I've arranged for a plane to take you to the States tomorrow morning at zero eight hundred hours. In the meantime, Major Judd will escort you to Miz Mabel's place, where you'll be able to rest until morning." He paused and glanced at the two. "I'm sure you and the major have a few things to discuss."

Liz quickly glanced down at her uneaten pastry to hide the instant flash of color suffusing her face. "Thank you, Colonel, er, for everything."

After the base commander left the building, Will touched the back of Liz's chair. "You must be exhausted. Let me get you back to Whittier." He helped her to her feet and led her past several well-wishers to the waiting military truck.

Moeshe stood beside the truck to help her climb into it. "Go with God," he whispered. "Till we meet again, my friend."

For some time, as the truck bounced over the rutted gravel road toward Whittier, neither spoke. A cover of fog rolled in off the harbor enveloping the couple in an intimate world of grays and whites. To the couple, the rest of the world had virtually disappeared. Occasionally, Liz cast a sideways glance at Will, who stared straight ahead at the road. And, at times, when she turned her face toward the passenger window, he did the same to her.

Never before had Liz felt tongue-tied in Will's presence, but the colonel's words hung between them. From the moment they'd met, they'd always been able to talk freely about anything. And now, when they needed to speak honestly to one another, no words came. At the edge of town, Will turned the vehicle left instead of to the right, which would lead them to Miz Mabel's place. He eased the vehicle to the side of the road and stopped. Liz stared down at her hands and tensely waited for him to speak. This was the moment she'd both dreaded and desired.

"The colonel is right, you know. You and I do need to talk." He turned partway toward her and placed his hand on the back of the cracked leather seat, barely touching her neck with his fingertips. Goose bumps skittered up and down her spine. His eyes were dark and filled with longing. "You and I, where do we go from here?"

Memory of the simple gold band beneath her glove burned into her conscience.

"Liz, the last thing I want to do is to put you on the spot, but I can't let you go tomorrow without knowing where I stand with you. I understand you spent the last few days with Alan. Has anything improved between the two of you? Is there enough of a marriage to rescue? If so, I'll retreat gracefully. If not—" He paused, and then took a deep breath. When she didn't respond, he continued. "I just learned I'm being transferred to Pearl Harbor, where I will establish a new communication grid to replace the one destroyed during the bombing. It's a plum of an assignment, but a long way from Seattle." His voice grew heavy with emotion. "They say Hawaii is nice this time of year."

Liz added lightly, "I understand Hawaii is nice any time of year."

"Elizabeth, what I'm trying to say is, you have had more of an impact on my life than I ever imagined possible. I can't let you walk out of my life without telling you how much I've grown to l—" He leaned closer to her for an instant and then retreated. "I know you are a married woman, and I've watched your growth as a Christian since you arrived in Whittier—just the kind of woman I would want God to design for me to marry. All the more reason we must ask for Divine guidance." He swallowed hard.

"Before I met you, I believed I had strong principles. Now, I'm not so sure. When you were alone with Alan in the wilderness, my moods went from worry for your safety to green-eyed jealousy. When I learned Lowell had abandoned you to the elements, it took Colonel Anderson and the entire 101st Army Corps of Engineers unit to keep me from hitching up a dog sled and hunting for you. It was only after the colonel sent Moeshe to find you that I could calm down."

She gazed down at her gloved hand.

"Don't be angry with me, Elizabeth. If I misinterpreted your feelings for me, if I misread the bond I believe we've established, please forgive me. But I don't think I'm wrong. I believe you feel the same about me as I feel about you." He turned to gaze out the side window.

Liz's breath caught in her throat. "I–I–I . . ."

"Wait! If I'm out of line, I really am sorry. But just for a moment imagine our life together in a Hawaiian paradise."

Incredibly strong emotions wrestled within her heart a second time in three days. Imagining an idyllic life with Will took little effort. She longed to throw herself into Will's arms and declare the love she felt for him. She longed for him to hold her, and together they might spin dreams of a honeymoon haven in Honolulu, of waving palm branches, of sandy beaches, of warm Pacific waters lapping at their toes as they ran hand-in-hand in the surf. A tear slipped down her cheek.

Will cleared his throat. "I've said too much, haven't I? I'm sorry. I have read too much into our friendship."

She placed her hand on Will's arm. "No, unfortunately you didn't. I have been fighting my feelings for you every step of the way. I don't know what would be best for us—and for my husband, Alan."

He glanced down at her gloved hand.

"Will, regardless of your passions, you're a man of high principles. I'm afraid that should we violate our convictions, in time you would come to resent me, which could destroy our love for one another."

He dropped his chin onto his chest. "I guess it all sounded too magical, like a fairytale, you and I running off to Hawaii, to paradise, letting the rest of the world go by. But life is no fairytale, is it?"

Her face softened; her heart weakened. "I confess it sounds so lovely. A little grass shack on the beach . . . walking on the sand in the moonlight . . . picking mangos off the trees for breakfast . . . Mangos do grow on trees, don't they?"

"Yes, I believe so." He turned toward her, his eyes dark and solemn. "Elizabeth, I do so want to kiss you right now."

From the deep recesses of her mind, Liz heard Grandma Keating's warnings, *"There is a line. If you abandon what you know is right, you will destroy the very love and respect you have for one another."* Gently, Liz shook her head. "I can't cross that line—not yet anyway. I want to, but I can't."

"Will you ever be able to cross that line, as you call it?"

"I don't know."

Will leaned his head back against the seat. "So where do we go from here? Is this all there is for us—a short, mild flirtation and goodbye?"

"I don't know," she whispered. "Yet I can't bear to say goodbye, knowing I may never see you again."

"Hey! Maybe I've been rushing things. Maybe you need more time to think about it. What if you went home to Seattle and finished up what business needs finishing while I visit my folks in Omaha for a few weeks, and then, I could head overseas to prepare a place for us in Hawaii? And after a few months when everything is settled, you could join me in Honolulu."

"There's a war going on, remember?" she reminded him. "Civilian travel is still limited."

"Fine! I won't go to Hawaii then. I'll get reassigned stateside in Oregon or in California if you like. The army is building bases all along the coast, and they need radio technicians."

She gave him a bleak smile. Will's boyish enthusiasm touched her heart as few others ever had. "It isn't as easy as that. I'm still married, remember?"

"I know! I know!" He paused a moment and then offered, "Look! I have enough money saved for you to live on in Mexico for six weeks until your divorce becomes final." As the dreaded word *divorce* escaped his lips, both caught their breaths.

She grimaced. "Divorce is a huge step to take. We will be forever marked by it."

"Liz, don't close your mind to the possibilities right now. Promise me you'll think about it. And if after a few weeks or months, whatever it takes, if you find your marriage to Alan just isn't working—" His words hung in the air between them. "Please promise you'll think about it."

Liz ached to say, "Yes! Yes! Forget the weeks, the months! Forget society's censure! Forget everything keeping us apart. I'll follow you to the ends of the earth!" Yet she hesitated. Could she throw aside her marriage, her family's approval, as well as the spiritual values she had been building over the last few weeks?

Gently, she touched his face and ran her gloved hand along his jawline. The agony in his eyes broke her heart.

She also realized Will could be right. She had no idea how things would go with Alan, if the man who'd vowed his love for her in the Alaskan wilderness would again become the cold, resentful, insensitive person she'd previously known. When his body healed, would he desire her as a wife? And what if he never recovered completely? Would he become even more embittered? Was she sacrificing a promise of happiness with Will for a life of possible misery with Alan? "OK, I promise I will think and pray about our possible future together."

His eyes brightened. Her lips parted. He leaned toward her. His eyes closed. A millisecond before their lips touched, she drew back. "One kiss and I'm afraid I would throw all caution to the wind." She folded her arms tightly. "I think you'd better take me to Miz Mabel's before there is no turning back and we both do something we'll later come to regret."

# Chapter 24: The Desires of Your Heart

*All things work together for good for those who love him,*
*who have been called according to his purpose.*
*—Romans 8:28 (NIV)*

## Seattle, Washington: Spring 1942

*"The truth will set you free."* Liz wondered whether she really wanted to know the truth. Sometimes the truth hurt too much. She watched the March drizzle form puddles on the walk outside her Seattle cottage. The solitude she treasured would soon be coming to an end once Alan returned home from the hospital the following day. As to the two men, one she needed and one who needed her, her heart remained divided. But by not making a clear-cut choice between them, she realized she wasn't being fair to either of them.

*The truth? Sometimes it's easier to go with what feels good, isn't it? Is that so wrong—to choose personal happiness, Lord? Didn't You say You delight to give us the desires of our hearts?* She threw her hands into the air. *I'm so confused and I'm so alone.*

Liz glanced down at the unopened envelope in her hands—the latest of a series of letters over the last three months, first from Nebraska and later from Hawaii. The familiar scrawl brought pleasure to her mind. When she touched the envelope to her lips, she imagined she could smell

Will's musky aftershave. The woman had coasted on the status quo of going to work every day, cleaning the house after work, grocery shopping, visiting her folks, never really making a decision. The arrival of Will's letters lifted her spirits.

On Monday mornings at the veterans' hospital, she never knew what she'd find. Some days her husband would be in high spirits; some days, flirty; some days, angry and would lash out at her viciously. On these days, she toyed with the idea of hopping in her forest green Hudson coupe and driving to Reno, the divorce capital for the Hollywood elite. One afternoon, she drove fifty miles south of Seattle before she changed her mind. On most days, she returned from the hospital, removed Will's growing stack of letters from her bureau, and tempted herself to read one, just one. As yet, each letter had remained sealed.

As she pressed the letters against her heart, nostalgia for her Alaskan interlude flooded her mind. But with Alan soon to come home, she knew she could no longer play her fanciful imagination games. She would either have to divorce Alan or put the memories and fantasies about Will forever to rest.

She knew that reading whatever was written inside the envelopes would make her vulnerable to breaking her marriage vows. Not reading them relieved her lingering feeling of guilt. Liz stuffed the latest envelope into her skirt pocket and crossed the parlor to her favorite Windsor rocker. Cozy flames of reds and yellows blazed in the fireplace, warding off the chill from the drizzle outside the cottage. She gazed at the cluster of keepsakes from her stay in the Inuit village, including Ludi's detailed sketch and Bjork's carved eagle on the mantel. On the needlepoint footstool beside the rocker, her Bible lay unopened. She closed her eyes and set the chair to rocking. The steady cadence on the dark oak flooring soothed her troubled mind.

In this room, she'd spent many lonely nights studying God's Word and praying for wisdom. In this room, her heart had longed for Will. In this room, the vow "For better or for worse; till death us do part" had strengthened her convictions.

After one particularly difficult bout with the petulant Alan, she sought out her Grandma Keating. "All I want is to be happy. Is that asking so much?"



"Honey-bunny, most people are only as happy as they make up their minds to be. Every marriage goes through tough times. And frankly, a happy marriage is all about learning just what you're willing to put up with." At first Grandma's advice sounded cynical, but Liz couldn't push it out of her mind.

Living with Alan would never be easy. The damage his dalliance with Trudy Dahl had done to their relationship wouldn't heal overnight, but in the months since the accident, she'd learned to forgive.

On that rainy afternoon, she glanced down at the envelope on her lap. Blazoned across her mind were the words, *"How long halt ye between two opinions? Choose ye this day . . ."* If she ever wanted to find real peace, she would have to choose. Alan's talk about wanting to try to have another child helped her make up her mind. Her relationship with her husband was real and legitimate. Her attraction to Will was becoming a pleasant memory of an inappropriate relationship.

Reluctantly, Liz gathered her stack of unopened letters, placed a kiss on the latest one, and then tossed them into the flames in the fireplace. Tears fell as the last envelope crumbled into ashes.

What was done was done! Setting her jaw, she whirled about and marched toward the kitchen. "I think I'll surprise Alan and make his favorite oatmeal-raisin cookies!"

★ ★ ★ ★ ★

## Seattle Space Needle: Spring 1962

Uniformed waiters, maintenance personnel, and kitchen staff piled into the small elevator cage, their faces eager and excited. To have been chosen to serve at the dinner celebrating the grand opening of Seattle's Space Needle was an honor to be treasured. The room would be filled with the brightest, the wealthiest, and the most influential citizens of Seattle's society.

When the well-known Elizabeth Ames stepped onto the first of the elevators that would take them to the top of the needle, the other passengers gave her a sly once-over. The women smiled and glanced down at her pristine white kid gloves. The men pretended not to notice, but everyone did. Anyone who read the local social or business pages of the *Seattle Times* immediately recognized the woman.

Liz caught a glimpse of her reflection in the mirrored walls of the elevator cab. Strands of gray had softened her once fiery red curls, now tamed in a sophisticated French twist, held in place by a silver comb studded with Japanese gray pearls.

Out of habit, she brushed a stray curl behind her left ear. The light from the elevator's crystal wall sconces shimmered off the bodice of her silver lamé dress and matching gray silk coat. When the cab jerked and began its five-hundred-foot ascent to the SkyCity Restaurant, the woman grabbed the nearest brass railing to steady herself. She eyed her souvenir copy of the evening's program, clutched in one hand. Though she'd read the pamphlet more than a dozen times before sending it to press, she browsed it again for possible typos.

> "The Space Needle elevator weighs 14,000 pounds each with a capacity of 4,500 pounds. The counter weights weighs 40 percent more than the elevator fully loaded. Each elevator can carry 25 adults."

Like every other passenger on board, she surreptitiously counted the number of people, decided she was safe, and then returned her attention to the details in the brochure. Though she'd been to the top of the tower several times during the building process, this was the first time she'd visited the Space Needle since it had been completed.

As the elevator slowed to a stop, she glanced at her watch—forty-three seconds—just like the brochure claimed. A bell rang and the doors glided open, revealing 360 degrees of spectacular cityscape. An unusually brilliant late-afternoon sun highlighted the city and the Cascade Range mountains beyond. As always, the scene took away her breath.

Liz strolled across the room to better appreciate the view of Mount Rainier hovering like a guardian angel over the city. "How lovely!" she murmured to no one in particular. "Tonight we'll be dining in the stars. Gorgeous, isn't it?"

"I assume you are speaking of me," her father whispered in her ear. The plush burgundy carpet had muffled the sound of his approach.

Like the good daughter she was, Liz turned, adjusted her father's bow tie, and smoothed the jacket of his tuxedo. "Oh, Daddy! You're such a tease." Once satisfied his midnight-blue satin cummerbund was straight, she turned to enjoy the scene beyond the window.

"It's all so unbelievable." Richard Bellwood slipped his arm around his daughter's waist. "So many dreams are about to come true for Seattle, for you. And the best is yet to come."

"Too bad Alan never got to see the building completed. He would have loved it." At the thought of her husband, she frowned. "Imagine, dying of a heart attack a week before the ground-breaking ceremony. Life isn't always fair, is it?"

Alan had been gone for more than a year. The project would have been her husband's crowning achievement. Because of his untimely death before he could see the project to fruition, she would receive the award and the acknowledgments made in his honor. "Too bad Mom couldn't be here too." Liz smiled and patted her father's hand.

Her father shrugged. "You know your mother. Katherine doesn't want to be seen in public since her last stroke. I can't even get her to go for short rides in the mountains with me. She used to love doing that."

"Too bad. She's missing so much. Oh, did I tell you I sent special invitations for Moeshe and his wife? I'm not sure Lita will be able to come, what with their fourth child due any day now. As you know, Moeshe has been a true friend to Bellwood Limited and a boon to the city of Seattle over the years."

Richard Bellwood nodded. "He's done mighty well in the process, setting up high-end markets for Native American art along the Pacific Rim. Out of the Deep Industries—that's what he calls his company, isn't it?"

She nodded. Liz was proud of her friend's accomplishments. "I've lost track of how many schools and medical clinics he's established throughout Alaska and Northern Canada from the proceeds. He's truly been a blessing to his people."

"And you, young lady, made a smart move partnering with him in his venture. I must confess, I wasn't so sure it was a financially sound idea in the beginning."

"Oh Daddy, I am hardly a young lady any longer, but thank you for the compliment." Liz couldn't hide her pleasure. Even at forty-seven, she basked in her father's approval.

"You'll always be my little girl. I can still see you as a five-year-old, determined to ride your first two-wheeler." He gave her a quick hug.

"And I must confess, you have a good head for business, my dear. You've never steered the company wrong."

Liz had moved up the ranks in her father's company from communications director, to marketing, to chief financial officer. Six months before, following her mother's illness, she gracefully made the transition to president of Bellwood Ltd., at her father's request. This kept Liz busy being both mother to her eleven-year-old son, Richie, and keeping the company operating in the black.

Suddenly, the idea of her son possibly antagonizing the dessert steward with a barrage of questions and/or the chef with helpful suggestions caused her to catch her breath. "Hey, where is Richie? Didn't he come with you?"

"Oh, he's with your sister and her brood. Don't worry. Anne promises to keep all the boys out of trouble." Liz raised one eyebrow. "Yeah, right! With three boys of her own, the woman hardly needs a fourth to corral."

"She's not alone. Her husband will help."

In front of the dais, the discordant sounds of musicians tuning their instruments brought a smile to Liz's face. The local group she'd hired to perform had been so eager for the gig. Using Seattle talent could only boost the city's growing reputation as the jazz capital of the Northwest.

"Mom! Mom!" The boy shouted from across the restaurant. "Look out the windows on this side. I can see one of Grandpa's ships in the sound."

"Richie! *Sh-sh-sh.*" She glanced about the waitresses lighting the candles and waiters placing water pitchers on the tables. The boy ran to her side.

"Sorry, Mom, I forgot. I'm supposed to speak quietly and not run in the restaurant."

Liz tousled his short crop of red hair. "Say Hello to Grandpa."

"Hi, Grandpa. Did you see your ship down there? I believe it's the *Mary Belle.*"

"Good eyes, son. But you'll have to ask your mother. I don't keep track of the freighters anymore." The older man glanced first one direction and then the other. "Is your aunt Anne around somewhere?"

"She took Ernie to the restroom. He spilled root beer on his tuxedo shirt. You know five-year-olds!" The boy rolled his eyes toward the ceiling.

"Let's go find her. See you later, Lizzy." The older man took his grandson's hand. "And stop worrying. Everything is going to go beautifully."

Liz watched her dad and his namesake stroll toward the restrooms. To watch the love of her life mature into such a competent young man brought tears to her eyes. Alan never had much time for the boy—to his loss. He spent his free hours poring over his architectural books and working on his latest building specs. Thanks to Liz's father, who ably filled in both before and after Alan died, Richie handled the loss with unusual grace and dignity for his age.

Elevators began depositing the evening's guests into the dining lounge. Their surprised gasps pleased Liz. With the sun setting over the sound and the soft evening light reflecting off the snow on the peaks of the Cascade Range, the evening couldn't have been more perfect. The woman sighed as she absorbed the magic of the evening.

The first bars of "I Can't Stop Loving You" drifted throughout the darkening room as multicolored lights blinked on across the city below. Reluctant to break the spell, Liz slipped into the "green room." There she would wait with the other dignitaries for further instruction. She had barely entered the small lounge and greeted a few of her friends when Richie burst into the room.

"Mom! Mom!" Richie whispered and tugged at her sleeve. "Uncle Moeshe is here. Isn't that neat-o?"

"I'm so glad he made it. And Aunt Lita, is she here too?" Liz laughed at the excitement in her son's voice. After spending two weeks the previous summer with Moeshe and his family in Anchorage, Uncle Moeshe had become one of the boy's most favorite persons in the world.

"No. Aunt Lita and the kids couldn't come, so Uncle Moeshe brought a friend with him. That's OK, isn't it? For him to bring another guest?" It was a by-invitation-only event.

"It's fine, son. I figured he might." Liz placed her hand on the boy's shoulder. "Could you please tell Uncle Moeshe that he and his friend are invited over to our place after the festivities? And then, I want you to find Auntie Anne and stay with her until we are finished here. Maybe you can help her corral the boys." Nothing harnessed Richie's overexuberance better than being given a responsibility.

"Yes, ma'am." The boy's eyes glistened in the dimly lit room. "Mama?"

"Yes, son?"

"You look very pretty tonight."

"Why, thank you, kind sir." She gave a little curtsy. "And you look utterly dashing in your first tuxedo, young man." She kissed him on the forehead. "Now, scoot! Go find your aunt and uncle. And stay with them!" Strains of the ever-popular "Some Enchanted Evening" from the Broadway play *South Pacific* drifted through the open door as Richie exited the room.

The lyrics to the song brought long-treasured memories to her mind. The door opened and the host for the evening led the dignitaries to their reserved places. Seated on the dais between the mayor of Seattle and the head architect of the Space Needle, she knew both men well enough that she would have no trouble making the appropriate conversation.

From the appetizer of smoked halibut and Tillamook cheese to the fresh green salad, to the succulent broiled salmon in Hollandaise sauce, to the dessert of huckleberry turnover à la mode, the Northwest cuisine served was superb. When the conversation at the table allowed her to mentally escape, Liz searched the crowded room for Moeshe and his guest. Once she thought she spotted her friend at a back table on her left, but she couldn't be sure in the candlelight.

Following a local comic's valiant attempt at humor, the awards and honors were presented. She thanked the committee and the city for honoring Alan for his work on the project. With her usual style, she kept her speech succinct. She'd attended enough awards banquets to know that by this point of the evening, the well-fed guests were tired and wanted to go home.

When she sat down, the band eased into one of Dave Brubeck's newest hits. Several of the guests began to dance. Recognizing her moment to escape, Liz slipped away from the table and made a quick stop in the ladies' room. Then she slipped on her kid gloves and set out in search of Moeshe.

Liz had taken barely two steps into the dining hall when Richie grabbed her hand. "Uncle Moeshe is looking for you," he whispered, tugging her toward the rear of the room. She spotted her father at a back table, talking with Moeshe and a tall stranger with his back to her.

"Moeshe!" She rushed toward her friend. "It is so good to see you. I'm glad you could make it to—"



Liz's breath caught as Moeshe's guest turned slowly to face her. Her hands shook. All color drained from her face. Her French heels wobbled beneath her feet, causing her to stumble like a colt taking its first step. Unceremoniously, she slumped toward the floor. Instantly, the man caught her by her elbows. "Elizabeth."

Twenty years faded into nothing. And though his hair was a trifle grayer at the temples and thinner on top, Liz recognized the questioning arch of his left eyebrow, the twinkle in his eyes, and his teasing grin. She opened her mouth to speak, but words wouldn't come.

Richard Bellwood stared in surprise. It had been decades since he'd seen his highly polished, poised daughter unnerved by anything or anyone. Whether challenging a government politician on a legal loophole in the latest import-tax bill or outbullying the CEO of an international conglomerate, her adversaries wilted when confronted with the woman's cool, professional demeanor. "Lizzy, are you all right?"

Richie stared as well. "Mom? What's wrong? Are you OK?"

*Breathe!* she told herself. *Breathe!* Dots like tiny fireflies darted before her eyes. The candlelight in the room swirled like a whirling carousel. She blinked to steady herself. Her evening bag slipped to the floor. Again, she tried to speak but couldn't.

"Elizabeth, maybe you'd better sit down." Moeshe slid a chair behind her knees. "I had no idea that my surprise would startle you quite so much."

The three men lowered her into the chair. Her father, concerned that his daughter might be having a medical emergency, asked, "Are you sure you're all right, honey? Should I call a doctor? Dr. Burdick must still be here somewhere."

"Here, Mom." Richie picked up his mother's purse and placed it on her lap.

"No, no thank you, I'm fine." She shook her head but continued to stare into the eyes of the stranger. It was as if everyone in the entire world had disappeared, everyone except Will Judd. Finally, she recovered enough to gasp, "Will, I don't know what to say. I'm so embarrassed."

Standing protectively behind her chair, Richie whispered in his grandfather's ear, "Grandpa, who's Will?"

Though Richard Bellwood had never met William Judd or heard his name since his daughter had returned from Alaska, the father quickly sized up the situation. He placed his arm around his grandson's shoulder.

"We'll talk later, son. In the meantime, we need to find your—"

"But, Grandpa—"

"Come on, Richie," Moeshe urged, taking the boy by the other arm. "Did I tell you that your aunt Lita sent you a box of your favorite bear claws—you know, the ones she makes with the sticky caramel on top?"

But the boy was not to be deterred by bribery. "Mom?"

"It's OK, son." Liz glanced toward the boy. Her face felt hot, as if she'd been in the sun too long. Tears glistened in her eyes. "I'm fine. Honest."

The boy glanced back repeatedly at his mother as he allowed himself to be led away.

"Will—" Liz searched for something brilliant or profound to say, but could only repeat his name.

The old, familiar grin spread across his face. "Is that all you can say—'Will'? Not, 'It's nice to see you'? Not, 'How are you?' Not, 'What are you doing here?' Just 'Will'?"

"Will—"

"There you go again." Without taking his gaze off her face, he lifted one hand to his lips. The gentle kiss sent shivers up her arms and into her hairline. "Elizabeth, I've missed you so much."

"Oh, I'm sorry." She struggled to regain her composure. "Of course, it is nice to see you too. How are you? And what else did you want me to ask? Oh, yes, what are you doing here?" She continued to hold on tightly to his hands as if fearful if she let go, he would disappear into the ethereal northwestern mist.

His laughter brought back a wave of treasured memories for her, memories she'd tried so hard to forget. "Now, let's see—yes, it's nice to see you too. As to how I am, I'm finer than I've been for at least twenty years, give or take a day. And the reason I'm here tonight is to see you, but you already figured that out."

"But how—how—?" A pesky curl had escaped from her French twist and tickled her neck.

"Have you developed a speech impediment since I last saw you, woman?" He tenderly brushed the errant curl away from her cheek. "I've always wanted to do that—brush a curl from your cheek. Did you know that every time you become flustered, you brush away a curl?" Tenderly, he lifted her fingertips to his lips a second time. "I hope I'm not taking unwanted liberties . . ."

"But, but, but, what are you doing here? Tonight?"

Drawing up a chair, he sat down to face her. "As you may or may not know, Moeshe and I became reacquainted several years ago. When he told me about tonight's event, I begged, pleaded, and bribed my way to see you again. By the way, I was truly sorry to learn of Alan's passing. I know the pain that comes from losing a spouse."

"Thank you. I'm not sure I'd admit this to anyone but you. Except when it came to rearing our beautiful son, Alan generally kept a distance in our relationship. So I built a life for Richie and me, often without him. And yet, in time, I learned to love him again."

For a moment, she stared into the gathering darkness outside the nearest window. She couldn't believe how much she'd revealed about her life to this virtual stranger. And yet, Will wasn't a stranger. Seeing him again was as if the intervening twenty years had never happened. She took a deep breath.

"So tell me about yourself. Where do you live? What do you do?" It pleased her to note that his ring finger was bare.

"OK. Here's the abridged version. I took the assignment in Honolulu. And when it was obvious you weren't coming, I dated and married Inez. She didn't take well to military life. Three years later, when I was transferred to Camp Pendleton in California, she left me for the owner of a used car sales lot in Bakersfield, California. In all fairness to Inez, I sometimes wonder if she suspected that she never really had all of my heart. Despite everything, I was saddened when I heard she had died of lung cancer."

"Oh, Will, I'm sorry."

"No, don't be. Doesn't the Good Book say, 'How long halt ye between two opinions'?" He brushed away a tear slipping down her left cheek. "I've learned that love is an all-or-nothing proposition. But it took me years to discover that."

The pain evident in his eyes tore at her heart. He continued, "I wrote to you for several months . . ."

She nodded. "I know. But I didn't let myself read your letters. I knew if I did I'd—"

"I figured as much." He swallowed hard as he traced his finger over the hand he still held. "Anyway, after Inez left me, I devoted myself to my career—first the military, and I was stationed all over the world. Since then, I've held several government posts in Washington, D.C. Currently, I am the government's cultural liaison to Southeast Asia. That's how I reconnected with Moeshe, through his Out of the Deep Industries."

"Whoa! Talk about miracles," she breathed.

Will glanced about the empty banquet room. The guests had vanished. The music had stopped. The waiters were clearing the dishes from the tables. "Do you have to stay here, or can we go someplace where we can talk?"

There was nothing Liz desired more. "I do have a houseful of company at my home even as we speak, but I am sure my father, my son, and my dear sister can fill in for me while you and I take the scenic route home." She withdrew her car keys from her sequined purse and dangled them before his face. "Would you like to drive, or shall I?"

Will shook his head and cast her a teasing smile. "You'd better drive, my dear. I will be so busy staring at you I might get us into an accident. And that's not the way I want to end our first evening together."

The headlights from Liz's silver Corvette pierced the mist on the ten miles of winding road to her home. She'd never before driven the familiar route home quite so slowly. As she drove, his left hand gently caressed the back of her neck, teasing tiny curls out of their carefully coiffed hairstyle.

The flames sparked twenty years before in the remote Alaskan village of Whittier were quickly stoked back to life. As they rode in the darkness, they shared a bit of laughter and a few of tears. Outside a giant wrought iron gate, she brought the car to a stop. At the end of the long tree-lined drive, an array of festive lights shined from the windows of the large mansion, high on a hill overlooking the sound.

Instead of activating the remote control to open the gates, she turned off the ignition. Her voice grew husky as she stared straight ahead, her hands clutching the steering wheel. "I can't believe this is happening, Will. I can't believe you're really here. There's a part of me that feels it was only yesterday you deposited me at Miz Mabel's boardinghouse, yet, so much has happened; so much has changed. We're not the same people we were so long ago."

"I know. You're right. A lot has happened since I saw you off on that twin-engine plane headed for Seattle. I do hope I'm not misreading you, Elizabeth."

"I am so confused," she admitted. "And you should know, I am a woman who is seldom confused about anything!"

"Do you believe in second chances?" He lessened the space between them, staring intently at her profile.

She could feel his breath in her face. "I don't know."

He exhaled sharply. "I admit I am out of practice when it comes to romancing a woman, but I do so want to kiss you right now."

She unwittingly moistened her lips. "Don't worry, Will, you're reading me with precision."

"After imagining this moment for the last twenty years, I don't want to mess it up."

Breathless with anticipation, she turned her face toward his. "Isn't this where we left off on that road outside Whittier, your wanting to kiss me? So please do it. Kiss me before my analytical nature returns." She cast him a teasing grin, but he missed it. His eyes were closed as he skillfully drew her face closer until their lips touched, first lightly, like a brush of a butterfly wing, then with an ever-increasing intensity that startled them both.

"Whoa!" He released her shoulders and leaned back against the seat.

Liz blinked in surprise. "Whoa?"

"Yeah! Whoa! I'm glad I didn't kiss you twenty years ago. I would never have let you leave me, at least, not without a fight." He laughed.

"Nor I, you."

Her hair tumbled about her shoulders as he loosened the comb holding her French twist in place and then buried his face in her curls.

Like a hummingbird hovering over honeysuckle, his lips teased her neck. She tossed back her head to better enjoy the sensation. He touched his lips to her throat. "Why, Elizabeth, my dear, your heartbeat is suddenly accelerating."

He kissed the tip of her chin and then captured her lips once more. At the end of the kiss, she inhaled sharply. "You make me feel like a lovestruck teenager. I better warn you, William Judd, I am a woman of exquisite tastes. And I am accustomed to getting what I want." And then, she begged, "Kiss me again."

Suddenly, as if a switch went off in his brain, Will leaned back against the leather seat and wiped his brow. Bereft of his touch, she cried out, "What? What happened?"

"Elizabeth, I'm sorry, but I must stop. I don't want to ruin everything between us by running ahead of ourselves or of God. I consider Him to be the center of my life." He paused. "You need to know I'm not playing around here. For me, this is no weekend fling. During my flight to Seattle, I vowed that if I had even a slim chance to win your heart, this time I would play by the rules, God's rules. And I can see now that we have more than just the two of us to consider—such as your son's acceptance of me, career adjustments for both of us, and whatever personality quirks we may have developed over the years."

"Quirks? What quirks? I have no personality quirks except for an overwhelming urge for you to kiss me again!" She leaned hungrily toward him.

Will chuckled. "I know this sounds strange at a moment like this, but God promises to give us the desires of our hearts when we trust Him to lead us. And personally, I recognize the desire of my heart when I see her."

"Will, I don't know what to say." She pushed her hair behind her ears.

"Elizabeth, the way I see it, you and I have waited twenty years to be together, we can certainly wait another day or two to do things right."

"A day or two?" A look of incredulity filled her face, followed by a wave of hysterical laughter. "I am the least spontaneous human being on planet Earth. Forgive me, but I have to ask, are you proposing to me or propositioning me?"

Will grinned and caressed her neck. "Definitely proposing. I can't believe I'm saying that. Maybe I'll wait a week or a month for you to make up your mind, but no longer. I'm not getting any younger, you know."

"I'm flabbergasted!"

"So what do you think? Are you willing to give us a try?"

"But we know so little about each other. And if you're talking marriage, weddings take time to plan."

"What do you need to know? I roll my toothpaste tube from the bottom as I use it. If you're a squeezer, we'll buy a second tube. I usually sleep on the right side of the bed, though that is negotiable. I prefer to read the comics in bed on Sunday before I start my day with a cup of Seattle's best java. And every other morning, I run five miles on the beach. What else do you want to know? Oh, and I virtually melt over fresh corn on the cob." A lazy smile teased the corners of his lips.

"You're right, we are rushing things. It's too incredible! Plus, this entire scenario sounds like the plotline for some B movie out of Hollywood. You do realize if a scriptwriter proposed turning our romance into a feature film, she'd be laughed out of the producer's office."

"I don't care what a hypothetical author or jaded movie producer thinks. You and I are real people. And I believe God has given our love for one another a second chance to flourish."

"Yes, but aren't we being a little rash?"

A quirky smile teased the corner of his lips. "Elizabeth, my patience only stretches so far. If you don't agree to a short engagement, I'll have to kiss you into submission."

She arched an eyebrow and shot him a devilish grin. "Sounds fair enough to me. But you should know it will probably take a ton of kisses to convince my executive committee and me to your proposed merger. And I can be very stubborn." She puckered up and closed her eyes.

"Your executive committee? What executive committee?" As he leaned forward to claim her lips, he suddenly stiffened. "The drapes on your plate glass windows just opened to reveal a sea of curious faces. Could they be members of your executive committee? And can they see us from there?"

"Who knows? Maybe with that floodlight shining in the windshield they might. But I am over eighteen."

"*M-m-m,* deliciously so. Besides, I'm here for the duration, however long it takes, as long as you need me. But in the meantime, I'd better get you inside before your father sends out the Alaskan huskies."

"The black labs," she giggled, pressing a button on the vehicle's teak dashboard. As the gate swung open, the sports car leaped forward.

"Huh?"

Again she laughed. "The black labs—Brutus and Bartholomew."

"Great." He sighed in mock exasperation "I not only must win the hearts of your father, your mother, your sister, her husband, your nephews, and most of all, your son, Richie, but a couple of black labs as well? Impossible!"

"True. You should know Brutus and Bartholomew are trained attack dogs. Given the opportunity, they'll bowl you over and lick you to death." She maneuvered the sleek craft into the four-car garage and killed the engine. Before hopping from the car, she planted a quick kiss on his cheek. "Come on 'fraidy-cat. Face up to the challenge. Besides, I predict it will take no time at all to win over the entire clan and the company board members. Remember, I fell for your charms in a lot less time than I'd care to admit."

"Not as quickly as I!"

"You wanna bet?"